Edge of the Rings

The EDGE Trilogy
Book 3

by

Andria Stone

To
Jude and Leo
with all my heart

Copyright @ 2018 by Andria Stone
All rights reserved.

No part of this publication may be reproduced, stored or transmitted in any form, or by any means whatsoever, including electronic, mechanical or otherwise, without the prior written permission and consent from the author.

This book is a work of fiction. Names, characters, places, businesses and incidents are either products of the author's imagination or used fictitiously. Any resemblance to actual events, locales or persons, living or dead, is entirely coincidental.

PROLOGUE

After the last war, most democratic countries on Earth united and combined their forces into one universal military. This led to a pooling of military funds, resulting in the construction of a new space station, spacedock, and shipyard. The military quickly became the primary spacefaring entity.

The moon, now officially named Luna, was colonized with three underground military bases. Next, world leaders elected to discard the old nomenclature "Earth" meaning dirt or soil, formally christening the planet Terra, with Terran Military Defense (TMD) as humanity's dominant armed forces.

The Martian Military Command (MMC) colonized Mars with three underground bases. Domed cities were built above each one, followed by a Martian Space Station.

While attending a scientific symposium on Mars, our six visiting Terrans help spoil a Martian coup. They returned home intent on uncovering a plot by another branch of the same treacherous enemies—to conquer the outer reaches—*leaving Terra vulnerable to new apocalyptic technology.*

As the life of one of their own literally hangs in the balance, so does the future of space exploration for humankind.

Table of Contents

Chapter 1 1
Chapter 2 13
Chapter 3 25
Chapter 4 35
Chapter 5 49
Chapter 6 60
Chapter 7 71
Chapter 8 82
Chapter 9 92
Chapter 10 101
Chapter 11 109
Chapter 12 120
Chapter 13 132
Chapter 14 143
Chapter 15 157
Chapter 16 169
Chapter 17 180
Chapter 18 193
Chapter 19 206
Chapter 20 217
Chapter 21 227
Chapter 22 238
Chapter 23 248

Chapter 24 260
Chapter 25 270
ACKNOWLEDGEMENTS 284

Chapter 1

Kidnapping a sleazebag in the middle of the night; that was the plan.

Their spacecraft landed on a moonless night, less than sixty miles below the Canadian border on a stretch of Montana's frozen tundra. Arctic wind swept across the barren tract of land, buffeting the ship.

Doctor Mark Warren jumped from the hatch into subzero temperature, on a hard-packed, icy surface. He, and two more intruders on this land, wore snow-white, self-contained, armored suits, which emitted no bio-signatures, thus they were shielded from any known surveillance device. Each one carried a pulse rifle plus a full pack of explosives. They could take out a city block or survive for a week without assistance—though none planned to be on the ground for more than an hour.

This was a covert surgical strike, planned and executed by a team of three private citizens—who were also former members of the Terran military—a cybernetic scientist and two sergeants of the elite armored division.

Warren and his friends were acting on a dying declaration from an informer. They were hunting for specific criminals, the goal to dismantle a league of three corporations trafficking in human clones. The mission: to take the head of the snake, leaving the other two vipers easier to eliminate. Rescuing any prisoners was a bonus.

They ran for cover in a nearby stand of Douglas-firs. With the woman, Kamryn Fleming on point, Mark, and Axel Von Radach broke away at a slight southern angle. Less than a minute later, their suits had auto-camouflaged in the ambient lighting to flat black. In silence, they hid among the trees waiting for the targets to file past. Their helmet's green-hued

HUD optics soon picked up an approaching trio of thermal images—local security guards on patrol around the exclusive compound. inclination

As the guards passed Kamryn, she stunned the last man in line with the gun built into the arm of her suit, rendering him unconscious. She caught him before he hit the ground. Into her helmet's comm she whispered, "One down."

Both the remaining guards continued, oblivious to the fate of their colleague.

Axel delivered a knifehand strike to the jugular of the guard following the leader. "Two down."

Seconds later, Mark took out the lead guard with a driving blow to the temple. "Three down." The guards were face and fingerprinted, then given an extra dose of heavy stun to keep them incapacitated before the three intruders advanced.

A week's worth of drone intel programmed into their HUD provided a detailed path to the lodge. Sound-absorbing soles on their boots muffled footsteps to barely audible. They advanced toward a two-story structure set in the middle of a clearing. Interior lights spilled from a dozen windows, smoke billowed from chimneys. Thermal imaging detected one large dog with nine adults on the bottom level and sixteen smaller humans on the second level. Within moments the software in their helmets had biometrically identified the primary target. His image turned red, all others remained green.

Near the dwelling, they separated to check the entire perimeter for additional humans or guard dogs. When none were found, Axel strategically placed field-dampening devices at each corner of the building. These devices canceled electronic emissions, including internal security systems.

Mark and Kamryn cut small holes at the bottom of every other window. Together, they moved around the exterior, firing egg-sized shock grenades into the holes. Small explosions detonated in rapid succession throughout the ground floor. The inhabitants collapsed into unconsciousness, where they would stay for at least an hour with no permanent damage.

In unison, Axel breached the front door as Mark took the back. They made a beeline for the body emitting the red image. Axel confirmed his identity while Mark face and fingerprinted everyone else.

Mark eyed a golden retriever on the floor. It was the spitting image of Zeke, his own boyhood companion. Jerking a man out of a recliner, he laid the dog there with a gentle pat, then set about dousing the fires. After retrieving the spent grenade shells, he went outside to recover the four field-dampening devices. Mark lifted his faceplate and exhaled a toasty cloud of vapor into the December night. He took in a deep breath of frigid air before contacting their ship's Captain. "Malone, the party's over. Time to go."

***

Bypassing the men, Kamryn headed to the second floor, straight for the younger, imprisoned people. She ran to the farthest room where her helmet showed a group of heat signatures. With the strength of her armor, she pulled the door off its hinges to find sixteen young girls in faded brown uniforms cowering in fear against the back wall. Their room held bunk beds and piles of blankets on the floor, but none of the creature comforts that adorned the first level.

Kamryn thumbed up her faceplate and smiled at the girls, motioning them to come forward. "Follow me if you want to be free."

No one moved.

"It's all right. We're here to rescue you."

Still no movement.

Could there be a language barrier? *"Hablas Español? Français? Deutsch? Hindi?"*

A light flickered in the eyes of several girls.

Naturally—since they were from India. Kamryn chinned the inside of her helmet. "Translator, broadcast the Hindi word for freedom."

In less than a nanosecond, the helmet chirped, *"Aajaadee."* She put on a big smile, again holding out her hand.

With considerable trepidation, the tallest girl stood. Moments later all were on their feet leaving the sparse room behind. They trailed Kamryn through a dimly lit hall, down the elaborate wooden staircase, past the motionless bodies, and out the front door. Ohashi and Petra Deering, both former military cyber experts, dressed in silver, ballistic-proof bodysuits, ushered them into the ship hovering thirty feet away. The cybers led them to the passenger cabin and showed them how to strap into the plush blue chairs.

Kamryn removed her helmet, finger-combed her dark spiky hair as she monitored the girls from the doorway. On the edge of her peripheral vision she caught sight of Axel carrying their prisoner into the ship's small, onboard exercise room. She'd join him for the interrogation after takeoff, once they settled the girls. She looked at them, noticed the leader staring at her with rapt attention.

All races were represented, from blue-eyed blondes to bronze-skinned brunettes. Except now she detected a glimmer of hope in their eyes where abject terror had been earlier, part of which was her fault.

"Ohashi, it seems they only speak Hindi," Kamryn said. "Use your tablet to translate, please: Do not be afraid. I'm sorry for scaring you. We will not harm you." Kamryn paced back and forth, holding their gaze one at a time. "You are no longer the property of anyone. You are free. We are taking you to live in a beautiful place with many other children. Lots of wonderful people are there to keep you safe." She dropped her gloves into her helmet. "Ohashi, since New Zealand's your home, add whatever else you think is necessary so it won't be a total shocker when we open the hatch."

Moments later, the interior lights dimmed to dark blue, the ship rose without a sound, turned toward their next destination and sped southwest toward the Pacific Ocean.

After liftoff, Petra treated the girls to hot chocolate and cookies which brought smiles and an undercurrent of happy murmurs. Ohashi waved a medical scanner over the girls to confirm the absence of contagions or health problems.

"Make sure they each get a quick shower and new clothes," Kamryn reminded everyone. "And make sure to keep them quiet. I'll be in the shark tank." After changing into black exercise togs, Kamryn padded barefoot into the combination Medical/Science Lab to collect a vial and syringe. She attached a brown band around her neck, sliding the one-inch disk of the voice synthesizer directly over her larynx. She hummed, dialing the disk as she did so to customize the pitch until it came out sounding like an androgynous robot's voice. "Testing, one million gigawatts, two dozen terabytes, a googolplex of silver scarabs." Satisfied with the results, Kamryn joined the men, more than ready to begin the interrogation.

The prisoner sat in the darkened room, strapped to a weight bench with tape over his eyes. Dirty-blond hair plastered to his sweaty skull, sculpted features, broad-shouldered, hovering around mid-forties. If he hadn't been such a despicable excuse for a human being, he might have been attractive—in another life, maybe. Today, Kamryn considered him to be just another Terran puke—one of the worst, really.

She keyed up engine room background noise on her tablet to further add to his disorientation. First, they'd try interrogation while he was conscious. If he didn't cooperate, she'd give him a vein full of Quazar, their version of truth serum, and he'd be questioned in a more receptive state. A couple people had died after being given "Q" but they'd chalked it up to preexisting conditions. Although, the exact cause of death was uncertain without an autopsy. "Are we ready?"

With nods from both men, Kamryn snapped open a vial of the stimulant AZ2 under the prisoner's nose.

His mouth flew open as he coughed, choked, and wheezed. Struggling against his restraints, he sputtered, "Where am I? Who are you?"

Axel stepped up to slap him with a gloved hand like a lioness would an errant cub, not to cripple, yet strong enough to teach a lesson.

"Wade Fulton, answer me, or you will die," Kamryn said, pleased with the artificial tone of her voice. "How many clones have you purchased from Samar Padhi in Mumbai?"

"I don't know what you're talking about." Wade licked his split lip. A trickle of crimson spilled down his chin.

Axel struck him twice as hard on the opposite side.

Fulton's head snapped to the left, a ribbon of blood spurted across the room, but again Axel didn't break anything.

"You have thirty-three vertebrae, dumbass. I will crush every one before I space you unless the next word out of your mouth isn't a number confirming what Padhi has told me."

Fulton's chest heaved with gulps of air as he answered, "One hundred and forty-two."

Mark validated the number with a thumbs up.

"Where are the clones?"

His rapid breathing slowed. A sardonic grin played on his pale, sweaty face. "Halfway to Ganymede, by now I'd guess. You can't stop them, you know, it's way too late for that." He took a deep breath before continuing as if he enjoyed the opportunity to one-up his abductors. "Humanity is evolving. Humans begat augments and clones. Robots generated cyborgs and AIs. We did things one way in the past, we'll do them differently in the future, whether it's us or someone else."

This nihilistic revelation staggered Mark to the core. He gestured to get the others' attention, signaling with a clenched fist—sign language for freeze—then stepped into the hall. They followed.

"Something's wrong," he said once they were together. "Not sure what it is yet, but I'm getting a bad vibe. He doesn't want to be hurt, but he's not scared. Why not? He knows something we don't. I need to physically examine him—he has to be unconscious."

Wide-eyed, Kamryn asked, "Really, Mark? You want to do this now? I was beginning to make some headway."

He raised an adamant eyebrow. "Trust me. I'm right. I can feel it."

"Okay," she relented, "but this better be good."

"I'll take care of it." Axel's wicked smile put a gleam in his eyes. He walked back to Fulton, stood for a moment, still grinning, and delivered a knockout punch with his human right hand. The augmented left would have killed him.

Fulton's head rocked sideways and dropped to his chest. His shoulders wilted.

***

Mark ripped the tape off Fulton's eyes, pried them open to check the pupils, took his pulse, peered in his mouth, patted him down for any kind of device, then as an afterthought, checked behind his ears for a slight bump. "He's chipped! Shit, shit, shit! He's being tracked." Mark commed Ohashi. "We need you in here pronto—Fulton has a geolocator chip."

When Ohashi joined them, her first words were, "Not to worry, I've got it covered. Nobody's tracking him because nobody's tracking you three—or this ship, either. Since we're all supposed to be with Eva at the International Terraforming Symposium in Vancouver, I tweaked our new SRVL system before we left. I created a loop—kind of like an echo—so your signals are emanating from the hotel's spa. It won't look suspicious to the TMD as long as we're back before morning. That's when the signal starts to scatter." She tucked an errant lock of dark hair behind one ear while giving Fulton the once-over. "His geolocator signal went dark the minute he came aboard, but there's no way for me to find out who's monitoring him. I only know his signal just vanished the minute Axel brought him across our threshold."

Mark's inquisitive brain needed more data. "What happens when we let him go? How long before his signal is released? Can we remove the chip? What happens if we do? Isn't it illegal for him to have one?"

Axel didn't care. His moral compass had two points: guilty or innocent. "All that's BS to me. I vote we fill him full of Quazar, interrogate the hell out of him, then I space him. It's not as if he doesn't deserve it. We have enough evidence to prove he's guilty of treason, cyberwarfare, and human trafficking. What do you want to bet that not a single clone volunteered for the trip to Ganymede—if that's even where they're going?"

"Let's find out." Kamryn expertly administered a dose of Quazar into Fulton's left carotid artery, waiting several seconds before giving him another whiff of AZ2.

Fulton's eyes popped open, bloodshot, with brown pupils big as moon rocks.

As usual, the men took their places flanking Kamryn to record the interrogation on their tablets. Ohashi faded into the corner.

"Wade, honey, wake up!" She clapped her hands in front of his face.

He tried to focus, but one eye drifted outward. Each person reacted differently to Quazar, a street drug Kamryn had appropriated—or misappropriated—during her time as a DEA agent. A full spectrum analysis had shown it was more potent than any current psychoactive drug in use. It had proven most effective in turning recipients compliant, almost eager to volunteer information.

Except for two prisoners who'd died for no apparent reason while under the influence, so it was a crapshoot.

"Wade, pay attention. We don't have all day." Kamryn gave him a little love slap to get his attention. "From whom did you acquire your geolocator and when?"

Fulton shook the cobwebs out of his head, blinking rapidly. "Uh...Lotus Chang inserted the chip last month."

Good to know, Mark thought, Chang happened to be another snake on their list. Now they were forewarned she also had a chip.

"Do you have clones on a ship bound for Ganymede?"

"Yes. Four hundred clones on three ships."

Stunned at the number, Kamryn glanced at Mark and Axel to confirm they'd also heard his answer. "Name these ships."

"*Fultronics, Kailani, Stellaria.*" Fulton's head drooped. Saliva mixed with blood dripped onto his rumpled khaki shirt.

After another hit of AZ2, he perked right up. "When did the three ships depart for Ganymede?" Kamryn prompted. "How many people were on board?"

"My ship left a week ago with a crew of two hundred. *Kailani* and *Stellaria* left a couple days ago, twenty-four hours apart."

"What is your mission?"

"To claim Ganymede and all its resources as a corporate holding. My company is in charge of mining operations for harvesting rare metals and minerals. Chang will establish laboratories for the production of clones, AIs, and cyborgs. Stepanov will manufacture bio and nuclear weapons for our security."

Kamryn hesitated, overwhelmed by the sheer scope of Fulton's revelations.

Mark drew her off to the side, handing his tablet to her. Moving in front of Fulton, he asked, "Does Stepanov plan to produce nuclear or thermonuclear warheads?"

"Both, I think. Powerful enough to glass an asteroid or moon." A spasm rippled through Fulton, followed by an aftermath of facial twitches.

Mark suspected the drug's effects were wearing off. He needed to get the most critical answers before Fulton blacked out. "What types of bioweapons?"

"Uh...Sorix, NuroKac, and Zdeth."

"Detail the clone production."

"Genetically enhanced humans—stronger, faster than organics. Devoid of congenital disorders—designed to withstand disease, aging. Better than the Indian models by a factor of ten. From cell to maturity in a nanite chamber or nanotank, in less than...seven...months." A fit of uncontrollable laughter escaped Fulton. It ended with repetitive eye blinking and more saliva dribbling onto his shirt.

Mark rushed to get the last bit of information. "Detail the AI production."

"Chang has six functioning prototypes...they'll be replicated to accelerate technological progress. In less than eighteen months, Ganymede will become our hub to—" Without warning, Fulton's facial muscles tightened, he coughed, choked, then lapsed into full-body tremors before slumping forward.

Mark checked his pulse. Still alive.

Axel took a few steps forward. "Now can I space him?"

Kamryn shrugged. "Fine by me."

"Alive, he would be extremely useful to the TMD," Mark reminded them, "but to Mars, in particular. If he has additional information which would directly impact them, since Ganymede is closer to Mars than to Terra. Depending on the speed of the last two ships, the Martian military might be able to detain them." Mark whipped around, searching for Ohashi. "We need data on the ships Chang and Stepanov sent. Also, are the owners aboard, or did they remain here, as Fulton did?"

Ohashi pulled a tablet from a pocket in her cargo pants and delivered her findings. "Both ships are smaller than Terran Warships, show a maximum complement of a hundred seventy-five, with no visible weapons. At top speed, Kailani is close to the rimward side of Mars. *Stellaria*, however, is approaching Martian space. Personnel manifests include both owners and crew, but no additional passengers, which means neither one includes clones. The inventory manifests also do not indicate either ship is carrying bioweapons or anything remotely nuclear. Uh...personally, I think spacing is too easy. How about roasting him—"

"No spacing, no roasting, no tar and feathering," Mark interrupted. "As planned, we're leaving him on a deserted island in the Pacific and sending his GPS to Axel's buddy, Nik Roman, who will turn the data over as an anonymous tip to the TMD."

Axel snorted. "So General Dimitrios can have Fulton picked up and halo interrogated for days until he's reduced to a puddle of horse pucky. Your conscience will be clear because the TMD will be responsible for his lobotomy."

"That's an urban legend, they don't lobotomize." Mark waved a dismissive hand. "Anyway, we're no match for these people. They have three ships. Crews totaling upwards of eight hundred people. Plus, god only knows what kind of radical bioweapons, designer plagues, weaponized pathogens, or genetically modified viruses they're carrying. The Terran and Martian militaries have ships all over the system that are infinitely better equipped to deal with this kind of threat. We're private citizens now. Putting ourselves in harm's way, doing this on our own dime and our own time. If we keep pushing our luck, we're going to get caught—and then there'll be hell to pay."

Chapter 2

Axel knew Mark's decision to let Fulton live was the right call, but that didn't mean he had to like it. He hated this guy for so many reasons—the first being clone trafficking, the original reason for hunting Fulton. The other crimes were icing on the cake. Terran Space Command had recently awarded *Fultronics* a contract to supply electronics for the new Europa Mission. But once General Dimitrios learned of Wade's collusion with Chang and Stepanov to develop bio and nuclear weapons, Axel hoped for a full-scale retaliatory strike to dismantle their holdings.

From Axel's stint in the TMD, he knew the military to be heavy-handed with any entity it perceived as an enemy. They wielded considerable power, freezing the assets of all three companies, indicting everyone in positions of authority. Corporations, however, were structured similar to the military, and with the leader eliminated, the next in line took command. No doubt, some would attempt to flee with hidden money. Others might try stealing proprietary data to sell on the black market, then slink into obscurity.

Dismantling *Fultronics* would delay the Europa Mission while giving the three ships headed for Ganymede a healthy lead to establish a colony on the frontier. Not good for Terra or Mars. There had to be a way to detour or stop the last two ships. Fulton's abduction had been to locate and save clones. That wouldn't happen now—maybe never would.

A slight change in their flight pattern interrupted Axel's thoughts.

Captain Malone commed, "Heads up everybody. Touchdown in thirty seconds."

The crew prepared to offload the youngsters into the secluded hills outside Greymouth, New Zealand. A few minutes later, the hatch opened to the sweet smell of a late summer evening. Four Anglican sisters of the Holy Cross convent waited on the newly paved tarmac behind the outbuildings. The nuns welcomed the girls with hugs and ushered them down the pathway to the dormitory to join the other young clones liberated from Mars.

One girl, the leader who'd first stood up at the house where they'd been rescued, broke away. She ran back to Kamryn, bowing in respect while clasping her hands together. "I want to be like you," she said in broken English before she returned to the group.

"You've got a fan," Axel said, standing beside Kamryn. He watched nuns comfort the more fragile girls along the winding path.

Kamryn snorted. "Ha! Better she stays here, gets married, and has babies. These kids have so many strikes against them already with no ID, no family, used as slave labor—or worse. These are the lucky ones. It will be a miracle if any of them overcome what they've lived through so far."

An older, heavyset woman with her gray hair pulled back into one long braid came forward as Ohashi stepped out of the ship. "Mother Superior, I'm sorry to arrive so late."

"Nonsense." The nun smiled, the wrinkles around her eyes crinkling. "It's not late. I haven't gone to bed before midnight in years. I thought you were bringing more children, dear."

"We were," Ohashi said. "But learned moments ago they were shipped out."

"To where?"

Ohashi's whole body slumped. "Ganymede."

"You, sir," the old nun poked a stiff finger against Axel's chest, "will bring them back."

"Yes, ma'am, if we can. On the way here, we learned they're on three ships that left for the frontier days ago."

The nun insisted on poking him several more times to emphasize her words. "Rescue those being led away to death; hold back those staggering toward slaughter."

Axel's violent past as his neighborhood's enforcer, years as a Phoenix cop, then a TMD armored assault soldier had cemented his position on Santa's naughty list. Yet he still recognized a quote from the good book when it was drummed into his chest. "Or die trying," he replied, tipping his head with a fist to his heart.

"You work for a higher power now, my son." She graced him with a warm smile and a mischievous glint from her tired eyes. "He will not let you fail." The nun turned, taking Ohashi's arm to lead her off a few paces. They spoke in hushed tones before saying farewell.

Axel had become Ohashi's silent partner in providing a home for the clones since he'd liberated Valerie Parker's funds. Of course, this had happened before Axel had ended her life because Valerie had murdered his woman. Ironic to use Parker's money to free and rehabilitate the clones she'd bought and traded as pawns in her failed overthrow of Mars. He forced the lingering images of her body burning in the fires of hell from his mind, bringing himself back to the more pressing matters at hand. After the crew boarded, the ship became airborne within seconds, speeding toward a small Pacific atoll on which to leave Fulton.

On an encrypted channel in the pilot's cabin, Axel contacted Nik Roman, an old friend and former intelligence agent who now ran his own Terran Intercontinental Security firm. Nik's dominant facial trait was a forelock of white from his widow's peak combed back against jet black hair.

"Nik, we need a favor. I'm sending a GPS with an interrogation vid. We'll be dropping a prisoner there any minute. What I need you to do is claim one of your TIS operatives intercepted the intel by accident, then turn it over *fast* to General Dimitrios at TMD Headquarters. No link to us, or there'll be epic blowback."

Nik's brows knitted together. "You used to ask for piddly things. Now it's all this counterintelligence BS. You'll owe me big time for this one."

"I'm good for it. Oh, and tell your mom I send my best."

"I will. She still raves about the lasagna you made for her birthday years ago." He smiled, sketching a casual salute. "Nik out."

Next, Axel faced the captain, "Malone, how long do you estimate before a TMD shuttle picks up Fulton?"

"Sir, we've been scanning for military traffic. Identified three ships with the ability to respond within fifteen minutes."

Nguyen, the female copilot, said, "The DZ is about thirteen minutes away. Palmyra. It's an uninhabited equatorial atoll—lots of open space, no obstacles. Be a good idea if we dropped him off ASAP and got the hell out of here."

Ohashi wandered in. "Personally, I think we should neuter the SOB."

"Or lobotomize him," Petra offered, also squeezing into the cabin. "We could do both, ya know." She giggled. "We have a MedLab."

"Uh-oh," Nguyen muttered, "we've got company...a Flamestar-380, portside coming up fast."

"I see it." Malone's jaw tightened. "Everybody harness up, this looks like trouble."

"What kind of trouble?" Petra asked as Axel propelled her out of the cabin.

Through clenched teeth came Malone's answer. "Pirates."

Axel steered the women to the passenger cabin in time to see Kamryn tightening her harness. "Where's Mark?"

With an impish grin, she gestured toward the Lav.

"In the shower?"

She nodded.

Axel ran to the door, jerked it open, and shouted, "We've got problems. Grab your pants and get out here."

***

Mark barely managed to get leather pants yanked up over wet skin before he joined the others.

"Buckle up buttercup," Kamryn teased, flashing him an evil grin.

As the interior lights dimmed to deep blue, he grabbed the straps to chinch himself in. "What's happening?"

"Pirates."

Mark knew about space pirates. Everyone did. They preyed on easy targets, stealing anything of value, including ships, under the right conditions. To them, *MAVREK* must've looked like a new toy; a sleek, bronze, business-class ship with a fancy logo of royal blue wings emblazoned on both sides. Little did they know both its pilots were former Terran Space Command warship astronavigators, capable of out-maneuvering damn near anyone, no matter what kind of ship they were flying.

Malone and Nguyen had cyborg parts due to war wounds, the same as Axel. Their certifications to pilot military ships had been revoked, but they could still fly—better than most. Without hesitation, Mark had hired them. Since he'd designed cybernetics for the military, he believed they were as good, if not more capable, than full organic humans. Axel was living proof.

Nguyen broadcasted, "They think we're easy prey, so we're gonna teach 'em a lesson. It might get a little squirrelly back there. Hope nobody ate recently."

Mark scanned the four faces around him. They were smiling. He realized they'd all seen space combat aboard ship except for him. "I didn't eat…uh…but I had a cookie, or two."

Kamryn tugged on her harness, grinning. "You puke, you clean it up."

The sound of Nguyen's cackling drifted out of the cockpit, followed by, "Okay ye pirates, come to mama."

Then the bottom dropped out. The ship hurtled toward Terra like a runaway comet. Mark's stomach wasn't inside his body any longer. Wherever it had gone, he hoped the cookies stayed safe inside. His brain weighed five hundred pounds, he couldn't swallow, tried hard not to pass out. Seconds later, he almost felt normal, until the ship inverted and they rolled upside down. These maneuvers went on for so long he lost all sense of direction. When the ship started shuddering from stem to stern, Mark expected pieces to start flying off. After an old-fashioned roller coaster double barrel roll, they came to a full stop. The interior lighting returned to normal.

Malone's voice broadcasted, "Ride's over. We're on Palmyra three minutes ahead of schedule. Time to drop off the prisoner."

Everyone but Mark scattered. He made sure no bits of chocolate chip cookies were decorating the ceiling or walls before he unstrapped. Axel carried the unconscious Fulton to a midway point on the atoll. Mark jumped through the hatch into the predawn hours of a salty sea breeze. It wafted over him with the faint noises of surf breaking on the shore. He longed for time to soak up the simple life. *No rest for the wicked*, his grandma Hilde used to say. Mark had learned the hard way there was no rest for those who *hunted* them, either.

Malone and Nguyen joined him outside to stretch out the kinks and get a breath of fresh air. The lanky, sandy-haired pilot stood at least a foot taller than his diminutive copilot. In the cockpit, however, they were a match made in spaceship heaven. Malone rubbed his right eye, the same one that had been disintegrated by shrapnel and replaced with an undetectable cybernetic eye, aided by a tiny neural implant at the base of his skull.

Nguyen slipped off her shoes to reveal blue painted toenails. She immersed both human-looking feet in the sand. They'd been severed at the ankles in a crash, but still she'd sent a Mayday which resulted in the rescue of all seventy-eight soldiers aboard her ship.

Axel returned at a run, motioning for everyone to get inside. "Okay, he's resting comfortably. Let's get back to Vancouver. I'm looking forward to time in a steam bath before the night's over."

With the successful completion of their mission, an air of excitement spread throughout the ship. Although their plans never quite materialized the way Mark imagined, as long as no one got shot or captured, he considered it a victory. He commed the pilot. "Malone, any sign of the pirates?"

"No sir." The pilot let out a derisive snicker. "But we just picked up a TMD shuttle that changed course to navigate on a vector straight for Palmyra. It seems Dimitrios received Roman's message and ordered a ship to pick up Fulton. Looks like your plan worked, but we'll continue to monitor their progress while we're airborne."

Mark signaled Axel that Fulton's recovery by the TMD was right on cue.

Kamryn said, "You didn't puke."

"I have never regurgitated on a ship."

She waved a finger at him. "There's always a first time."

"Sir," Malone commed with an update, "the military shuttle landed on Palmyra, then departed on trajectory straight to TMD Headquarters in Virginia."

Seven hours after *MAVREK* had left Vancouver, it touched down behind a warehouse complex on the outer fringe of the city. Their covert comings and goings necessitated an obscure landing area away from prying eyes. A prearranged limo waited for them upon touchdown. Within thirty minutes, the early morning ride dropped them back behind their hotel. One by one, the crew unobtrusively filtered in through a service entrance, weaving down back hallways to a steam room, fitness center, sauna, or massage treatment room, as if they'd never left.

An hour later, they met Dr. Eva Jackson, a Molecular Nanotechnology scientist and the last member of their team, for breakfast outside the hotel's dining room. "I'm so glad everyone's safe," she whispered to Mark. "Is it done?"

"Yes, but there's a wrinkle." He took her arm, slowing to walk alongside to a table near the rear.

"Isn't there always?" Eva's whole five-foot frame slumped. Her sweet bronze face pinched together. "Wasn't this supposed to be one of those easy-peasy jobs?"

"No such thing as easy anymore, Eva. We discovered most of the clones were gone—shipped off to Ganymede." Mark filled her in on the rest, finishing with, "Oh, yeah, and pirates chased us coming back."

Shocked, Eva's mouth fell open as she clasped a hand to her chest. "Pirates?" Not quite a novice space traveler, there were many situations Eva hadn't yet experienced.

Before he had a chance to explain, Mark's tablet vibrated. He checked the caller. "Hi, mom."

The image of Leslie Warren, her blonde hair piled high, standing in a living room wearing mauve dentist's scrubs, filled his screen. "Hi honey. I'm getting ready to leave for the office, but I wanted to catch you early."

"How's everybody?"

"Great, great. There's fresh powder on the slopes. We're inviting everyone to spend a weekend here before the holidays. *This weekend.* It's all arranged. I'm not taking no for an answer. Love you, Mark. Bye." She waved as the screen went dark.

He held up the tablet, replaying the call. Everyone except Eva had met his family on a previous trip to Portland. Not quite a year ago, Beth Coulter had sent a cyborg to attack Mark's father in the hopes of coercing Mark into giving up his classified military cybernetic research. The elder Dr. Warren almost died. The military had sent their team, including Dr. Torance and a unit of armored soldiers, to apprehend or destroy the cyborg. They succeeded, however, Kamryn became the second casualty when she was shot in the neck. She'd nearly died as well. This would be an emotional trip for each of them.

"Great. Can we go skiing?" Petra asked.

"How about rock climbing?" Kamryn sounded enthused.

Ohashi leaned forward. "Doesn't your sister have a yoga studio?"

Axel watched the others as he smoothed the stubble on his jawline.

Mark nodded. "Yes, to everything. The only catch being you'll have to show up for dinner and help trim the tree."

A sad-faced Eva raised her hand. "Oh," she moaned. "I can't go. I've been asked to speak at another conference in Buenos Aires—tomorrow. Someone fell ill, and they needed a substitute, so I volunteered. I leave in three hours." She brightened. "But you can't go visit Mark's family empty-handed. Presents are in order. Let's head to the hotel gift shop after breakfast."

***

A chill crept down Kamryn's spine. She pivoted right then left, searching for the cause. Nothing stood out as unusual. Nevertheless, she committed random faces in the crowd, clothing, and body language to memory. Her friends were within sight; busy shopping, testing perfumes, trying on ski goggles. Everything seemed normal.

Five minutes later, the same cold uneasiness wormed its way into her chest. Caressing the knife handle strapped to her thigh, Kamryn sought out Axel. "Something's hinky," she mumbled in an undertone.

He did not question her. Instead, they exchanged knowing looks. He veered away to the left.

She strolled to the right, around displays and groups of people. They wandered in an expanded spiral pattern, acting as shoppers, but scanning for anything out of the ordinary. Although nothing was found, Kamryn couldn't shake the eerie sensation.

As a pragmatist, Kamryn lived in the present, yet she understood the tightening in her gut came from years of exposure to a myriad of hardcore, perverse, lifelong criminals. She knew a few, from personal experience, who couldn't meet the classification of humans. The nervous, crawly feeling hadn't faded, and she vowed to remain vigilant.

***

With Vancouver's International Terraforming Symposium concluded and purchases in hand, they checked out of the hotel. Rather than returning to their home base in Lexington for a couple of days, a unanimous decision made Portland the next destination. The ship sped south with the team eagerly planning various forms of winter R&R.

"My sister, Gina, is meeting us with a van at the spaceport," Mark said. "She has two spare bedrooms, and my parents have three, so figure out who's going where."

Surprised, Petra said, "Really? We get to stay with your family? I assumed we were going to a hotel."

Axel walked by to drop his old military duffel bag in front of the hatch. "I'm staying at your house. I hope your mom remembers she gave me keys to her kitchen."

Mark nodded. "She never forgets anything."

By the time *MAVREK* landed at the Portland Spaceport, Kamryn had shelved her earlier apprehension, at least for the time being. Along with the others, she looked forward to a long, enjoyable weekend. A mountain of duffels and gift bags crowded the passenger cabin. It took two hover trolleys to transport the crew with their baggage to the security checkpoint.

Kamryn had spent most of her first trip to Portland in the hospital, so she didn't recall much about Mark's family. But, when she noticed a young blonde woman in a plum-colored parka waving the minute she caught sight of Mark, Kamryn knew they were siblings. Mark was a tall, good-looking, blue-eyed blond who'd transformed from a first-class scientist to a kick-ass soldier in less than a year. Gina, on the other hand, was a glamorous, effervescent, smaller version of her brother, with big blue eyes and long, honey blonde hair. They even shared the same dimples.

The siblings hugged, and Mark introduced everybody. "You remember Axel…"

"I sure do," Gina said, hugging Axel.

Kamryn thought the hug lasted a bit too long. It could have been little sister hero worship, but Kamryn's suspicious nature told her it might be something else.

"You all look so…off-world," Gina gushed as she eyed their edgy clothing.

Kamryn scanned the crush of teaming voyagers in the spaceport terminal. She had to agree. The style here appeared more mountain casual—colorful parkas, capes, caps, snow boots. Not long, dark leather coats and guns.

Outside, the mighty snow-capped Mt. Hood stood as a sentinel. Their breath condensed into white clouds in the crisp air of a bright, clear morning as they loaded the van, then piled inside. Gina drove them past her studio, Beyond Yoga, on the way to the Warren's family home. She rattled on about Portland's coffeehouses, microbreweries, their mom's dental office, and their dad's child psychology practice. "He's scheduled to testify this afternoon in a custody dispute. He hates testifying in court. Why don't you surprise him, Mark? Meet him for lunch—he'd love that."

Gina veered down a street which turned into a cul-de-sac and aimed for the sprawling, two-storied house sitting in the middle of the curve. It featured arched windows, double front doors, with snow-clad fir trees bordering both sides. She pulled up into the side driveway. "We'll drop your things here. I'll take Petra and Ohashi to my condo, and you three can have the van."

On the road again to Gina's condo, she answered a zillion questions on everything from Portland's nightlife to skiing conditions. After unloading, Gina tossed the key to Mark. "We'll grab lunch and squeeze in some shopping before going to the studio for my afternoon session. Meet you back at the house for dinner?"

Chapter 3

Mark led Axel and Kamryn into the subtle, peach-toned waiting room of his father's clinical psychology office. Doctor David Warren, PhD, was a specialist in Childhood Psychological Assessment & Intervention. He shared the office with two others psychologists—a woman who specialized in addictions, and a man who specialized in phobias.

They sat in silence with several people until a young girl came walking down the hall. A woman rose to meet her, and they left. Seconds later, a mature, fair-haired man with intense blue eyes walked toward them.

Mark stood. "Hi, Dad."

David beamed when he saw Mark, a smile spreading from cheek to cheek as he rushed forward to greet his son. The Warren family had never been inhibited about showing affection. Two years ago, Mark's brother, Eric, an astro engineer, had been killed on the Europa Mission as a result of sabotage by Beth Coulter. Earlier this year, his father had sustained life-threatening injuries resulting from a cyborg attack by the same Beth Coulter—now deceased. Conscious of his own mortality, Mark saw no reason to withhold displays of affection in public.

Amid back clapping and handshaking, Mark introduced Axel and Kamryn.

"Oh yes, it's Sergeant Von Radach, isn't it? I remember you from the hospital in Virginia. And Sergeant Fleming, I'm so happy to finally meet you. Mark admires you both so much. We're delighted you've come to visit for a few days." He grabbed an overcoat from a hook by the door on the way out to his car. "Let's have lunch downtown. I have to testify at the courthouse afterward—it won't take long—then I'll bring you back. I still have a few patients to see this afternoon."

They stuffed themselves with Mexican food at Pedro's Hot Tamale Kitchen, always one of Mark's favorites. Since he hadn't eaten there in years, Mark ordered the Combo Plate of enchilada, tamale, chile relleno, two tacos, beans, and rice, with chips, guacamole. And two beers. The conversation focused on their recent trip to Mars, omitting the scary parts in deference to Mark's father. When Mark's food arrived, it came served on a what looked like a turkey platter. Axel and Kamryn poked fun at him the entire time, but it didn't slow him down. When he pushed the plate away, only a few uneaten bites remained.

After their meal, they walked several blocks to the courthouse. "I'm sorry, you're not allowed inside." David explained, "Because the victim is a minor, these are restricted courtroom proceedings. Please wait here." He waved at benches lining the walls. "I'll be out presently."

Mark sat on a bench next to the double doors to the courtroom. Tilting his head from left to right, he picked up bits of conversation between the attorneys and clients as they maneuvered through the corridors. Mark had been shot less than a month ago. A few centimeters to the left would have left him a corpse. He'd lost an ear—regrown with nanites, but surgery had replaced his auditory canal with an augmented one. His friends had christened him with the moniker "Old Cyborg Ear." He was still fine-tuning the intricacies of using it to his advantage.

Kamryn elbowed Axel. "He's eavesdropping," she whispered.

"No. I prefer to think of it as learning how to use a new toy." Mark filtered out the soft hum of the heating system, shuffling footsteps, intermittent coughing, sneezing, and sniffling noises to concentrate on voices.

Within seconds, two loud male voices came from the inside the courtroom, overpowering everything else. A gavel banged repeatedly. More shouting ensued. Two males, the stepfather and his teenage son, denied allegations made by the girl's mother.

Mark's acute hearing picked up sounds of a scuffle. Footsteps approached the door. "Uh-oh." He signaled for Axel and Kamryn to flank the doors. "Bad guys on the run."

One door opened. An angry, bearded man in a tweed jacket erupted into the hall, pulling a teenage boy along by the sleeve.

An alarm blared in the corridor. Other courtrooms opened. Spectators crowded into doorways.

People from David's courtroom yelled at the man, Mr. Grant, to stop.

A bailiff caught up with them. He grabbed the kid by his free arm, trying to pull him away from his father. Grant turned and sucker punched the bailiff square in the nose. He fell backward, taking the attorneys behind him down as well.

Grant jerked his son around, heading left toward the exit.

Axel dove at the dad's midsection, tackling him with the force of a freight train, and brought him down. Sprawling along the smooth floor, Grant lost his grip on the boy's sleeve.

The son abandoned his father, bolting toward the front entrance. That's when Kamryn flung her long black coat out over the kid like she was casting a net. The heavy leather blinded him long enough for Kamryn to dive for his legs, knocking him off balance. He tripped and fell. She pounced on him, putting a knee between his shoulder blades while she grabbed both his wrists and brought them together in the back.

The onlookers applauded. Seconds later, four guards arrived with guns drawn. Two helped Kamryn untangle her coat from around the kid as they cuffed him.

Trying not to smirk, Axel stood with the heel of his left augmented leg placed on the carotid artery of Grant's neck with a pressure of fifty pounds to hold him in place. If Grant blinked, Axel wouldn't hesitate to exert the entire 1,500 pounds of which he was capable. No wonder Axel's prisoner looked terror-stricken, his eyes big as moon rocks.

The other guards rushed to haul the submissive Grant away in cuffs.

Mark approached the two heroes. "No blood or broken bones, and you didn't shoot anybody—I'm shocked."

"No guns, we left them in the van, remember?" Aware of people staring, Axel smoothed his stubble and straightened his clothing. "Blood's a little hard to explain in broad daylight, especially with an audience."

"Besides, the Police Station is around the corner," Kamryn added. "I have no intentions of spending any portion of my Holiday in a private sector's version of the stockade."

David came forward to congratulate them. "I'm so sorry this happened. But you were amazing, just amazing," he said, shaking their hands.

A woman in a black robe approached. She tucked a few errant gray hairs back into her bun. "I'm Judge Beckman. You have my eternal gratitude. This could've been a complete disaster. Thanks to your quick reactions, it wasn't. A dozen different cameras recorded everything." The judge twirled her finger in the air, pointing to ceiling cams. "Our statements will corroborate what transpired," she motioned for the bailiff, "but Dwyer, here, will need to copy your IDs."

"Yes ma'am," all three chorused. They handed their blue data chips over to the bailiff.

Judge Beckman noticed the color; blue indicating former TMD personnel. "I suspected you were military. Both my daughters are TMD shuttle pilots stationed in San Diego." She smiled, turning to leave. "You're released. You may go."

***

After leaving the elder Dr. Warren's office, Axel felt as if he were being watched. He became hypervigilant, glancing over his shoulder, alert to every sound, motioning for the others to be quiet with a finger pressed to his lips.

Mark squinted at Axel. "What's wrong?"

"Don't know yet, but take a roundabout route back to your house."

"I felt it, too, in Vancouver," Kamryn said, peering out the window. "I thought someone might have recognized me—maybe related to an arrest from my past with the DEA."

Mark zigzagged through the suburbs for half an hour while they monitored traffic for anyone or anything following them.

Nothing.

"What are we looking for?"

"Not sure. I'll know it when I see it." Axel glanced at Mark's puzzled face. "Maybe coincidences happen to other people, but not me. Not Kamryn, either. We've spent our whole adult lives stopping bad guys—one way or another—from here to Mars and back. War, police actions, off the book missions. It adds up. We've made a lot of enemies. You have, too. We're all in the same club, except *our* enemies want control over some part of Terra, *yours* want to rule the galaxy."

"Sad, but true," Mark agreed as he pulled into the driveway. "Good thing the TMD installed that upgraded surveillance system in the house after dad was attacked. We'll be safe here."

Inside, a message waited on the vid for Mark from his mom saying Axel still had keys to her kitchen, and to have the tree up in front of the window when she got home.

They grabbed axes from the garage and went out back to 'thin' the Warren's grove of fir trees as opposed to paying an exorbitant price for one from a lot.

"I've never had a real Christmas tree," Axel said in a wistful tone, eying the freshly cut six-footer with reverence.

Mark traded glances with Kamryn. "Well, you will this year. We'll put it in a stand. Get the boxes of decorations to trim it later."

While Kamryn set up the tree, Mark chopped wood for the living room fireplace.

Axel donned the red BBQ apron he'd worn before in the Warren's kitchen. Despite his ominous premonition, Axel's mood lightened as he prepared chicken cacciatore for dinner. Still, Colonel Maeve Sorayne's beautiful face hovered just out of reach every once in a while. Dead, yes, but very much not forgotten. Eva said the visions kept insinuating themselves into the present because he wasn't ready to let her go yet. Axel had killed Maeve's murderer, thus ending that chapter of his life. Now he waded through the aftermath.

Moments later, Gina barged in with Ohashi and Petra

"Look," Petra said, "we went shopping."

They wore new ski gear in metallic-neon shades, ready for fun in the snow tomorrow. A festive atmosphere swelled with both Warren siblings plus the four Mavrek women breezing in and out of the kitchen to sample Axel's cooking.

"Drop that fork," he said, threatening Petra with a wooden spoon, shooing her away from the food. On the surface, Axel seemed to enjoy it. Granted, being in a real house for the holidays with people he considered his family presented a new sensation—unfamiliar, but heartwarming.

Before long, Mrs. Warren arrived with hugs for everyone. The commotion rose to party level, with everyone talking at once. Mark tended the fire while the women congregated in the kitchen to comment on the mouth-watering aroma of food and hunt for snacks.

When David Warren entered, everyone converged on the dinner table.

That's the same time Axel's tablet buzzed. Nik Roman, from TIS, did not look happy.

"What's up, Nik?"

"You know what's up." Nik stared into the screen as his forefinger pointed at Axel. "General Dimitrios is holding my feet to the fire until I tell him exactly how my operative got that intel."

"Well, I don't care what kind of whopper you tell him as long as my name's not attached to it. That was our deal."

"Do you really think he's going to believe Santa dropped it in my stocking as an early Christmas gift?" Nik snapped.

Axel lowered his voice. "Look...tell him you were working a cyber-spying case involving a *Fultronics* competitor who's got a hard-on for Wade Fulton because he underbid them for the TMD's electronic contract on the Europa mission. To those corporate types, losing a multimillion-dollar contract is more than enough reason to kill someone. We both know you can lose your life for a lot less on the streets. Fulton's lucky to be alive."

Nik arched a brow. "You think Dimitrios will buy it?"

"Why not? Especially if you let it slip the target you were following used half a dozen aliases, then disappeared somewhere the TMD isn't welcome—like China or Russia."

"Okay, that's a line of BS I can sell." Nik cracked a smirk. "You know, I got a spot for ya here whenever you want to make a move. You can bring Fleming. I heard she's hell on wheels."

"Yeah, she is that." Axel winced at a vivid memory of Kamryn delivering a roundhouse kick to his chest when she'd stopped him from going rogue to hunt for Maeve's killer on Mars. "I'll pass your offer along, but I like where I am."

"I heard you were on Mars when their so-called revolution broke out. That true?"

"We were there so one of our scientists could attend a Terraforming Symposium."

"Ah-ha, I get it. So, if I see news media covering a political hot spot or corporate corruption, I'll know you're not too far away. Tip of the spear, all that shit. Gotcha. Nik out."

Axel had to admit, Nik's assessment was accurate.

***

Every bowl, platter, and plate sat with scant remains of the chicken cacciatore, zucchini, a loaf of crusty garlic bread slathered in butter, plus two empty bottles of wine.

During dinner, Mark's father had entertained them with his account of the excitement in the courthouse. "You should've seen them, Leslie. It looked like a powerfully choreographed ballet. Violent—but without a broken bone, or drop of blood. Simply astonishing. And over in seconds." He snapped his fingers.

Seeing apprehension in Mrs. Warren's eyes, Axel said, "Not a big deal. We didn't even work up a sweat."

"Personally, Dr. Warren," Kamryn chimed in, "I enjoyed it more than spending time in the gym onboard our ship."

David gestured to Kamryn. "You were the soldier in the hospital room next to me here in Portland, right? The one who got shot hunting down the thing—the cyborg—who attacked me?"

"Yes, sir."

"You have my endless appreciation, as well as my heartfelt apologies. I'm so sorry the injuries you suffered caused your retirement from the TMD. It changed your life."

"True, I almost died. But because of the nanite protocol, I healed perfectly. Yet, due to the way the military rated my injuries, I couldn't return to my Armored Assault Unit as a Sergeant. So, I chose a different path."

"And you, Axel, I will forever regret that you lost two limbs while trying to save my son's life. Your sacrifice means more than I can ever express."

"I understand why you feel that way, Dr. Warren, after losing Eric on the Europa Mission. But the day I met Mark, one of my men died. As his sergeant, I was responsible for the lives and deaths of my people. I volunteered to re-up if the military gave me the assignment to guard Mark for the opportunity to catch the person responsible.

"Truth is, Mark saved my life less than fifteen minutes after Coulter's merc shot me. We're even. No one owes anyone anything. As it turned out, I helped him dispense justice to Coulter. I'd come close to dying twice before, so my luck was running out. The armored division is equivalent to the Rangers or SEALs of Old Earth's military—harder to kill, but we still die. Kamryn and I are exceptions to the rule—we're alive. As for my cyborg arm and leg…well, they make me stronger and faster than any human. I came out of the operating room better than I went in."

The sound of doorbell chimes interrupted the conversation.

David rose. "I'll see who it is."

People started clearing the table, until David roared, "Mark!"

Everyone rushed into the archway to the living room.

The opened front door framed three TMD soldiers in gray uniforms—a tall, thin major with tired eyes flanked by two sergeants built like tanks.

Mark and Axel hurried to join Mark's father.

"Dr. Mark Warren," the middle-aged major said, looking directly at Mark. "We've been sent by General Dimitrios. May we have a moment of your time, please?"

Axel and Mark eyed each other, trying to look as innocent as possible. There weren't enough soldiers to arrest everyone. Could this be related to the Wade Fulton incident? Nope—not a chance.

With reluctance, Mark motioned for them to enter.

The sergeants remained standing in the frosty darkness while only the major stepped inside and closed the door. After a quick glance at the eight other people staring at him, he lowered his voice. "This is a classified matter, Dr. Warren. May we speak in private?"

"It's my father's home. What would you have me do? Ask them to leave?" With a sinking feeling in his gut, he ushered the major to the farthest corner, and waited for him to speak.

Chapter 4

"I am Major Steffen Brandt, Assistant Director of the Terran Military Defense's AIRED, Artificial Intelligence Research Engineering & Development Program. I'm sorry to barge in on your family's holiday gathering, Dr. Warren, so I'll get straight to the reason I'm here. The TMD received vital new intel today on the production of what they're calling 'super cyborg' and 'ultra android' prototypes the military has never seen. Based on your cybernetics specialty, General Dimitrios is requesting you accompany me back to HQ, where they're assembling a global team of experts to decipher this new data."

Mark wondered if the military suspected him of being involved. He decided to play dumb. "For what purpose? Specifically?"

Brandt opened his mouth, but stammered for the right words.

"Never mind—don't tell me. He's just been hit with new technology, which puts the military behind the private sector, so the general wants us to reverse engineer versions for the TMD. We'd be playing catchup on a *galactic* scale. Is that about it?"

The major responded with a sheepish grin and a shrug.

A definite nonverbal indicator of "yes." Good. Since Brandt hadn't implied Dimitrios suspected Mark of being part of the intel's acquisition, he breathed an internal sigh of relief.

"I'd be very interested in examining this new technology, Major. Take a look under the hood, so to speak. But, as you can see, we were about to engage in a family tradition of decorating the tree. Besides, everyone in my team has plans to visit their families as well."

"You misunderstand, Dr. Warren, this is for you alone."

"I'm afraid *you* don't understand, major. Where I go, my team goes."

"Check your contract, Captain Warren." Brandt's posture straightened, a tense, determined look transforming his face. The mister nice guy tone changed to deadly serious. "I've been authorized to institute an active duty recall for your services. As per TMD Directive 1352.1, this is deemed a national emergency. It's perfectly legal. You are hereby ordered to report to Norfolk tonight. Please collect your personal items— *now*—and follow me. Four others are waiting on the shuttle. We need to make the meeting on time."

It took every ounce of Mark's willpower for him not to toss Major Brandt out of the house, trapped in a waking nightmare. Mark would never be rid of the military ordering him to do things against his will. He'd been chipped and sent to the moon; his dad and Kamryn had almost been killed; his best friend had lost two limbs; he himself had lost an ear! Now they were forcing him back into a uniform.

Mark gritted his teeth, staring at Brandt with an ungodly loathing.

The major didn't blink.

As Mark's anger raged, he stole a glance at his family. His dad looked worried, mom nearing tears, sister jaw-dropping dumbstruck, the anxiety written in large letters on everyone else's face stopped him from losing his temper. Not here. Not now.

So be it.

His anger faded with the realization some battles were just not winnable. Mark knew when he was beaten, yet underneath his waning anger, resentment festered by a factor of ten. In the past, he'd outmaneuvered the TMD, gaining four spaceships with millions in scientific equipment as spoils from the BioKlon seizure. Mark would follow orders—again—while waiting for an opportunity to work this to his advantage, but there would be a day of reckoning for this latest reversal of fate.

Mark stood, turning toward his worried family and friends. "I'm being recalled. It's a matter of national emergency. They've come to escort me to Norfolk tonight." He hugged his mom, her cheeks were wet as she whispered, "Stay safe." Hugging his dad, Mark exchanging a knowing look with Kamryn and Axel over his dad's shoulder. Gina hugged him around the waist, making little whining noises.

He took the stairs three at a time to retrieve his gear.

Upstairs, Mark commed his team. "So far, they don't seem to think we had anything to do with Fulton's intel. I should've realized they might want my help, but didn't think it would happen like this. It would be nice if someone monitored my chip while I'm gone, to make sure I don't wind up in a supermax somewhere above the arctic circle. Guess I'll see you when I'm released, whenever that is." Not having the heart to prolong the goodbyes, Mark charged down the stairs, tossing a "Merry Christmas" and a half-assed salute over his shoulder before he bounded out the door with a lump in his throat.

The cold hit Mark like a slap in the face. If the waiting sergeants were cold, it didn't show, except for the cloud of white vapor being expelled from their lungs into the frigid night air. In silence, they sped through light evening traffic straight to the spaceport. With military clearance, the car bypassed security and delivered them far downfield on the tarmac.

Mark's stomach squirmed when he spotted a soldier standing guard outside the shuttle, holding a BDX-97 plasma rifle. Shaped like a boxcar, the black, transport-class ship had a slanted front, twin side nacelles, two torpedo tubes, with a side hatch. Imposing, but unattractive. The large red TMD insignia of eagle's wings surrounded by a circle of stars made certain no one mistook it for a civilian ship.

He took one last look around before climbing into the ship. The hatch clanged shut with the hollow sound of a cell door. Liftoff occurred less than a minute after they'd boarded. Interior lights dimmed to a steel blue, playing havoc with onboard shadows.

When Mark's eyes adjusted to the darkness, he noticed a handful of soldiers harnessed in between four other civilians, thus eliminating small talk among the scientists. Three men and a woman, all middle-aged, with dour expressions, dressed in clothing for temperate climates, not freezing temperatures. They must have come from a much more southern locale, making Mark the last person to board before heading back to TMD Headquarters in Virginia. One small, dark-skinned man in particular seemed familiar; Dr. Omar Chakir, a specialist in Molecular Architectonics Research. Mark recognized him from an Artificial Intelligence Conference several years ago. No doubt, these scientists had been rounded up for the AI portion of the military's mandatory reverse engineering project.

An experienced space traveler now, Mark stretched out to doze until the shuttle landed. The soldiers herded the five PhD's off like prisoners of war through a labyrinth of gray corridors to an auditorium overflowing with the people pouring into it. As if they were enemy combatants, everyone underwent fingerprinting, faceprinting, DNA and retinal scanning. This amounted to a no-frills command performance—rather frightening to any neophyte scientist.

On the raised stage, a bear-like form walked out from between red curtains and approached the podium. It was none other than General Eli Dimitrios—commanding, heavy-set, silver at the temples, in a pristine gray uniform trimmed in crimson. The five stars embedded in his tunic glistened in the overhead stage lights. He swatted the microphone a few times. It pinged in protest.

A hush fell over the crowd. People scattered to find seats. Tension surged through the room like an electric current by the time he began to speak.

"I am General Elias Dimitrios. I will not mince words. You've been told why you're here. We have a national emergency, the magnitude of which the TMD has not faced before. The military has obtained prototypes of what's being labeled Super Cyborgs and Ultra Androids from the private sector that far exceed any current models in our Research & Development Divisions."

An unseen gust of surprise mixed with dismay wafted through the audience.

"You are some of the brightest minds on Terra, which is why we've summoned you here: to reverse engineer this technology, and do it in record time, or humanity will undoubtedly suffer the consequences." Dimitrios paused for effect before delivering the bombshell. "Our entire planet is faced with not only these two technological threats, but a host of bioweapons including Zdeth, Sorix, and NuroKac. Plus, the genuine possibility of a nuclear or thermonuclear attack."

A shockwave of disbelief rumbled from every corner of the room. Learned scientists were either staggered into silence or jolted into frightened babbling. Not a single smile could be seen anywhere.

"Three privately owned Terran firms have joined forces to send ships laden with this apocalyptic technology to the frontier—Ganymede, to be exact. Your guess is as good as mine which way they'll be heading once they control the frontier."

Dimitrios slammed his meaty fist on the podium hard enough for the sound system to pick up the echo, bouncing it off the walls.

Half the audience visibly flinched.

The General's ruddy face clashed against his graying hairline like fire on ice. "My predecessor, General Gregory Richmond, coined the phrase, 'Annihilation is visited upon the naïve.' If there is one among you who thinks these new enemies won't turn toward Terra and burn us to the ground—or worse—blackmail us into subservience while they still have the upper hand—then you are a fraud, and your presence here is rejected. You may leave now." He pointed to the door through which Mark had entered.

Out of the entire roomful of scientists, no one budged, much less breathed.

"This has officially been labeled Operation Crossfire. The Prime Council has approved a communications blackout for TMD Headquarters until further notice. Specifically, because we cannot afford to have any outside entity become aware of the precarious position these companies have put us in. Thirty-seven countries depend on us to defend them, and defend them we will—with your help."

A fervent hum of approval greeted this last piece of information.

"Very well," he continued in a conciliatory tone. "There is no latitude for error here. I have work to do, and so do you. The clock is ticking. Let's get to it. Dismissed." Dimitrios took a moment to probe the faces staring at him before moving his bearish presence off the stage.

A blanket of silence descended over the audience. Not so much as a cough or sniffle was heard until Major Steffen Brandt approached the podium. "All scientists specializing in Artificial Intelligence please use the left rear exit. Cybernetic Specialists use the right rear exit. Bioscience specialists, please stay and take a seat to my left," he said, motioning with his arms. "Nuclear on my right. We have special briefings for you people."

Low-level chatter grew as civilians unaccustomed to following orders scurried out the assigned doors.

A baby-faced officer approached Mark. "Sir, would you be Captain Mark Warren?"

"Today I am," Mark replied bitterly.

"Right. Well, I'm Lieutenant Craig Foster. Your quarters are being prepared, sir. In the meantime, your lab's this way. It's not far."

"Who's in charge of this lab?" Mark asked, following Foster.

"Uh..." The young man checked his tablet. "That would be Major Edward Whitley."

"Needlenose Whitley?"

"Ha-ha." The lieutenant looked mortified for laughing. He struggled to correct himself. "At the moment, Major Whitley *is* the ranking officer in your section of Cybernetics." Foster lowered his voice. "Though, I've heard a colonel from Luna is slated to take over." He slowed down, stepped up to a retinal scanner for a quick check, waited for the *click*, then opened the door.

They entered a large lab. The door closed with a soft hiss. Foster led the way, searching for Whitley. As Mark walked down the center aisle, heads turned in his direction. With his blond hair almost reaching his shoulders and still wearing off-world clothes under a long, russet colored leather coat, he presented an uncommon sight. Some individuals looked annoyed, others insulted at his unwanted presence.

"Who the hell is he?" asked a small, potbellied major standing with his feet widespread, arms crossed over his chest.

The lieutenant gestured toward Mark. "Captain Mark Warren, PhD, Cybernetics."

"*Captain?*" squawked Major Whitley, his arrogance not veiled in the least. His moniker *was* well-deserved. "He looks more like a mercenary in those off-world clothes and long hair. He's not working in my lab dressed like that."

Mark raged inside. After being recalled by the military, forced to travel 2,100 miles in a barebones TMD shuttle, and crammed like a sardine into a stuffy room for much too long, Mark was in no mood to be badmouthed. He slipped into the bad guy alter ego "Kell" persona he'd used on Mars.

Bearing down on the portly officer, Mark got inches from Whitley's face. "I designed the synovial joint bioware module that's used in every ankle, elbow, and knee joint replacement in the current version of over 6,400 TMD soldiers. I can also shoot the eye out of a moving cyborg and bench press three hundred pounds. So, if you want my help, give me a white coat, then get the hell out of my way." Mark finished his performance with a treacherous sneer for Major Needlenose.

Whitley sputtered unintelligibly before disappearing in a huff.

Someone offered Mark a lab coat. He turned to see a captivating brunette with sapphire blue eyes.

"I am Désirée Bouchard," she said in a soft, earthy voice laced in a French accent.

Ironically at a loss for words after his tirade, he only managed, "*Enchanté*, Désirée." Mark was a sucker for French women, or redheaded women, or a nice derrière, or—

No-no-no! Mark's friends had rated the moral fiber of his last female conquest as worse than crappy. Being a red-blooded male, he might entertain lecherous thoughts of this drop-dead smoldering woman, but under no circumstances would he invite another round of humiliation by engaging in any amorous indiscretions or allow her to affect his work here.

At least, he'd *try*.

***

The skiing and indoor rock-climbing Kamryn had scheduled before heading to Calgary to spend the holidays with her father and step-mother were on hold. The TMD's unexpected move had derailed everyone's plans. Ohashi was torn whether to leave for Christmas in New Zealand where her sister and parents were waiting. Petra had three younger siblings and a widowed mother expecting her in Saint Louis. Axel and Eva, the two members without families, were splitting a vacation in the Caribbean, where she'd relax on the beach drinking exotic concoctions with little parasols in them while he went deep sea fishing. As of a few minutes ago, everything had fallen apart—totally FUBAR.

Leslie Warren sat on the couch staring into nothingness, looking hurt. Gina sat next to her with an arm around her mother's shoulders for comfort while the girl cursed the TMD under her breath. David Warren was slumped in a chair, elbows on his knees, cupping his head, looking deflated, as if all the air had gone out of him. Their happy holiday plans—trashed.

Axel took charge. "Since problems usually come in three's, let's find a way out of this one before the next disaster hits. We're heading to Virginia. If Mark's released soon, we'll be there to pick him up. Then everyone can go on with their holiday plans."

"I'm on it." Kamryn commed the ship with orders for Captain Malone to prepare for liftoff while Axel retrieved their gear.

After saying their goodbyes to Mark's parents, Gina took them to the spaceport. She reached for Axel's arm before he entered the terminal.

"I wanted to thank you for what you did. You know, when you were here before." Her eyes brimmed with tears. "Except now I need to ask another favor, Axel. Please bring my brother back. I don't want to jinx this, but I have a bad feeling about the way they came to get him." She clung to Axel's arm.

He wrapped her in a reassuring embrace, murmuring words of comfort.

Kamryn watched the touching interaction between them. *Interesting*, she thought.

The undercover work she'd done for the DEA had sharpened her skills at reading body language. These two clearly shared a private connection. Kid sister worship? Maybe, but not Kamryn's business. Still, she wondered if Mark knew of this bond. It must've happened when she was in the hospital in Portland.

A comm from their pilot interrupted her thoughts. "Okay everybody, Captain Malone's ready for takeoff. If you don't want to be left behind, it's time to go." She herded the team through the terminal to their ship.

As they boarded, a small flash of light drew Kamryn's attention. That creepy sensation returned. She looked up to see a glint in the night sky a hundred feet above—a gray drone with two unique red markings. At once she remembered seeing the same exact model at the Vancouver warehouse location where *MAVREK* had been hidden.

She caught Axel's arm and whispered, "We're being monitored. Drone. Over my left shoulder. Capture it—*don't* kill it." Kamryn tossed baggage inside the hatch while pretending not to follow his movements.

He ducked below the ship, coming out on the other side behind the drone. Axel aimed at it and fired. Two silent shots of his pulse gun disintegrated its flying capabilities. The housing with the transmitter and receiver plummeted toward the tarmac. He sprinted to catch it. Like a fly ball, it fell into his hands.

Kamryn commed Ohashi. "Bring Eva's terraforming vault on the double. We have a new drone for you to dissect."

She appeared in seconds, holding out the specimen box—a unique twelve-inch square, tri-layered, glass-plastic-glass apparatus. Axel dumped the case in. Ohashi locked the lid.

After liftoff, everyone followed Ohashi to the lab. In case of an emergency, Kamryn kept a pulse gun handy as she oversaw the work on the drone.

First, Ohashi attached the transparent box to a small computer which showed readouts for every conceivable type of gas or toxic matter. Once the drone's readouts showed no evidence of harmful substances, decryption and transfer of data to an old tablet were completed. As the tablet rumbled to life with the sound of an Old Earth racecar engine, Ohashi set about dissecting the drone. Wearing a headband with magnifying visor, her dark bobbed hair tucked behind her ears, she used microelectronic tweezers to dismantle the circuitry. Her small hands covered in blue, wrist-length gloves, she worked with surgical precision to examine the minutiae of the parts for any identifying characteristics.

At last, she looked up. "Generic components, but an expensive camera."

Kamryn frowned—not the information she wanted to hear. They wouldn't know more until the data was analyzed.

Ohashi removed her headband apparatus. "Where did you begin to notice the drone?"

"Vancouver. At the warehouse location, near the *MAVREK*."

"Are you sure it's the same one?"

"It had the same configuration, color combination, and markings."

Axel bent down to peer at the remnants strewn over the work station. "It obviously followed us to Portland. I never saw it, but I felt something behind us after we left the courthouse."

Petra had been observing the dissection. No longer able to contain her curiosity, she asked, "You think there's a connection to one of your old DEA cases? Shouldn't all those people still be in jail?"

"Maybe, one of their relatives recognized you at the hotel," Ohashi offered. "Could this be some kind of grudge or payback thing?"

"No way of knowing, yet," Kamryn said. "Petra, come with me. I'll make a list of my arrests. You can verify they're behind bars, crosscheck for any of their family members living in the Vancouver area."

"Oh, yay," she groaned, trudging behind Kamryn. "I get to hack into the Justice Department's Bureau of Prisons encrypted system, slog through scumbag files checking on drug lords and violent offenders, to make sure they're locked up nice and tight—*then* search for their lowlife relatives. Lucky me."

Ohashi called after them, "As soon as I'm sure there's no self-destruct protocol, I'll start analyzing the data."

***

In the pilot's cabin, Axel leaned against the bulkhead in back of Malone, waiting for him to confirm landing coordinates. Axel's thoughts ran the gamut of everything from who'd been tracking them to a curious feeling of something he couldn't quite name about Gina Warren. He'd sort that out later. Axel smiled as his thoughts turned to Mark. The kid—Axel always thought of him as "the kid," although he was only a year younger, with a PhD. Mark disliked being told what to do, especially by the military. Nevertheless, science was Mark's true element and he'd do his best, no matter what the circumstances. His attitude might get him into trouble, but never the quality of his work. Axel flexed his two augmented limbs. He was a walking testament to Mark's genius.

Beeps from Malone's console broke the silence. When the copilot's navcom captured the new heading, Nguyen double-checked the data. She entered a slight course correction, which redirected the ship toward its new destination.

Malone advised, "I found a private tarmac less than ten miles from TMD Headquarters. One of my old Star Command buddies opened a flight school and said we can park there, no problem. Touchdown in thirteen minutes."

Axel left the pilots to check on progress with the drone. In the lab, he didn't waste any time. "Ten minutes until we land, Ohashi. I need a sitrep."

"I'm ready." After spending four years as the top cyber in Axel's TMD Armored Unit, she'd done this hundreds of times. "The drone had a satellite-based tracking mechanism pinpointing its exact location in real-time. Plus, it relayed flight and activity data with a return-to-home function that sent out a loss of signal or out-of-sight crash longitude and latitude coordinates. It notified the sender of the exact crash site," she said, holding up a finger to halt any interruption. "But since the tarmac is no place for a drone, anything could have caused the crash. Under the shield of our SRVL system, all outgoing or incoming signals are blocked. It ceased to exist." She took a breath and continued. "The drone came from Vancouver. Specifically, our hotel, The Grand Imperial, so, it must've been one of their employees who sent it to follow us. Do we know who yet? Have you checked with Kamryn and Petra?"

Axel accepted that shit was hitting the fan from three different sources: Fulton, TMD, and Vancouver—Vancouver being the most important to the people on this ship. For now, they'd concentrate on the drone, who'd sent it, and why.

Chapter 5

In the Cybernetics Lab, seventeen scientists, including Mark, were crammed into drab six-by-nine cubicles, each one studying a 3D holographic replica of the 'super cyborg' in front of them. Tuning out all extraneous noise, Mark focused on the multi-layered transparency rotating in a 360-degree circle. His fingers swiped away contrasting colored layers of synthetic skin and alloys until the synovial joints were exposed. He enlarged, rotated and inspected them, before muttering Axel's pet phrase.

"Well, shit on a blue moon. They couldn't make a better one, so they stole my design." Both flattered and irritated, he resumed his inspection. "Okay, turnabout's fair play. Let's see what I can steal from you."

Energized, Mark peeled away holo layers around the skull, squinting at what lay beneath.

Every scientist, even young ones, knew reverse engineering was a euphemism for just plain copying. Mark had been doing it since childhood, much to the chagrin of his family. It began with his sister's toys, graduated to a myriad of kitchen appliances, and ended with one of his father's prized electronics. He discovered that to build something without design specs, you dismantled it, duplicated the parts, and built another one. Easy-peasy. But, if you wanted to build a better model, it became a little harder.

The one thing that stumped Mark about cyborgs was that none of the previous models *spoke*. They received and executed commands like robots or drones, yet he'd never heard any of them utter a sound. This one could. It had a talking module which emitted a natural sounding human voice—not an androgynous-toned one. Scaled down six inches to normal life-size, it featured a plain, nondescript face, brown hair and similar eyes, which made it indistinguishable from organic humans. He concentrated on the skull, stripping off holo layers, tracing how the wiring configuration joined the voice module to the lower jaw or mandible to the mouth. Ingenious. He recognized a remarkable breakthrough in joining bioware with software housed in the machine's body, except this cyborg could now converse with humans as well as each other. Mark spent the next few hours scrutinizing the intricacies of sensory networks in the cyborg's hands and feet.

This machine was nowhere near the new AI he'd seen earlier, which featured deep neural networks and complicated mathematical systems capable of learning complex tasks. As humanity and technology became integrated, the mysteries of artificial life were collapsing at a phenomenal pace.

Out of nowhere, an ominous thought occurred to Mark: Wade Fulton's embedded geolocator chip. What if something similar had been hidden in the two physical units undergoing analysis in the TMD Headquarters? Could such a chip be so undetectable that scores of military experts hadn't found it yet?

What might it do if found? Self-destruct?

Holy shit.

Spurred to action, Mark probed between the layers of cybernetic matter and biomolecular structures. He searched for an anomaly—any tiny device secreted among circuitry—just waiting for an accidental trigger to, worst-case scenario, *explode!*

Suddenly, Mark's cybernetic ear picked up an unexpected snippet of conversation coming from the corridor outside his cubicle's wall.

"…Chang, Fulton, and Stepanov are visionaries of our future…the semi-literates here are nothing but a bunch of wannabe scientists…"

The names spoken shattered his concentration like a bolt of lightning. A distinctive male voice had been praising the three people plotting against Terra while disparaging him and his peers in the process.

Mark grabbed his tablet. Not too many people were awake at 1:35 am. He was out the door within seconds.

Shit. On the left, he saw two men in TMD uniforms walking away. On his right, father down, were four men in white lab coats. Mark turned left, following the uniformed pair, now at least thirty feet ahead of him, hoping to overhear the same voice.

The shorter man looked back, straight at Mark. A few seconds later the taller man turned and glared at Mark, with a look that said *'Are you following me?'*

Frustrated at being discovered, Mark turned off into the nearest T section of the hallway and collided with Lieutenant Craig Foster.

The young officer stumbled backward. "Uh…my apologies, sir."

"Foster, there are two men in the hall. Follow them. Find out who they are. But don't get caught."

"Sir?" Foster asked, wide-eyed.

"That's an order, Lieutenant," Mark snapped, pointing after the suspects. "Go."

"Yessir." Foster scurried around the corner and out of sight.

Mark waited until the hall looked empty before making his way back to the main AIRED lab where the prototype cyborg and AI were being kept. He scanned the roomful of white coats for a familiar face. "Dr. Chakir," he said, approaching the Architectonics specialist. "I'm Mark Warren. We arrived on the same shuttle last night."

"Oh, yes." Chakir nodded, standing only shoulder-high to Mark. "I thought I recognized you. Umm, cybernetics, isn't it?"

"It is," he said, gratified the doctor knew of him. "Sir, I may have new information pertinent to your research. Is there a place...?"

"Certainly." Chakir's face sagged with exhaustion as he looked for a suitable location for a private discussion. "I must admit, it's past my normal bedtime. I need to sit down for a minute. Will this do?" He motioned to a six-by-six corner cubicle stuffed with a hodgepodge of spare lab equipment. As Chakir sank into a chair, relief spread over his face.

Mark snatched another one and straddled it, facing Chakir. "During my tour in the TMD, I was stationed at CAMRI, a classified Research & Development installation in Canada. After a sabotage attempt, the military embedded a geolocator chip in my neck before transferring another scientist and myself to Luna. Do not ask why I suspect that Wade Fulton, the man currently being interrogated by the TMD, also has a geolocator chip in his neck—implanted by, I might add, the person who designed the two units in our possession. My personal knowledge and experience dictate that any entity capable of designing such a chip, plus these units—which have exponentially surpassed ours—can also hide a self-destruct mechanism or a trigger of some sort...to..." Mark flung his hands in the air, fingers widespread. *"Boom!"*

Watching Chakir's dark features transform from alarm to outright fear, Mark hesitated to divulge the last item he surmised was true. Nevertheless, he delivered the *coup de grâce*.

"If what you've just heard isn't enough to make you paranoid, as of a few moments ago, I believe our enemies have supporters, or at the very least, *sympathizers* in our midst. I followed the suspects. When they spotted me, I sent a young officer to track them and came here instead."

The color had drained from Chakir's face, leaving a pallor of total shock. Seconds passed as the scientist struggled to grasp the harsh reality Mark had presented. In a soft but decisive tone, Chakir said, "Our first priority is human safety. We must sequester these units in a containment field before they can do any harm. I'll inform Colonel Harrington, our AI Project Manager, and the new Cybernetics Manager, of your hypothesis. I'm sure they'll notify the TMD's Director of AIRED. When can we expect an update on the suspects you've had followed? You're aware this is time-sensitive?"

"Yes. The officer will contact me as soon as he has verifiable information. Do you know who the new Cybernetics Director is yet?"

Chakir produced his tablet. "As of twenty minutes ago, we learned Colonel Falana Ongaru has arrived from Luna. Excellent credentials. Somewhat of a maverick, I hear. She's in briefings now." Chakir rose in slow motion, as if struggling under a colossal burden. "Stay here...I'll return with Colonel Harrington."

The phrase 'excellent credentials,' reminded Mark of Beth Coulter, who'd migrated to CAMRI with the same kind of list, and yet she'd turned out to be the harbinger of death and treachery. He also picked out the word 'maverick', the name of his company being Mavrek Enterprises, and etched into the side of his ships.

Mark missed his ship. He missed his friends, although at the moment he missed Ohashi and Petra more than anything. They could've done deep background checks on this new Colonel Ongaru in a matter of seconds. Upon touchdown at Headquarters, he'd been relieved of his comm unit and gun at the security checkpoint, but allowed to keep his tablet and vest. Thanks to Axel's extensive knowledge of the military's restrictions, the ceramic knives hidden in his boots had not been detected. However, the dampening field over the AI/Cybernetic section cut off communication to the outside world. No webnews, no netchatter, and access restricted to scientific applications only as they related to your specialty.

Chakir burst into the cubicle, speaking so fast he dropped words as he gasped for breath. "Harrington's missing...hasn't been heard from for hours...notified the authorities...requested immediate containment fields..."

Mark pressed him into a chair. "Slow down, doctor. Take a deep breath. Now tell me if anyone's notified General Dimitrios."

The small, dark man acquiesced, using the back of his lab coat's sleeve to wipe sweat from his brow. "Yes, he's on his way here with the AIRED Director and your new Cybernetics Manager. I'm certain you'll have to explain everything to them, as you did me. I don't understand how this could happen. We're in the safest place on the planet."

"Not quite," Mark muttered as memories of Colonel Olivia Rushing shooting him and Dimitrios in the general's office flashed through his mind. "I'll speak to the general. You concentrate on making arrangements for the containment field."

A commotion erupted in the lab, many people talking over one another. Mark stepped out of the cubicle to see if Harrington had returned.

General Dimitrios, flanked by four armored soldiers and trailed by numerous important-looking uniformed officers, cut a swath through the maze of white coats.

Dimitrios spotted him. "Warren, why am I not surprised to see you in the thick of things."

True, Mark had been 'in the thick of things' twice before, notably saving Dimitrios' life a few months earlier. "General, sir, a pleasure to see you again, too. You're looking well."

"I was having a good week until this morning, then everything fell right into the crapper. Somebody's going to end up in deep shit when I find out who started this whole mess. Where's Dr. Chakir? He reported Colonel Nash Harrington as missing."

"I arrived on the same shuttle with Dr. Chakir last night. He's in here, but there's a few things you need to know first," Mark explained. "Remember the neural implants that were hijacked and caused problems on the Europa Mission? Well, sir, it's my opinion the designers of these two units could have hidden similar devices—or programming—which could cause explosive repercussions."

Dimitrios studied Mark's face for any hesitation or doubt. "You sure about this?"

"As sure as I can be, sir, without proof."

The general spun on his heel and bellowed, "Clear the room! And get a containment field around these units!"

The nearest armored soldier escorted Dimitrios out the door to safety.

Flocks of people in white coats moved in an orderly fashion toward the lab's only exit.

Mark snagged Chakir's sleeve, hustled him through the bodies into the hall, and dragged him left, toward the Cybernetics Lab.

One moment everything was quiet, the next…

A stupendous blast erupted in the lab.

The building rocked with a horrific, ear-splitting noise.

An invisible shock wave blew the lab's door off its hinges into the hallway. The explosion radiated outward, shoving everyone and everything away at a phenomenal rate of speed. A blast wind of negative pressure sucked it back in toward the center.

The force slung Mark against the wall. Chakir fell from his grasp. Mark's head slammed against the wall, his vision clouding as he dropped to the floor with a heavy *thump*.

The lights went out.

***

Mark opened his eyes to a sporadic flickering of dim light and the feeble whine of a klaxon. The blast had knocked him unconscious. He was deaf in his right ear, but his augmented ear heard a groan. He rolled over to find Chakir curled up in a fetal position on the floor, his breathing raspy and uneven. Mark checked his vital signs, diagnosed a concussion, various bloody shrapnel wounds, possible internal injuries, too.

Orange flames billowed out of the AI Lab, followed by a haze of acrid smoke. Five blood-soaked bodies lay strewn on the floor like disjointed marionettes. The walls were studded with metal projectiles. Carnage in both directions. It looked like a Saturday Night Massacre—everything wrecked, disfigured, burned, or scorched.

Flashbacks sprang to mind of death and destruction from the attack on CAMRI. For an instant, fear immobilized Mark, but he hadn't died there, and he wasn't about to die here—if he could help it.

Despite bouts of dizziness, Mark struggled to stand. Every muscle in his body cried out in pain. He strained to get a lungful of air down his parched throat. His eyes stung. The part of his brain that still functioned screamed, *Get out of the building! Get out of the building!*

He somehow found the strength to lift Chakir in a fireman's carry, intent on taking him to the hospital in the adjacent complex. Clinging to the wall, he maneuvered through the smoke-filled corridor. Finally, he turned toward the Cybernetics

Lab on his way to the exit. A mutilated door lay on the ground, hinges ripped off at deformed angles. Those still able to walk stumbled into the hallway.

Mark glanced inside. The explosion had demolished most of the wall separating the two labs. A dark layer of smoke hung chest-high. Charred bodies littered the floor.

Désirée Bouchard lurched through the opening—disheveled, with blood-matted hair, her lab coat singed. One arm hung limp, the other outstretched as if striving to keep her balance.

Mark shifted Chakir's weight across his shoulders and reached out for her. "Come with us."

She exhibited no signs of recognition, yet clutched his arm, walking along beside them in a trance.

Now feeling responsible for getting both people to safety, Mark picked up the pace as the exit door came into view.

The second explosion erupted in a deafening roar. Everything around them shook—the walls, the floors, the ceiling.

Mark hung onto Chakir with all the strength he could muster and shoved Désirée to the floor as he dove for cover, bringing Chakir down with him.

A mega-wave of heat passed over them, followed by flying bits of shrapnel that stabbed into the walls with a speed and force that would kill any human standing. He closed his eyes and hung tight to Chakir and Desiree, holding his breath while it passed.

Farther away from the blast's epicenter this time, Mark escaped being rendered unconscious. After taking in a lungful of toxic fumes, the voice of self-preservation again yelled at him to get out of the building before something else happened.

He rose, inch by inch, first to his elbows, then his knees, holding onto Chakir and pulling Désirée up with him. He saw the exit, moving toward it, one footfall at a time, as if each step were through quicksand.

Bodies lay crumpled near blood-smeared walls, the victims of blunt-force trauma after being hurled through the air by hurricane-force winds. Weak human cries filled the air. Lethal bits of metal had found their targets.

At last, he pushed on the door.

It didn't budge.

He panicked. Despair washed over Mark. Hope vanished. He'd come all this way only to be held prisoner by a simple metal door. But desperation is a funny thing. It can stop you in your tracks, or send you headlong into an abyss. Now, it spurred a flashback of Kamryn delivering a roundhouse kick to Axel's chest that had sent him flying.

Mark gritted his teeth. Summoning every ounce of energy speeding through the universe, he channeled it into his leg and kicked his way to freedom.

The door sprang open.

Enveloped by a cloud of smoke and fumes, Mark hauled his two injured peers outside into blinding white floodlights. The ground rumbled with the sound of heavy footsteps. He squinted into the light. *The Cavalry*. Armored soldiers had come to save the lab rats once again, though not soon enough. Many more had lost their lives this day.

Platoons of soldiers in beautiful gleaming armor raced toward him. They were trailed by dozens of medics in gray, ballistic-proof bodysuits. Several converged on Mark to lift Chakir off his shoulders. Another pried Désirée's hand from his arm and led her away. Mark's head pounded as he bent over, hands on his knees, trying to get fresh air into his lungs. He turned to see a medic folding the Chakir's arms across his chest.

No, not possible.

Mark dropped to the ground, grabbing Chakir's wrist to check for a pulse. The skin was still warm, yet no heartbeat throbbed beneath it. Mark hung his head, clasping a fist to his chest, according Chakir the same respect as a fallen soldier as he fought back tears, or maybe his eyes were watering due to the smoke. He'd tried so hard—*so hard*—to save the little scientist. Chakir hadn't been a friend, but he could've been. He was a brilliant scientist who'd devoted his whole life to making the planet a better place in which to live.

Sickened at the loss of another admirable soul, Mark added him to the revered list of his brother, Eric Warren, and Maeve Sorayne, two others who'd given their lives for Terra. For a moment, three of their ghostly images hovered close enough to touch, then faded away.

"Sir. Sir?" the medic said, trying to get Mark's attention. "Please follow me to the triage center."

"I'm not leaving him."

"But, sir, you're bleeding. I need to move you to triage."

Incapable of moving, Mark shook his head.

"Okay," the medic relented. "Have it your way, sir." He jabbed a knockout battlefield cocktail of pain meds and nanites into Mark's bicep.

"Aw, shit," Mark mumbled just before he passed out.

Chapter 6

"Out of all the bad guys you helped arrest, Lucien Gérard is considered the worst, and the only one not currently incarcerated." Expecting a volatile reaction from Kamryn, Petra shifted uncomfortably before adding, "He escaped."

Kamryn stared at her in utter disbelief. "What the hell do you mean he *escaped?*"

Petra kept one eye on Kamryn while reading the hacked prison files opened on her screen. "He's classified as a Level 8 Violent Offender: convicted murderer, high escape risk, with a lengthy record. They sent him to Hámark Institution, a Canadian penitentiary on Prince Edward Island in Nova Scotia. A riot there last month lasted three days. The body count came to fifteen, including guards. At first, due to extensive damage, they thought Gérard was among the dead. But the autopsy proved otherwise. He's gone—in the wind—just disappeared."

Usually, Kamryn didn't drink anything stronger than beer, except today was as far from normal as she'd been in a very long time. She grabbed Mark's prized bottle of scotch and poured herself half a glass.

Desperate to find any good news, Petra's search continued. "Several people with the last name of Gérard work at The Grand Imperial. Hold on a minute…I'm checking birth records to see if there's a connection to your guy." Petra's face scrunched up. "Uh-oh…we have a match. There's one employee named Étienne. Lucien Gérard has a son of the same name."

Kamryn looked up to see Axel and Ohashi crowded in the doorway. She'd have to tell them. They were all at risk now, even the pilots. That painful episode had to be made public. "Take a seat. You're in danger, and it's my fault."

In two gulps, she emptied her glass, shuddering as the liquor burned its way to her gut. "Five years ago, I helped take down Lucien Gérard—better known as "Ghost"—for drug trafficking and murder. He made Vancouver his base of operations. Bigtime drug dealer for 'Gold Dust,' a euphoric, Glistrobrixmide-3V. Cheap to make, extremely addictive. Not afraid to get his hands dirty, either. Credited with murdering five of his rivals. He's smart, and he's vicious.

"I worked undercover as a girlfriend of a competitor he killed. Gérard took every one of us as part of the 'spoils' he was entitled to. A week later, a nasty little puke blew my cover. Gérard would have killed me if the DEA hadn't broken into his stronghold and arrested his whole crew." She poured more scotch. With much more to tell, Kamryn needed all the courage she could get. "Gérard knows how to use a knife. He's an expert. Could cut you fifty times, and you'd bleed, but you wouldn't die. My testimony nailed his ass to the cell door." Kamryn took a swig of scotch, remembering her unadulterated joy at the Guilty verdict.

Petra ventured a question in a small, soft voice. "I'm assuming you were the recipient of his blade, right?"

Kamryn rattled off the answer she'd given lots of times. "More than a hundred stitches, not counting staples and surgical glue. The nanites worked their miracles. Not a single physical scar—anywhere. Had some mental ones. Therapy taught me how to deal with those. Because I couldn't work undercover any longer, I left the DEA. Had something to prove to myself, so I joined the TMD and volunteered for an opening in the Armored Unit."

"I knew you were in the DEA," Petra said, "but I thought you were a detective. I had no idea exactly what you did. No wonder you joined the Armored Assault Unit. It must've seemed like a vacation."

Axel pulled them back to the present. "The drone came from our hotel. Étienne works there. He's Lucien Gérard's son. Okay, let's say the father contacted his son—he's looking for payback. Since Vancouver was your last known location, the search started there. Because we made reservations, your name is in their system. Simple to include your image in the hotel's facial recognition software—it's tied into law enforcement to ID anybody with outstanding warrants. Here's the part I have a problem with…coming back to Vancouver strikes me as a dumbass move for a big-time drug lord trying to avoid the law. You actually think Gérard would return to Vancouver right after escaping just to hunt for you?"

"Yes. My testimony about what I'd seen and heard, plus what he'd done to me, sealed his conviction." Kamryn finished off the last bit of scotch. "He threatened to kill me." Her hand trembled. She gripped the glass tighter, forcing her muscles to contract before someone else noticed. When the spasm passed, she got up and walked out, not about to let anyone view a Kamryn Fleming full-blown meltdown.

She headed straight for the onboard gym. A workout would harness her emotions into a force she could handle. Better to get a grip on herself now than let things spiral out of control. After shedding her jacket, Kamryn attacked the heavy bag as if it were Gérard, delivering five or six frantic kicks before the door opened.

Axel entered, locked the door, and dimmed the lights.

An eerie silence filled the room.

He began with a simple question in a calm voice. "What aren't you telling them?"

They stared at one another for a while before she answered.

"A lot." She knew how Axel worked. He didn't quit until he had all the answers—sometimes violent and non-stop, sometimes gentle but persistent. She'd seen him in action too many times.

Axel picked up a pair of martial arts sparring gloves specifically designed for partner training and impact absorption. He tossed them at her, peeling off his shirt before putting on a pair himself.

They circled each other, Axel's eyes never leaving her face. His soothing, husky voice zeroed in. "How long were you really with him—in his stable—before your cover was blown?"

Kamryn threw a quasi-friendly combination to Axel's chest. Not hard. Not soft, either. "Seventeen days."

He should have blocked, yet didn't. "And how did that happen?"

An overload of memories brought everything back. "Donnie Cooper, a mealy-mouthed scumbag I'd previously busted in a low-level sting, recognized me. Gérard paid him a five grand bonus." Rage coursed through her body. Cooper was a despicable, pint-sized troll, not five feet tall, and rumored to be a perv who liked young boys. Kamryn fought to erase his vile image from her mind.

"And how long did Gérard carve on you?"

"I don't know!" Kamryn snapped, then unloaded a flurry of quick, hard jabs at Axel's body.

He let a few of them connect, then parried left. "What else did he do?"

"Everything!" she screamed, delivering a blitzing side kick to his torso and a knee strike with the opposite leg.

Unfazed, Axel stepped in, folding his arms around her like a vise, squeezing until she quit resisting. "We'll get 'em, Kam," he whispered in her ear. "Don't worry, we'll get 'em."

Axel had everything now, plus a few bruises for his trouble. The release of secrets she'd kept hidden brought the sting of tears to her eyes, but Kamryn pushed them back. She'd rather slit her own wrists than wallow in self-pity. Instead, she allowed herself to wallow in loathing for Lucien Gérard. Her dark side had fantasized about slicing off his dick and stuffing it down his throat so far he choked to death. She held on to that thought and let it soothe her.

***

Two hair-raising klaxon screeches rang out of every speaker on the ship.

"Alert! Alert! Alert!" Malone roared over their comms. "Reports of explosions at TMD Headquarters!"

"Strap in!" Nguyen barked. "Liftoff in five…four…"

Axel pulled Kamryn out of the gym, running straight for the passenger cabin. The overhead lights switched to deep blue. Emergency walkway lights glowed along the floor.

Ohashi and Petra rushed in from the opposite direction, scrambling for chairs and harnesses. Both cybers attacked their tablets. Petra began tracking Mark's geolocator chip, muttering, "Come on, come on…"

Ohashi hacked the TMD system through a series of patches to a backdoor she'd planted before leaving the military for just this kind of emergency. It gave her access to real-time updates on the Damage Assessment Team's response—threat level, which complex had exploded, body counts, alerts to ground forces, and Space Command, should a retaliatory strike be deemed necessary.

Once airborne, Axel ran to the pilot's cabin. When it rains, it pours. The first Christmas he was actually looking forward to in years—canceled. Surveilled by a common hotel drone—from Vancouver, no less. Kamryn admitting an escaped drug kingpin—surely on Canada's 10 Most Wanted List—is out to kill her. And, to top it off, Mark was in the middle of a shitstorm—*again*. Icing on the cake.

Nguyen gave him a nod, pointing to the forward viewport. Axel took the jumpseat behind her.

Cool as ever, Nguyen studied her console, tapping away while she spoke. "Headquarters is Prohibited Airspace for civilian ships, but we can still skirt the edges. From this altitude, we'll get a general idea of what's happening. Be prepared for some tricky flying."

Axel looked out on a clear, dark night. A thousand feet below, Xenon searchlights swept over buildings in a crisscross pattern. Giant plumes of smoke rose above one building. People the size of ants covered the ground. Red emergency beacons dotted the open areas.

Although enemies had attacked other military installations, never Headquarters with its multi-layered safety protocols. Instinct said it must be connected to the Fulton intel they'd sent to General Dimitrios. Fulton won the electronics bid—maybe he'd planted collaborators or associates within the military to ensure his success.

Things started to fall into place. Fulton's partners designed weapons, AIs, and cyborgs. Axel needed to know what blew up, worried now that Mark—*no*, Axel refused to speculate in the negative. Mark was smart. He knew how to handle himself. Except the uneasiness didn't leave, it just burrowed deeper.

Beeps from Malone's console broke the silence. Sweat beaded on the pilot's forehead. His eyes were busy scanning for TMD ships while he guided *MAVREK* in a sweeping perimeter around the mission control nerve center of the entire Terran Military Defense command.

Before long, everyone had crowded in beside Axel.

"There were two explosions," Ohashi blurted out. "Cause unknown. Preliminary reports say the blasts originated from inside the AIRED Complex."

Petra's face grew pale as she clutched Kamryn's arm. "That's where Mark would have been."

"Hang on," Malone warned, taking evasive action. "Two warships spotted us."

The crew grabbed handholds along the bulkhead.

"I got it—I got it." Nguyen coded in a new 180-degree vector and swung *MAVREK* around on a path toward Richmond, Virginia.

Malone accelerated away at a velocity rivaling their escape from the pirates a few days before.

Petra's tablet pinged. "Yay! Mark's alive!" Her fingers danced over the tablet's screen. "Uh-oh…he's in the TMD hospital's Neurological Unit."

A collective sigh of relief filled the cabin.

Axel smiled at the news. To ease their concerns, he joked, "Don't worry, he's been hit in the head lots of times. He'll be fine. Probably got nurses fawning all over him." He ushered everyone out of the cockpit except for Kamryn. "Malone, when it's safe, head back to the flight school. We're not getting anywhere near HQ until things calm down." To Kamryn, he said, "This would be a good time to brief the pilots on the Gérard situation. In the meantime, I'll get our cybers to pull up data on Canada's Violent Fugitive Task Force, then widen the search parameters to known family and past associates. We'll be in the conference room when you're finished."

Axel veered toward the galley for caffeine and chocolate cookies, the lifeblood of his cyber sleuths.

Petra joined him. "How's Kamryn?"

"Strong."

She nibbled on a cookie. "Did you know about her…past?"

Axel shook his head. He identified with Kamryn one hundred percent. She hadn't shared the intimate details of her torture because it made her vulnerable. Axel also kept his past sealed shut. Volunteering personal intel was against his code of ethics, which included: protect your own, and kill the enemy before they kill you. Period. He'd protect Kamryn, as he had Mark, even if it cost him another arm and leg.

"I suspect this surfacing now is a complete surprise to her," Petra added. "No doubt it brought up memories she thought were long dead. She might need to talk to someone. Will you tell her I'd like to help—before things get, you know…out of control?" Her big eyes pleaded with him to say yes.

He turned to give Petra his full attention. Under normal circumstances, Axel wouldn't bother trying to explain Kamryn's state of mind. Instead, he spoke from his heart.

"When Kamryn and I wore armor on the battlefield, you couldn't tell us apart. We were equals. She can give orders and shoot as well as I can. Out of armor, I fight harder, but she fights smarter. We may not always agree, but we always respect each other." Axel crossed his arms and took a step closer. "Gérard violated her in unforgivable ways. She hates him. If we find him first, he *will* die. Do you understand?"

Petra pressed her lips together, nodding as large tears spilled over her cheeks. "A year ago, I might not have understood. But here, I've seen what the 'bonds of friendship' really mean." She sniffled, used a napkin to mop her face, and took the tray of cookies to Ohashi. Axel carried the carafe filled with steaming coffee.

Kamryn sat between them, compiling a list of known contacts. Petra started her search inside the Canadian prison system to locate or eliminate associates. Ohashi focused on Gérard's son.

Nguyen appeared in the doorway, signaling for Axel to follow her. "I know this has been one hell of a day, but there's another wrinkle."

"What now?"

"Malone got a comm from Donovan King. Someone's been asking strange questions about our ship. We need a more secluded place to land. Not a good idea to return to Lexington—home base may not be safe either."

Entering the pilot's cabin, he asked, "Does the flight school have surveillance?"

She grinned, sliding into her chair. "Keyed up, ready to view."

Axel watched a screen on her console. Two large men, one dark, one light, questioned the owner's young assistant about the *MAVREK*. Their features looked unusually similar, except for the color of their skin. The kid kept saying he couldn't tell them anything because he didn't know anything. After hearing his response for the umpteenth time, the men walked away with blank expressions on their faces. They left no business card or message. They did leave clear closeup headshots, perfect for the super processor in the Science Lab called Hercules. It had state-of-the-art deep neural network algorithms for planetwide facial recognition.

"Send that clip to Hercules, please," Axel said. "Now, if you don't mind, I'm going to stay up here until we land."

Malone swerved out over the ocean, nosing the ship south along the Virginia coastline. He winked at Nguyen. "See if you can find us a nice quiet spot, one not too far from a Chinese takeout or a burger joint. I've got a hankering for comfort food after all this excitement."

"No," Axel warned, with a jolt. "People are looking for us, and *I* don't want to be found. Set a course for Arizona, the Sonoran Desert region, south of Phoenix. I know that area.

Hiding there will make us a hard target. Kamryn's got an escaped killer after her, and we just missed two trackers by less than an hour." He placed a hand on Nguyen's shoulder. "Let me know when you get there. Petra and I will pull the first watch while everyone else gets some shut-eye. And send that flight school clip back to Hercules, wouldja? I need to check on something."

Axel planned on being awake until morning, so he showered first, the hot water acting as a lubricant to his tired muscles. Dressed in black workout togs, he visited the gym to perform specific routines for his cyborg limbs before padding barefoot into the conference room.

Petra sat alone staring at the large screen, her short, pink-tipped hair disheveled, signs of weariness in the creases under her eyes. Nevertheless, she continued to poke at images from the clip. "Everybody else is asleep. What a day, huh? It hasn't been this crazy since we were on Mars."

Axel circled around to sit on the other side of her. That's when he saw her small pulse pistol on the table. He felt a twinge of conscience. Maybe she thought he could no longer keep her safe. "You scared?"

"Nope, I'm prepared." She made a funny but determined face. "I remember the evac in Brazil when you saved my life. Then in Ecuador when I got separated from the squad with no comm or tablet and you still found me. That's when I was an inexperienced newbie. I know better now. I'm a veteran. Been off-planet. Got shot. Got a tattoo." She smiled, the fatigue fading away. "I'm fine. Was kinda looking forward to spending the holidays in St. Louis with my family, but this is my home away from home. You're my extended family, so I'm good with being here." She glowed with satisfaction. "Besides, I have a surprise for you." She swiveled the screen for him to see. "Ta-da!"

Axel leaned forward to inspect the biometrically mapped faces. Both had been turned from 2D images into 3D morphable models covered with red grid lines. Up close, they were identical, including a detailed map of their eyeballs. When he'd first seen Nguyen's clip, he'd suspected they were cyborgs. Not anymore.

"AIs. Human-looking AIs," he muttered.

"Yes!" Petra nodded, unable to contain herself. After she attached the holographic equipment to her screen, they watched as a hazy cloud coalesced, suspended in midair above the table. It fused into an image then split in half, each becoming a separate form. The figures shimmered like a mirage while materializing more than a foot tall. She cued the hologram to play in 3D from the moment they started questioning the kid, but without the sound, zooming in on their upper bodies. She turned to Axel and watched his reaction.

More to himself than her, Axel said, "They're breathing. Blinking. Swallowing."

"You got it! Now listen to their voices." She tapped the screen to cue up the conversation. "Every human voice is unique because of the size of our individual vocal chords and articulator use patterns—or how each person learns to speak. Watch their speech wave displays on the spectrograph."

On a split image, two separate graphs showed blue lines rising and falling within the exact parameters without a single fluctuation.

"This is *humanly* impossible." Petra beamed, then popped the last cookie into her mouth.

Chapter 7

A few hours before sunrise, Malone landed their pale bronze ship in the Arizona desert. It rested near a rock outcropping in the southwestern corner along the Mexico border. Axel jumped out to drape tarps over the fifteen foot royal blue wingspan, covering the *MAVREK* logo emblazoned on both sides. Sitting on his haunches, he picked up a handful of sand, feeling an immediate connection as it drained through his fingers. Surprised by how much he missed the desert's wide-open landscape, Axel soaked up the desolate silence, the complete lack of light pollution. He looked skyward to stare at the crescent of Luna against the dark expanse of a gazillion visible stars. From far away, the night carried sounds of two coyotes talking to each other. He smiled.

Ohashi poked her head out of the hatch. "There's an update on the explosion at HQ."

"On my way." He followed her in to the conference room, surprised to see the entire crew, pilots included, waiting for him. "Let's hear it."

As she had in the military, Ohashi remained standing to give her report. "After the TMD interrogated Fulton, they located a pair of fully functional prototypes, which were transported to HQ's AIRED Complex. Both units were scanned for all known hazards. Holographic copies were made—twenty-three for the AI lab, seventeen for Cybernetic's. Five hours later the prototypes exploded within minutes of each other. They were booby-trapped. As yet, no one has figured out how. The blasts nearly demolished both labs. Thirteen fatalities so far, fifteen injured by burns, shrapnel, and toxic gas."

Ohashi bowed her head and brought a fist to her chest in a TMD ritual of respect for the souls lost, as did everyone else.

Seconds passed before Ohashi continued. "TMD is calling it a staggering loss of world-class scientists. Less than an hour after the explosions, the Prime Council issued a unanimous directive: Dimitrios and General Carmen De Palma of Space Command have orders to apprehend the three ships on their way to Ganymede by any means necessary." Ohashi's voice dropped an octave. "Also, there's been a flurry of super-encrypted messages sent to Mars. It would take us hours to decrypt them. I can confirm, however, that three Martian warships left their exosphere on a vector toward Ganymede."

Ohashi sank into her chair with a sigh of relief.

Malone nodded to include Nguyen. "We researched the Terran ships. *Fultronics* is a Goliath-class hauler, big and slow, perfect for transporting mega rig drilling equipment. Not fast, by any means, unless Fulton poured money into it. I'm told it's also carrying two hundred or more people. That means lots of food, water, and supplies. I bet they're jammed in so tight if one person farts another one gets blown out an airlock."

Kamryn snickered, then caught herself. "Sorry."

Nguyen added, "Both *Kailani* and *Stellaria* are Pathfinder-class ships; smaller, faster, maximum payload of a hundred seventy-five people all—squished in with supplies, science equipment, and electronics. Not what I'd call a comfy ride. In South America, I saw this model turned into a paramilitary ship fitted with black market weapons. It was dangerous." She waved a dismissive hand. "But I was deadly."

"We have news of Mark," Petra said. "He's out of the Neurological unit. Near as I can tell he's in a Recovery room, classified as walking wounded."

A beep sounded.

Everyone's attention focused on Petra's tablet. She stared at the screen as an image of a white-haired man in blue scrubs appeared, none other than the head trauma surgeon from their old base in North Dakota. "Major *Torance?*"

"Yes, my dear," the doctor whispered. "A call went out for surgeons after the explosions at HQ, so I hopped on a shuttle. I'm in Norfolk."

"Have you seen Mark? Is he okay? We've been so worried."

"Oof, he'll be good as new in a couple of hours. I'm with Warren now. He's coming off heavy sedation from this morning. No worse than what he's done to himself with alcohol." The doctor chuckled. "Nanite protocol's almost finished. He got a little banged up, but the vest saved his life. It was riddled with shrapnel. He did get a snoot full of toxic gases though. Might have destroyed a few brain cells. He has plenty, so no permanent damage. He's lucky. Many weren't."

Petra spoke up. "When Mark's released from the hospital is he still under orders to stay, or can he leave?"

"The research is continuing. They've set up new temporary labs. Scientists from across the planet are volunteering for the project. TMD wants the technology that blew up their house and they'll do whatever it takes to acquire it. I can assure you since Warren's a survivor, his knowledge is considered essential. I doubt he'd be allowed to leave. What's more, I don't believe he'd *want* to."

"Major, this is Von Radach."

"Axel, how are you, son?"

"Good, sir. I'll get right to it. We have intel vital to the current situation."

"Oh, hells bells." The doctor grimaced. "What is it now?"

"We have proof there are human-looking AIs walking around in the Norfolk area." Axel added, "Two were tracking our ship."

"Proof?"

"Yes, sir. Video and holographic."

"Very well, send it to me." Torance stifled a yawn, wiped his eyes. "I'll walk it up the chain of command immediately. Where are you now?"

"Far away, sir. That's all I can say. Contact us when you have news. Good luck, Major—oh, and tell Mark to get his lazy ass out of bed."

Axel looked to his left. "Petra?"

"Already sent," she replied, a smug grin tugging at her lips.

Axel stood. "I'm ordering a good hot meal for everyone. The night watch will get some rest while Kamryn takes the day watch and Ohashi hunts for the Canadians."

***

Mark felt like shit. He tried to remember where he was, but his brain refused to cooperate. Had he gotten drunk?

"Captain Warren?"

Mark's eyes popped open. In the span of three nanoseconds, he remembered everything: the explosions, Chakir, Désirée, death, and destruction. Everything.

"Where am I? How long have I been out?"

"You're in HQ Hospital's recovery room—been here for three hours." A youthful male nurse in green scrubs stood at his bedside. The name on his chest ID badge identified him as Jared O'Connor. "How do you feel, sir?"

"Like the morning after my cousin's bachelor party when we ran out of tequila and started drinking scotch." The hospital's antiseptic fragrance exacerbated his throbbing headache, although Mark was thankful he now had hearing in both ears.

"Hmm, that bad, huh?" O'Connor watched multicolored graph lines waver across a nearby machine's screen, receiving data from the wireless electrodes on Mark's chest and forehead.

"You're recovering from shrapnel wounds and toxic fume inhalation." O'Connor tapped a message into his tablet as he spoke. "Your doctor, Major Torance, said to notify him when you regained consciousness."

"*Torance?* Is he here?"

O'Connor nodded. "Within minutes of the second explosion, all senior TMD Combat Trauma Surgeons with recent battlefield experience were ordered to respond to the disaster. Major Torance arrived in the first wave. He mentioned you'd been a patient—several times."

Mark frowned with memories of Torance treating his dislocated shoulder, broken hand, pulse gun wound, and various injuries from Coulter's torture. "Where is he?" Mark asked, pressing a button on the small device attached to his bed which self-administered pain meds. Nothing happened.

"Left over an hour ago. Didn't say when he'd be back."

Mark pressed the button again. No response. "Don't take this personally, but where are the pretty nurses?"

O'Connor chuckled. "They got off shift just before you woke up."

"Well, since I don't get to look at any cute little nurses, you need to give me a painkiller for this headache."

"How bad is it on a scale of one to ten?"

"Twelve."

"We need to wait five more minutes. While you were unconscious, they did neuroimaging to check for injuries and inserted more nanites to counteract whatever the toxic gas nanoparticles might have done. You can't get more pain meds until the nanites run their course."

"Why did you wake me up if I can't have female nurses or pain meds?" Mark snapped.

"Because I said so."

Major Torance's voice preceded him. The white-haired doctor breezed in wearing fresh blue scrubs. His suntanned face held a broad smile and pale blue eyes.

"You always were a cranky patient, Warren." He did a quick check of the machine's readouts. "Okay, O'Connor, I've got this now."

"Yes, sir."

When they were alone, Torance said, "I have news."

"I do too, Major. Mine may be related to the explosion. I overheard a conversation between two officers that sounded as if they were sympathizers of Wade Fulton's plans." Mark related the entire incident, then tucked the hair behind his cybernetic left ear, offering to let Torance inspect it.

"Excellent work," he remarked. "I read in your chart the operation was done here a few months ago…at the exact time Dimitrios got shot. Rather coincidental, wouldn't you say?"

"I can't say." Mark tried rubbing away his headache. "We need to locate Lieutenant Craig Foster to find out where those men went and if he identified them."

Torance produced his tablet, then tapped in a query, showed the image to Mark. "Is that Foster?"

Mark nodded.

"Okay…I'll check to see if he's a patient first in case he got caught in the explosion. If not, I'll send a request for him to report here A-*SAP*. Be right back with your pain meds."

"Wait. There's a woman…"

Torance gave him a lopsided grin. "Isn't there always?"

"Désirée Bouchard, another scientist from the Cybernetics Lab. I helped her out of the building. Please check on her, too, sir."

"Be right back."

Torance did not come right back, and Mark's headache, if he could even call it an ache, had graduated to a fifteen. He grabbed the bed rails with both hands to keep from screaming obscenities.

A voice said, "Relax."

Blissful euphoria streamed through Mark's body. The pain level sank back to twelve, then ten as the drugs blocked pain signals from traveling along the nerves to his brain cells. Not realizing he'd been holding his breath, Mark heard himself panting, as if he were slowing down after running a marathon. He opened his eyes to see Torance holding an injector.

"The gases you inhaled were highly toxic. I'm going to release you in an hour, but you'll be fitted with a KorVu monitor. It has internal sensors to activate nanites already in your system. Until you rebuild a natural immunity, you'll be susceptible to the slightest exposure of any toxic substance."

O'Connor delivered a new uniform, the monitor, and Mark's old boots.

Torance waited for him to leave. He adjusted the black KorVu band, similar to an Old Earth physical activity tracker, around Mark's left wrist. Activating it, he said, "Get dressed while I tell my news. Your friends were close by during the explosions. They've since left." Torance related the intel given to him by Axel while showing Mark the footage on his tablet. "I had to show this to three generals before it got to Dimitrios, but he's seen it."

"So the brass knows there's irrefutable proof more AIs are roaming around out in the general population. And some are after my team?"

"Yes, but don't waste time worrying about them. Axel and Kamryn were adept at taking care of their troops way before you came along." Torance lowered his voice. "Dimitrios wants you to bring Colonel Falana Ongaru, the new Project Manager for Cybernetics, up to speed on your research."

"Why me?" Mark stood half-dressed in gray uniform pants. After confirming the two knives were still hidden away, he put on the boots.

Torance ticked off points on his fingers. "First, you alerted them that a containment field should have been in place. Second, you survived. As of now, you're one of the healthiest scientists left of the original cybernetics group. Three, putting you in the hub of activity increases opportunities for your cybernetic ear to be of value."

"You're turning me into a *spy?*" Mark asked in disbelief. "I *hate* spies."

"Suck it up, son. I know about Chakir…and Bouchard. How many more of your colleagues do you want to see die?"

"Is Désirée…?"

"No, she's recovering. I'll take you to see her before you leave."

Mark looked at the tiny pink shrapnel scars covering his arms, not yet healed by the nanite protocol. Sullen and headstrong, he said, "I want a vest, or I'm not leaving this room."

***

Kamryn leaped out of her chair. "Étienne Gérard is dead," she announced over her comm. "Apparently, in a freak accident at the hotel in Vancouver two hours ago. The hotel called for law enforcement to remove two drunken customers who were fighting. Étienne thought the officers were there to arrest him and he shot a cop. You don't get away with shooting a member of The Force in Canada. He was killed."

"Well, good. That's the end of the hotel drones." Axel clasped his arms behind his head, leaning back, looking pleased. "Is his father in the vicinity? Can we point the Canadians to any location where Lucien might be hold up?"

"Not yet," Ohashi replied. "We've been monitoring the son's communications and got nothing. Zip. Nada. He lived in an apartment with surveillance. I hacked into it and again got zilch."

"What about dead drops, third parties, smoke signals? Hell, I don't know." Kamryn chewed on her bottom lip almost hard enough to draw blood. "Mark would ask, 'What did Étienne do after his father escaped that he didn't do before? Like dentist or doctor's appointments. Eating or drinking at different places. Getting his hair cut in a new place.' You know, Mark's normal 'outside the box' thinking."

Simultaneous lightning bolts hit both cybers. After a flurry of screen taping, Petra cried, "Jumpin' Josephat! The son started going to a barber shop every other day once his dad escaped."

Ohashi tossed her a sidelong glance. "What's *gee-hose-a-fat?*"

"I don't know. My gramma used to say it. She lived in Ne*bras*ka."

"Okay, work backward from there," Kamryn said. "The owner, employees—widen the net to their families, crosscheck for any associates of Gérard, in or out of prison." Kamryn experienced a small dose of relief with hopes the drone situation had ended. Plus, Axel couldn't have picked a better place to hide their pale bronze ship than on the sand of the Arizona desert. Malone had assured them he'd found no roads, thermal heat signatures, or man-made structures for hundreds of square miles. Nguyen kept scanning for any potential threats from above.

Still, Kamryn hadn't slept. She'd been plagued by dreadful visions of Gérard torturing her friends the same as he'd done to her. She was coming apart, piece by piece. All her carefully stitched together innermost fears were unraveling in full view of the whole crew. She felt naked, vulnerable, exposed. Those sensations were so unfamiliar, she had trouble dealing with them.

Even after working out in the gym for an hour, peaceful sleep continued to evade her, yet the nightmarish visions returned. Kamryn had avoided caffeine and alcohol or anything else that might bring on another episode of hand tremors, afraid someone might notice. Self-medicating would eliminate that possibility—although, with Étienne dead, it meant one less threat. Lucien Gérard and human-looking AIs were enough.

Besides, Kamryn reminded herself, she and Axel were Armored Assault soldiers, the elite of all TMD units. They'd both been shot, were still alive, and had fought enemies before on two fronts in South America and Africa. Their ship was full of smart, courageous soldiers. On Mars, Axel demonstrated he could not only look the part of a criminal, but as act like one as well. Kamryn suspected his younger years were more than a bit shady, a definite asset in catching Gérard.

"Whoa boy," Petra breathed.

"I see it, too," Ohashi confirmed.

"What?" Kamryn demanded.

"Hercules confirmed a faceprint of Gérard clearing a checkpoint," Ohashi said, adding, "but he's changed his appearance. Skin color is dark brown, with wiry black hair and matching beard."

"Okay, so where is he?"

"Uh…San Diego."

Kamryn didn't know she had a panic button until this moment. "How did he get through that security point?"

"How do you think?" Axel rubbed his thumb over his first two fingertips. "Maybe he paid somebody."

"But it's less than two hundred miles from our current location." Now Kamryn's panic meter registered a six—and climbing. "How can you be so relaxed?"

"Don't worry, Gérard has no idea where we are," Axel said, tucking hands behind his head while staring at the ceiling. "What's the first gateway below San Diego? Panama. What's there? The Panama Canal. Boats. I'd guess he has a contact there who could help get him hired on a ship bound for Africa or Australia and off the American continent. Foreign flagged ships often 'forget' to check an employee's IDs or backgrounds to fill their maritime crew rosters, especially if the cargo isn't a hundred percent legitimate."

"We'll lose him down there." Kamryn glared at Axel, wondering how he stayed so calm.

"Ohashi, get Gérard's new image to Canada—by way of the TMD, of course. Put it on a Canadian Ten Most Wanted with a Murder warrant and a million-credit reward for information leading to the arrest of…you know the rest. Nah, make it *two* million. Blanket every security checkpoint south of San Francisco in case he tries to double back, including all land, space, and shipping lines in Panama." Axel looked at Kamryn with all the self-confidence in the world. "We'll box him in—no sweat."

Chapter 8

Torance escorted Mark to a hospital room with two beds. Curtains were drawn around the left one. Désirée, awake, was propped up in the right one wearing a pale pink hospital gown. Her whole face lit up at the sight of him. She looked gorgeous, even sexy with a white bandage above her temple, peeking out between strands of long, dark, wavy hair. Her eyes were the exact color of a sapphire he'd seen once in a jeweler's case while shopping for a Mother's Day gift. Sparkling bright today, they held no hint of the earlier horrors she'd gone through.

She motioned for him to come closer. "Captain Warren, I have been told you were my savior."

Mark's heart melted—but nothing below his belt did. Her earthy tone struck a definite chord in his libido. He managed to reply, "I just steered you toward the door. And please, call me Mark."

She offered her small hand. He enfolded it between both of his. Nanite protocols had nearly healed the shrapnel wounds and singed skin on both her arms. They were beautiful arms. He was hooked.

"You must call me Désirée." She pulled him closer. "I have seen the images they took of me. Without you, I never could have made it out alive. You helped someone else, too, yes? A friend? How is he?"

Mark's gaze fell. He shook his head. A deep sadness returned with thoughts of Chakir. Mark made a mental note to find out if the scientist had family, to send them condolences and flowers for the funeral.

"*Mon Dieu*," she said, a catch in her throat. "I am so sorry for your loss." She sniffled. "My lab partner, Lenard Bowman, is in Intensive Care. No one will tell me how he is doing."

Mark looked over at Torance, lounging in the doorway. The doctor nodded and walked off.

"But you are in uniform." Her eyes widened as if just noticing. "Are you released? So soon?"

"I'm a hardy soul," he joked. "This isn't my first explosion."

A nurse in green scrubs entered. Her hair was more salt than pepper, her disposition surly. "Sir, I need the room, please."

"Yes, ma'am, I'm leaving." He patted Desiree's hand. "A makeshift lab is up and running. The new Cybernetics Project Manager has ordered all survivors to report as soon as possible. I was on my way there, but wanted to check on you first."

"I will join you, Mark, when they release me, yes?" The lilt of her accent sounded musical.

"Perfect." Mark turned warm and happy inside. "What's your specialty?"

"Neurotech—Autonomous Systems Interface."

Well, crap. There's no way they'd be working together. Why did all the women choose Neurology? In the field of Cybernetics, his Xenobiology specialty of combining bioware with metals was at the opposite end of the spectrum from her Neuro-ASI field.

The dour-faced nurse moved into his space, hands on her hips.

"I'd better be going. Glad to see you're okay."

He cussed the nurse under his breath as he walked out. Halfway down the corridor, Mark joined Torance at the nurses' station.

The doctor's shoulders sagged with glum resignation. The doctor heaved a deep sigh. "They added Lenard Bowman's name to the list of fatalities three hours ago."

Mark hadn't known Bowman but his burden of sadness felt heavier at hearing another scientist had died.

"Report back here tomorrow before dinner. I'll check the data on your KorVu monitor." Torance lowered his voice. "I may have other news for you by then."

Mark squinted at him in confusion.

Torance mouthed the word, *Axel*.

"Sure thing, Major. I'll be here at 1800."

The elevator doors opened adjacent to the nurses' station. Lieutenant Craig Foster exited, bleary-eyed, but clean shaven, wearing a fresh uniform and a broad smile. "Captain Warren, I'm sure glad to see you. I didn't know you'd made it out until a few hours ago. I'm here to show you to the temporary AIRED facility. It's been set up in the Gym."

Mark introduced Foster to Torance as he motioned both men into the stairwell. "Foster, did you follow those two men?"

"Yessir, clear back to their offices. I have the information you wanted." Foster held up his tablet.

Mark handed his to the Lieutenant. "Transfer the intel to my tablet while you tell us what you found."

Torance relaxed against the wall with his arms crossed, not participating, just listening.

The young Lieutenant glanced from Torance to Mark. He looked flustered, but complied. "Majors Darren Ashley and Micah Whitaker are the men you ordered me to follow. They're assigned to the Defense Contract Management Division."

Mark's suspicions were correct. "Major, this substantiates the pro-Fulton conversation I overheard. Foster's new intel points to them being much more than sympathizers. Their department awarded the contract to *Fultronics* for the new Europa Mission. Money might have changed hands, which would elevate them to partners—and traitors."

Torance straightened, leaning forward with pinched brows, his mouth set into a hard line.

Turning toward the Lieutenant, Mark asked, "Did you hear any of their conversations?"

Foster's face took on a pained expression. "I knew you were going to ask me that, sir." He remained silent.

Mark grew impatient. "Well? Don't keep it a secret, Lieutenant."

Foster squirmed as if he were standing on hot coals. "I only got close enough to hear a couple of things. Ashley, the shorter one, said, 'I think it's time we sent a communique to *Kailani*.' Later, Whitaker said, *'knee vol-nush-sya.'*"

Mark's tone edged toward irritation. "What the hell does that mean?"

Foster backed away. "Not a clue, sir."

"Wait." Mark cued the translation app on his tablet, thrust it in front of Foster's face and nodded. "Translate into the English language."

Foster obliged by repeating the phrase.

Two seconds later the genderless translator's voice responded with, "*Ne volnuysya*, is the Russian equivalent of *'don't worry'* in English."

"That fat little SOB just verbally connected the dots to Fulton's cohort Chang, who's on *Kailani*," Mark gushed with excitement. "The other jerk who gave me the evil eye is speaking Russian, a solid link to Stepanov, who's on *Stellaria*. Both are headed to Ganymede. It sounds incontrovertible to me, Major."

"I agree," Torance said. "However, I caution you against assuming these two are the only ones involved. We have no idea yet how far this conspiracy may go. The guilty parties have no conscience. They're in it strictly for material gain. Treachery is a virus—easily spread, hard to wipe out."

"Foster," Mark asked, "where are these two men?"

"I don't know, sir, but I do know that since the explosions, no one's being allowed off base. Complete lockdown. The only people being allowed on base are the new scientists—although the security protocols are twice as stringent as they were when you arrived."

Torance placed heavy hands on the shoulders of the two younger men. "It's imperative neither of you shares this information with anyone. I mean *no one*. Consider that an order. I'll update our friend and advise you of their decision." Torance grabbed the stairwell's door handle. "Now go. I need to find a clean uniform and make another trip."

***

Axel had persuaded everyone to leave their desert haven for the unknown perils of Panama. As a youth growing up in Phoenix, he'd learned enough Spanish to threaten the bullies and sweet talk the girls out of their…clothes. True, he hadn't spoken it much since, but still remembered how to intimidate bullies. Besides, most business people spoke English.

Nguyen found a quiet spot to land outside Villa Zaita about ten miles north of Panama City, the land of high humidity, palm trees, and sunshine.

As a disguise, Petra (again) dyed Kamryn's hair blonde—a natural sandy shade this time, not the bombshell color she'd been on Mars. The balmy 85-degree weather made it difficult to pack more than a few weapons. They left the ship wearing vests, knives, a couple stun batons, and small pulse guns hidden under black exercise togs. Only Axel and Kamryn were 'boots on the ground' for this mission. Their comms would remain open, the cybers were tracking their chips, the pilots could pick them up on a moment's notice.

Edge of the Rings

The smell of food from an open-air market signaled a place to buy local clothing. They wandered past booths offering local food and, ones full of colorful apparel, listening to the locals trading in several languages. Axel bought an ugly blue shirt, worn open over a black tank to cover his vest with khaki pants, Kamryn a mustard and mauve flowered shirt over a black tank with black cargo pants. Dressed as natives in cheap tropical clothes, sunglasses, woven straw hats, and tan leather huaraches, they took a cab to the waterfront in Panama City, got out a block from a bar called *Los Navgante,* and went to work.

In a practiced, covert motion, Axel turned away from prying eyes to checked his comm. "Ohashi, Petra, are you tracking us?"

"Yes," Petra answered. "And I'm glad we stayed on board because the part of town you're in has the highest crime rate."

Kamryn wrinkled her nose. "It smells like dead fish baking in the sun here."

Axel needed Kamryn focused on the present, not distracted by her past. They did not need things to go wrong now. A simple trick that helped his troops take the edge off before battle might work. Axel began with a tease.

"I take you to the nicest places, and all you do is complain."

"Nicest places?" Kamryn spread her hands, looking down the narrow, winding street crowded with dives and other disreputable storefronts.

He answered, "Portland? Luna? Mars?"

"I got shot in Portland, arrested on Luna, clobbered by a cyborg *and* shot at on Mars."

"At least we got to blow shit up."

"I do enjoy pyrotechnics," she said. "Think we can blow something up before we leave?"

"I didn't bring any party favors."

She flashed a naughty smile. "I did."

"Well, then, Sergeant Fleming, we may just have to light that candle."

"Good idea, Sergeant Von Radach. I'm ready whenever you are."

They entered the worst saloon Axel had been in since the Dead Dog Bar on Mars. Although none of the dozen or so customers noticed, Kamryn and he were the cleanest, soberest, and best dressed people in the joint. Behind the bar, a string of green lights, every other one burned out, hung over a cracked, plate-glass mirror decorated with bullet holes.

Kamryn shuddered. "Whew."

"What's wrong now, Princess?"

"Dead fish," she croaked, flapping a hand to wave away the aroma.

He tried to hide a smile. "I thought you liked fish."

"Lobster and shrimp, on a plate, in a nice restaurant."

"We'll head to San Francisco when we're finished here, okay?"

"Is that a bribe?"

"A reward, and don't be so picky."

Axel showed Gérard's image to the bartender, saying the man was a missing friend.

He gave them a blank stare, then shook his head.

They ordered beers, faded into the corner shadows, eyed drunken patrons stumbling in and out for over an hour. No target spotted. On to the next watering hole, and the next, for five more hours. Given Gérard's drug history, Ohashi fed them data on bars with the highest arrests. For the most part, they concentrated on criminal haunts and drug dens. After a while, Axel saw the hopeless look settle over Kamryn's face. He also sensed a hollow feeling in his gut. They stopped for dinner at *La Sirena Azul*, The Blue Mermaid, which had a much better clientele.

A young, dark-skinned waitress who spoke English took their order. Something about her smile prompted Axel to strike up a conversation. She confided her that father worked as a cook at Bora Bora, a greasy spoon down the block. Axel showed her the newest image of Gérard on his tablet.

She bobbed her head. "Yes."

Surprised, yet wary of her powers of observation, Axel showed her images of Mark, Malone, Nik Roman, and Major Torance.

She shook her head to each of them.

He offered Gérard's image again.

"Yes."

"Where? When?"

"Bora Bora. Today at breakfast."

When the woman, Henrietta, got off her shift thirty minutes later, it was mid-evening, near dark in the narrow winding streets. They walked her back to the 24-hour hole-in-the-wall café where she claimed to have seen their target. Axel entered with the waitress, leaving Kamryn concealed outside in the waterfront's twilight. He learned from her father that Gérard had eaten there twice in the last forty-eight hours. Axel pulled out a wad of cash, and divided it between the girl and her father with strict orders to keep silent. To intimidate the old man, Axel bent a large cooking utensil in half with his augmented hand, then gave it to him. The old man unquestionably understood.

Outside, Axel joined Kamryn, tucked into a shrouded hidey-hole. "The cook identified him eating there twice—alone. Let's go topside. That roof across the way should give us a clear view of the entire street. You up for a little climbing?"

Kamryn was ecstatic now that two eyewitnesses had ID'd Gérard. "Thought you'd never ask."

He led her through an alley around behind the buildings. One rickety fire escape ladder from the last century led to the rooftop. "No easy way to do this."

"Is there ever?"

Axel laced his fingers together, giving her a boost to the fourth rung. She made it over the top with the grace of a panther. Kamryn crouched, scanning the alley while he jumped halfway up the ladder with his augmented strength, before joining her on the roof. It felt stable enough to set up surveillance.

He sprawled out on his stomach facing the street, placing his weapons on the surface of the roof, positioning them just so, as if he were arranging silverware before a meal. "Gérard's not a novice. Since he's out of jail, I'm damn sure he'll do whatever it takes not to go back. You said he was smart and vicious. Well, we're twice as smart and three times as lethal." Axel scooped up rubble, looked at Kamryn while crushing it into dust with his left hand. "When Gérard realizes every gateway terminal has a copy of his image with a two million credit reward, he'll get rattled. Rattled people make mistakes."

"So, we just sit here to wait until he shows?"

"This is an Old World police stakeout. Not much to do except…" He surveyed the street in both directions. "Ohashi, blanket this area with mini drones, you copy?"

"Read you 5 by 5, baby drones will be on their way in ten minutes."

"I want the tightest pixels you can set for facial recognition with the widest possible coverage. We need to know where Gérard's coming from and where he's going." Waiting for the drones, Axel rolled over onto his back and shut his eyes with one arm under his head, the other across his chest. "Stay frosty, Kam."

"Frosty? I've been sweatin' like a whore in church since we left the ship. Going from frigid to fry in the last twenty-four hours is taxing my exocrine system, and you're taking a nap."

Chapter 9

Kamryn sat next to Axel, listening to his breathing even out, watching as his chest rose and fell slower than normal. Power naps energized him. Kamryn thought she should take one as well. The roof might become their home for a while.

As for staying alert, it didn't take much for Kamryn to boost her already heightened state of awareness. She instinctively noticed more details of her surroundings, recalled specific information without effort. She remembered the waitress' chipped canine tooth, the antique gold band on her pinky finger, coming down heavier on her right leg so she favored her left. The eleven meandering blocks she'd walked into the squalid waterfront district hunting for Gérard held dives, gin joints and dens of iniquity populated by every fringe element in this Panamanian melting pot. The prevalent smell of dead fish, burnt circuits, stale beer and sweat—an overpowering stench of sweat—lay over it all.

Kamryn could identify Gérard just by his hands, or the sound of his voice, his syntax, the way he walked, even his posture. Blindfolded, she could pick him out of a lineup from nothing more than the sound of his laughter. Everything about him was seared into her brain. That's what torture does to you.

Her tablet vibrated with an update from the ship. A small army of drones, identified by blue dots on her tablet's map, were speeding toward her location. The blue dots grew in size as they closed in on her rooftop. Kamryn hung over the ledge, deploying each small drone separately. She moved the dots with her fingertips to strategic sites along the street. By double tapping the dots, she sent a code instructing it to find a pre-programmed type of solid surface. The drone adhered to it, thus activating its signal to a red dot. She remotely triggered all full-motion video feeds—FMVs—to stream directly into the ship. Only confirmed faceprints would be sent to their tablets. As usual, one drone refused to cooperate no matter how much fiddling she did. It was snagged on something.

Axel stirred, yawned, and opened his eyes. "What'd I miss?"

"Drones arrived, they're in position, but one's hung up. I'm going to fix it. I'll bring water back."

"I'll go."

"No, I have to pee—and I'm not peeing up here on the roof—so I'm going."

Kamryn shimmied down the ladder and dropped to the alley. She glanced up, spotted Axel standing as lookout. Passing around the front of the building, she walked south through an almost deserted street for half a block until she saw the malfunctioning device hung up in a massive spider web under the eaves. "Well shit," Kamryn muttered. She'd sooner go toe-to-toe with an enemy twice her size than deal with spiders.

Axel commed her, sounding edgy. "What's wrong?"

"Nothin'. Gimme a minute."

She climbed on the storefront's windowsill to shoot a narrow beam of plasma under the eaves. It not only cooked the spiders and the nest, but also burned a three-inch-wide hole straight through the roof. Once freed, the wayward drone fell into her hands, a little warm to the touch, but otherwise it looked okay.

"Got it." She returned to their building, tossing it up to Axel. "See if you can fix it. I'll be back in a minute."

Kamryn walked in the opposite direction looking for a clean business that might have a restroom. Not finding an acceptable level of cleanliness, she located a trash module. "I feel like a homeless person when I have to pee outside."

Axel chuckled over the comm. "It doesn't bother me."

She purchased bottles of water in a bodega, making sure the lids were sealed and sanitary, then joined Axel on the rooftop.

"Does it work?"

"Yeah, but it's not streaming the FPVs to the ship. It's coming straight to our tablets."

"Okay, we'll deploy it directly across from the restaurant. Maybe get lucky if Gérard walks in."

Tablet in hand, Axel steered the drone over the ledge, lowered it to just above eye level, and double tapped the blue dot. The obedient little device stuck itself to the wall of their building. Its dot turned red. A real-time vid looking into the Bora Bora's front window appeared on both their tablets. Perfect.

***

Mark and Lieutenant Foster walked through a veritable maze of corridors before reaching the temporary AIRED research site. The cavernous gymnasium had been split lengthwise, with thirty cubicles for Artificial Intelligence on the left, twenty-four cubicles for Cybernetics on the right.

Foster located Colonel Ongaru from the sound of her authoritative voice issuing commands to several new scientists. Not young, inexperienced, or amateurs by any means, they were profoundly uninitiated to the military's code of SOP, Standard Operating Procedures. Mark could see the blood pressure of each scientist had risen by a factor of ten as they hurried away from the Colonel's presence.

She whipped around, almost knocking Foster over.

"Sorry, ma'am, uh, Colonel Ongaru. I'm Lieutenant Craig Foster. This is Captain Mark Warren, one of the original Cybernetic scientists."

"Are you ready to go to work, Captain?" Ongaru's gray and crimson uniform was tailored to perfection over her athletic 5-foot-10 frame. A firm set to the jawline of her dark brown face contrasted with the soft laugh lines at her eyes, but not one black hair was out of place in her short military cut.

"Yes, ma'am, I'm more than ready." Saying it aloud intensified Mark's eagerness to make up for lost time.

"Very good." She guided them to a vacant cubicle where she posted Foster at the opening with orders not to allow anyone to disturb them. Ongaru perched on the desk's corner, the foot of one slender leg touching the floor, and gestured for Mark to take a chair. "Now, tell me exactly what you experienced from the moment you arrived at HQ."

He recounted everything, except the part about overhearing Majors Darren Ashley and Micah Whitaker.

She listened, nodding with genuine interest. "May I see your KorVu monitor?"

Mark pushed up his sleeve, offering her his wrist.

She studied it. "We must keep an eye on that, Captain. Can't afford to lose another one of our own." She stood, straightened her tunic. "I've seen your file. I know what you're capable of in the lab—and out of it. I'm appointing you as ranking officer of the Bioware Prosthetics Section's research." She held up a hand to halt any interruption. "Reason one—you're military, and most of the newcomers aren't. They can't tell a lieutenant from a general. Reason two—Dimitrios said I could trust you, and I need every trustworthy person I can find. There are some who don't take kindly to me be being here. It upset the status quo." She closed her eyes for a few seconds to massage her right temple.

Mark could relate to the pressure she must be feeling after experiencing his own inhospitable reception from Major Whitley. He wondered who Ongaru's detractors were, and how far they might go to derail her authority. Could this faction be tied to Ashley or Whitaker? Were there more Fulton sympathizers in hiding?

Ongaru opened her eyes, blinking away any distress before continuing. "Your PhD in Cybernetics and previous military experience make you the perfect candidate for Team Leader. Eight people who specialize in bioware will report directly to you—and you report directly to me. As of now, everyone's on a 24-hour clock. We need to make up for lost time. General Dimitrios is adamant about completing these projects before we're hit with another catastrophe. The military and Prime Council are under enormous pressure to apprehend the guilty parties and avenge the twenty-two deaths of Terra's irreplaceable scientists."

With a sad face, Ongaru brought a hand to her chest in homage to the souls lost.

"We will meet for briefings at 0700, 1230, 1800, and 2300. I don't usually micromanage, but every minute progress is not being made we fall further behind. This is your office, such as it is. Everyone has been updated. Their academic and employment files are on your tablet. Holograms were installed four hours ago. Questions?"

Mark's stomach grumbled. The combination of nanites and pain meds repressed hunger, but returning to normal had revived his appetite. He was starved. "Yes, ma'am, a few. Are you familiar with any of the people in my section?"

"No," she admitted. "I've been stationed on Luna for the last five months doing classified work for Space Command. You'll have to assess them on your own."

"On a more personal note," Mark said, "I don't know where my quarters are. Can't remember the last time I ate. Also…I'll need to contact my family. My brother died on the Europa Mission. I don't want my parents to go through that pain again—plus my business partners, just in case they think I'm dead, too," he smiled in jest, "and try to collect insurance."

Ongaru seemed too distracted to notice his comment as she worked her tablet. "Dimitrios tried to downplay the explosion, but that's no longer possible due to the fatalities. The TMD's Public Affairs division and the Prime Council have spun it so the military isn't culpable for the deaths. The exact number has not yet been released. However, the worst is yet to come. The true extent of the damage is being kept under wraps. It's a nightmare which will only be overshadowed by the enormity of the death toll on hallowed ground—*Headquarters* of the Terran Military Defense." She reached out to put a dark, slender hand on his shoulder. "Captain Warren…Mark…had you not warned Dimitrios when you did, I, along with many others wouldn't be here today. I've cleared you for minimal comm use to your family and business. Use it judiciously." Ongaru's tablet beeped. She turned toward the opening. "Lieutenant Foster?"

The young officer spun around. "Yes, ma'am?"

"Have someone deliver a tray of food to Captain Warren A-*SAP,* then find him a place to sleep—not that he'll get much." Ongaru moved to the cubicle's opening. "I have another meeting. Your first report is due at 1800, Captain Warren. Don't be late."

Mark executed a smart salute to his new commanding officer and crossed to his desk to power up the 'super cyborg' hologram.

***

At 0400, Axel sat on the rooftop, watching a drunken sailor stumble through the light spilling from the Bora Bora diner's window. It was the only street light for a block in either direction, except for a red porch light advertising an all-night brothel. Feminine voices peppered the silence with boisterous laughter as they catcalled the sailor heading back to his hotel.

Another lone figure drifted forward out of the shadows, edging along next to the buildings—a small man with his head on a swivel, keeping track of every dark sound along his path. Axel's instinctive reaction labeled him a perp—too small for muscle, so a thief, dealer or perv of some kind. Watching the man's furtive movements, Axel dismissed the thief likelihood. This man didn't have the finesse of a successful pickpocket or burglar, which left dealer or pervert.

With no one else on the street, Axel indulged himself by continuing to watch the man much like a lion would track unsuspecting prey. He entered the café, took the front table, ordered. Axel checked his tablet to see a clear, high-res image displayed on the screen. With his thumb and index finger, he zoomed in on the man's face close enough to count the pores in his skin.

Next to Axel, Kamryn awoke from her doze, yawned, and stretched. "Anything interesting happening?"

"It's been quiet. Cats chasing rats. Drunken sailors. Perp in the window." Axel pointed to the café as he offered the tablet.

Kamryn sat up and looked at the image.

Axel heard a sharp intake of breath, saw her whole body go rigid. Her eyes were the size of moon rocks, glued to the image on the screen.

"What's wrong?" He waited. "Kam?"

She dropped the tablet, jumped up, and ran for the ladder.

Axel was after her in a flash, catching her arm before she reached the roof's edge. Moving in front of Kamryn, he said again, "What's wrong?"

"That 'perp' is Donnie Cooper, the same scumbag who outed me to Gérard. I'm going to kill that little puke."

From his hand on her arm, he could feel the rage churning in her body. Still, he didn't move.

"Get out of my way, Axel." Her tone was icy.

He let go, then stretched out both his arms to block her path to the ladder. "Remember on Mars when the guy grabbed Eva's purse? You said not to kill him, or they wouldn't let us in the hotel. And when we found Barton with Sergeant Wong's body on the space station? You said not to kill him because we needed to interrogate him."

Kamryn wasn't budging, no matter how solid his reasoning. She exuded wrath like the sun radiated solar flares.

"Okay, look at it this way. If Cooper's here, Gérard's not far behind. We just wait for him to show or follow Cooper—see where he leads us."

She wavered for a moment. Axel lowered his arms. In the next split-second, Kamryn thrust out her hand, slamming Axel aside as she barreled past him, sprinted to the ladder, swung over the edge, and got half-way down before Axel made it to the ledge. He jumped ten feet straight to the ground, making sure to land on his augmented left hand and leg—he couldn't afford any injuries to his right extremities if he were to stop Kamryn. She dropped to the ground a second later, spun to face him.

Axel didn't want to do this. He *really* didn't. But time had come for what some people called Tough Love. He had vivid memories of being on the receiving end of hers on Mars. Karma's a bitch.

He twirled her around and shoved her against the wall, placing his forearm on her neck while his other hand grasped both her wrists. "No," he said calmly. "I didn't want to do it this way, but either you give me your word we do this together, or I'm taking you back to the ship, and we're *leaving*. Do you understand?"

Kamryn squirmed in silence.

Confirming his determination, Axel applied a bit more pressure with his forearm, squashing her cheek into the wall. "I want your word, Kam—on your honor."

After she relaxed, her breathing became normal. "Okay, okay," she groaned.

"Say it," he ordered.

"On my honor."

Axel eased away from Kamryn, half-expecting her to throw an elbow or knee. She peeled herself off the wall, turned to face him. Even the dark shadows couldn't hide the fire still burning in her eyes, but he also saw respect. Axel offered his hand. She paused for a long count of three, then clasped it in friendship. "Let's go set an ambush."

Kamryn tilted her head, reciting from memory, "Intel. Choose the ground. Spotters to tell you when the target's coming."

Axel nodded his approval. "Exactly."

They shared a conspiratorial grin before returning to the rooftop.

Chapter 10

In her lab onboard Kailani, Lotus Chang sat studying a bank of screens, performing a diagnostic on her ship's systems. She spooled through data searching for the cause of intermittent transmissions with the *Stellaria,* Fultronics, and Terra. When her tablet beeped for the third time in as many minutes, she finally answered it.

"Yes, Captain Torres?"

"Sorry to interrupt, ma'am, but we have a situation here."

"Can't you handle it?" she snapped, not in the mood for his petty problems.

"It's the Martian military, ma'am. They claim to have reports of pirates in this sector. An MMC vessel is on an intercept course with our ship."

"Why are we able to receive their comms and not *Stellaria's*?" Chang held no respect for Mars or its draconian military. Knowing they were in the area made them a prime suspect.

"They're rimward, between Jupiter and us, so the interference may be Sol. Nevertheless, the MMC is requesting permission to come aboard to check our cargo."

"Do they have a warrant?"

"These are Martians, ma'am. They don't need a warrant."

"If they want on my ship, Captain, they'd better damn well have a warrant."

"No, ma'am, they don't." His voice carried a grim resignation. "They have torpedoes, rail guns, and plasma cannons."

"But we also have weapons, Captain."

"We are no match for them, ma'am. Even if we were in their space, they wouldn't need a warrant."

"We're not in their space?"

"No, but—"

"Save it, Captain. I'll be right there."

Lotus Chang reached around under her hair to unplug the neural interface implanted in her occipital region to the peripheral devices surrounding her. She checked herself in a mirror by the door. Her reflection looked human—on the outside. On the inside, she was the first human-AI hybrid, or what she liked to think of as a techno-organic, a distinction she didn't mind keeping secret for a while longer. Chang adjusted her straight black hair, fixed an unwavering smile on her face.

Captain Hector Torres stood as Chang sauntered onto his bridge. She stepped up on the raised dais to stand beside Torres. Her lithe 6-foot figure towered over his pudgy 5-foot-8 frame. He fidgeted with the gold-trimmed neck of his brown uniform, a color slightly darker than his complexion. "We've identified the vessel as a Martian Warship, Invictus-class, advancing at full speed. As near as we can tell, they'll intercept us within the hour. We can change course and speed, but we cannot outrun them."

Chang scanned the three other bridge personnel. No one else had acknowledged her presence. They seemed engrossed in their duties, eyes glued to their consoles. Perhaps she made them nervous. If they only knew.

"Have you confirmed any pirate activity, or could the MMC be using it as a ruse to stop us?"

"Yes, ma'am, we've noted two recent instances of piracy listed in their crime reports."

"Where's *Stellaria*?"

"Solward by fifteen hours. We're still experiencing intermittent communication failures with them."

Wade Fulton's ship had passed through this sector without being stopped. Therefore, Chang doubted the MMC's veracity.

On the surface, she had nothing to hide, except 112 clones in cryopods—most everything else would appear completely legal. "I trust you have not sent a response."

"Correct, ma'am, but we should respond soon, otherwise I couldn't venture a guess as to what their next move might be."

"Give me a few minutes to prepare a response." Chang left the bridge. Rushing back to her cabin, she began to craft an innovative reason for stalling long enough to learn how to disable the Martian ship. A virus was the most likely candidate. Their encryption would differ from the Terran's, yet not be impossible to break.

But first, she had to get a message to Natalya Stepanov aboard *Stellaria*. That ship must not be stopped.

***

Mark paced within the confines of his dinky cubicle while listening to Piper Larsen postulate a theory about how to strengthen the cohesiveness of bioware with metals to at least rival, if not outperform the 'super cyborg.' At the end of his patience, Mark interrupted her.

"No-no-no, Larsen. What's Rule Seventeen?"

The young biomedical engineer squinted at him. "Seventeen, sir?"

"Rule Seventeen: Omit needless steps. Fewer parts mean fewer things to go wrong. We need an elegant design—strength without added bulk." He pointed to the opening in his cubicle. "Now go design one. Don't come back until you do."

She zipped past him with her head tucked down, clutching her tablet.

Mark returned to his own work, feeling guilty at his heavy-handedness with the young woman, and hoped he hadn't provoked her to histrionics. He'd treated her exactly as his professors had treated him years ago. Her degree more than qualified her for the project, but she didn't have much practical experience.

Well shit, she's volunteered knowing full well a lot more rode on what happened in this lab than grade points. Larsen would have to toughen up. She was playing in the majors now, no time for tears. As a civilian, they'd get her benched, or worse, cut from the team.

"Captain, do you have a minute?"

Mark turned to see Conrad Sellers, the senior member of his team—razor-sharp but unassuming, with a girth so wide his lab coat failed to close. "Sure, Connie, what can I do for you?" Mark motioned him in.

"I've completed my project." The grandfatherly figure opened his left palm, waving the hologram into the air between them while pointing out various sections as he spoke. "The new onboard electronics can now sense the environment and flex the joint or adjust the angle to match different terrains, a 15 percent improvement over the previous model. I included the option of programming it with a unique gait and natural walking pattern—couldn't resist adding a personal touch. Also, the learning algorithms automatically add power to the joints to make movement smoother when climbing, adding strength and stability for battlefield logistics, a 20 percent improvement."

Mark studied the holographic mock-up with amazement, inspecting every inch as he twirled the holo image 360-degrees. "Simple, well-designed…have you—"

"Yes, I conferred with Travis Moran and Désirée Bouchard at lunch. They're working on an interface to test its integration into the neural network."

Mark reached out to shake his hand. "Congratulations, Connie, you just earned yourself some face time with Colonel Ongaru. Come with me, I'm sure she'd appreciate good news for a change." As they walked, Mark added, "If you're a wagering man, there's a cyborg pool to see which section can complete their assignment first. Another one between us and AI to see who snags the grand prize."

"I'm already in." Connie grinned. "A little friendly intellectual competition gets the juices flowing, don't you agree?"

Mark glanced sidelong at him as they walked. "You sly old fox. I bet this was your idea."

Connie shrugged the question away, but the gleam in his eyes told the truth. In a confidential tone, he said, "I heard Piper sniffling in her cubicle."

"Damn. I don't mind admitting management is not my forte. Someone with your experience should be in charge instead of me. I have partners, not employees. Everyone has an equal say. Sometimes it gets heated."

"She'll get over it. Piper's tougher than she thinks. I'd like to mentor her, if it's okay with you."

"Sure, as long as you're the consultant and she does all the work."

"Of course. What I've learned over my lifetime helped me be of use here. What she learns here will help her over her lifetime. Oh, I wanted you to know I heard what you did for Désirée and Omar Chakir. I knew him. Not well, but in these circles, one knows *of* almost everyone else. He was a nice fellow with an extraordinary mind. He will be missed."

An audible sigh escaped Mark as he relived the failed attempt to keep Chakir alive. "I tried."

"I know." He patted Mark's shoulder. "We can't save them all, but we can save some."

Twenty feet from Ongaru's office Mark's cybernetic ear detected a high-pitched noise in a frequency range above what normal humans could detect. It stopped Mark in his tracks. He snagged Connie's arm, whispering, "Keep quiet. Go along with whatever I say."

The closer he moved toward the wall, the clearer the sound became. A drone or bot—either in the wall or ductwork. No way to tell without a scanner.

With his back against the wall, Mark whispered, "Bring back Ongaru and a 3D scanner."

Conrad Sellers gave a quick nod, then scurried off on his mission.

***

Natalya Stepanov sat facing the console in her quarters, drumming her fingers while bouncing her leg to a rhythmless beat. Her raging anger was a hair away from going supernova. Communications from her counterpart, Lotus Chang, had decreased to almost nothing in the last four hours, and were so degraded as to be unreadable. Because Natalya's payload was flat out illegal, Chang had gone ahead to run interference, or to remove any unforeseen obstacles. Given *Stellaria's* fearsome contents of bio and nuclear weapons—plus 117 clones— Natalya had reason to be alarmed about every action that deviated from their plan.

The scowling face of her ship's captain, Brisa Rylak, appeared on the screen. "Stepanov to the bridge."

Natalya made it in sixty seconds, tamping down her anger with every step.

Captain Rylak stood with her arms crossed, observing the four men in front of her, all busy at their consoles. The silver trim on her black uniform emphasized the streak of white hair above her right eyebrow while short, dark hair framed her hawkish features.

Natalya strained to sound more hopeful than disturbed. "What is it, a message from *Kailani?*"

"Mister Yancy is confirming that now." Rylak pointed with her chin to the bald man sitting to her left.

Eager to hear the interference had passed, Natalya asked, "Do we have comms again?"

"No," Rylak grumbled, returning to her command chair. "Their transmission were interrupted and scrambled. We're performing an analysis. The earlier messages sent by *Kailani* were encrypted. We had no problem decrypting them, but the most recent ones are corrupted beyond repair. The single word we can piece together is *Martians.*"

Natalya's mind raced through possible scenarios, settling on the most obvious. "We need to change course, Captain, go the long way around Mars. This will delay our arrival to Ganymede, but if Chang's encountered problems with the Martians, we must heed her warning. We need a decoy. Can you code a drone with our ship's signature to continue on our current heading?"

Rylak turned toward tactical. "Mister Boone?"

"On it, Captain."

"Mister DeSilva," Rylak said, "plot a new course around the far side of Mars."

Natalya reasoned if the Martians were monitoring *Stellaria's* course, she'd be safer taking a detour even without information on what they might find along this new path. If it came to a showdown, she had weapons and wasn't squeamish about ordering Rylak to use them. All the gods in the galaxy could not keep her from landing on Ganymede.

She bent over Rylak's shoulder. "Captain, my ship cannot be stopped, waylaid, or boarded—for *any* reason—by anyone. You agreed to these stipulations before we left Terra, pledging full allegiance to me in exchange my silence. Do not test me, Rylak."

Stepanov spun on her heel, leaving for the solitude of her cabin. Rylak should be exceedingly thankful she occupied a command chair onboard this ship instead of a metal cot in a stinking Terran jail. She had coerced Rylak into becoming captain by threatening to release evidence which would put Rylak on death row. Stepanov's one requirement had been to deliver her to Ganymede, and the evidence disappeared—forever—and Rylak would be rich beyond her dreams.

Likewise, every crew member of her ship had committed blue-collar, white-collar, or in some cases, heinous crimes, the knowledge of which was used to recruit them for this voyage. Every last man and woman were criminals, and sworn, as Rylak had, to get *Stellaria* to its destination in exchange for a share of the riches and a return trip to Terra.

Chapter 11

Axel and Kamryn sat perched on the roof, devising a plan to gather intel while watching Donnie Cooper shovel food into his mouth. Axel's stomach growled. "I'll bring back water and food. You keep an eye on the café."

A short time later, Axel left the bodega with a full shopping bag just after two men walked past. He followed them for a short time until Kamryn commed him in a strained voice.

"I got visual. That's *Gérard*. You're following Lucien Gérard!"

Damn. Axel almost veered off...until he saw this as a gift. Axel didn't believe in coincidences, so this was pure, unadulterated destiny. In the shadows, a devious grin spread across his face. Axel turned his head away to mutter, "Don't move. I've got this."

Axel slowed, careful not to crowd the men in front of him. It gave him time to do a visual check for weapons. Both were smaller than Axel, dressed in loose-fitting clothing which showed no sign of concealed weapons, but that didn't mean they weren't carrying. The man on the right strolled along as he spoke casually to his companion. He also fit the most recent description of Gérard—dark-skinned, wiry black hair and matching beard. The heftier man on the left had short, straight hair, never spoke, only nodded in agreement. His behavior relegated him to an employee or hired hand, not an equal. When they entered the Bora Bora café, Axel followed.

Kamryn had watched in silence. Seeing Axel enter the diner, she told him to leave—pronto. When Petra and Ohashi heard Axel had entered the café, even they were on his comm, urging him to leave.

The two men joined Cooper, the solitary customer at this hour. Axel took an empty table against the wall, turning his head to growl, "Comm silence," at the women in his ear. He looked around in time to notice an unnatural bulge under the mystery man's shirt at the small of his back. Okay, at least one of them was carrying—a good chance the others were, too.

Henrietta's father had left long ago. With no waitress, the relief cook came to take the new orders. Axel pretended to doze, as if he'd just gotten off shift, while listening to the conversation from Gérard's table. None of them gave Axel a second look, no doubt assuming from his cheap clothing and grubby appearance he must be a poor local. Their hushed voices blocked most of the exchange, but they spoke in English, making it easier for him to piece together words and phrases.

Gérard wasn't searching for a way *out* of Panama, he planned to open up a new drug business *in* Panama. The mystery man was muscle; Cooper, the contact for a local supplier. This new intel sped up their plot to ambush Gérard. More people involved meant more problems.

Axel finished, left the café, and hurried back to the roof while mentally running through different scenarios of taking them out. He squatted on the ledge next to Kamryn, kept a bottle of water, and handed the bag to her. "Did you hear any of their conversation?"

"Some," Kamryn said, grabbing a sandwich. "Enough to understand he wants to set up a new shop here. That's Gérard—escape prison to jump right back into the drug trade. We need to take them out before this snowballs." Kamryn took her shirt corner to wipe sweat from her face and neck. "Man, what I wouldn't give for a real snowball right now." She bit into the sandwich, groaning with delight as she chewed.

Axel stated the obvious. "We can't afford to draw this out. It's quick and dirty. I'm thinking you want payback, but it's not going to happen. There's no time."

"Fine with me," she mumbled around the food. "Dead is dead."

Axel tore his eyes off their targets in the window, and turned to her. "I want your word you won't flip on me at the last minute—try to draw things out."

Kamryn wiped the back of her hand over her mouth. "You're getting real technical in your old age, Axel. Far as I'm concerned, we're still soldiers. We kill our enemies, and make no mistake, Cooper and Gérard *are* the enemy. Don't know the third guy, but he's clearly not a priest, so he's guilty by association."

"That works for me. Check your gear. It'll be light soon." Axel pointed at the café window. "They came under cover of darkness. They'll scurry back before daybreak, just like roaches."

He and Kamryn tightened vests, examined knives, confirmed placement of stun batons, and inspected pulse handguns. He'd decided on an ambush.

"You remember Veracruz?"

"I do." Kamryn pouted. "Who's the bait this time?"

"It's my turn, isn't it?"

Her pout switched to a grin. "Absolutely."

***

With Ongaru and Connie huddled off to the side, Mark programmed the scanner to detect electronics before climbing on a chair to pass it over the wall. In less than a minute, the red light on top of the scanner started to blink as it pinpointed an object in the ductwork behind the wall register. He climbed down, joining the others to inspect the 3D image.

Colonel Ongaru studied the impression. "It's a Strategic Infiltration Bot, an SIB-25. I saw the specs for one on Luna last month." She passed the scanner to Sellers.

"I thought the 25 was still experimental." Connie rotated the image, then handed it back.

"Apparently not anymore," Mark said. "Are we being monitored, ma'am? Or is someone from the outside spying on us?"

"It's not the TMD," she declared, tucking the scanner under her arm. "We need to notify Internal Security and the Cyber Division."

"Not from this room, ma'am. Where there's one, there might be more."

"Right." She pointed to the AI section. "I'll inform Colonel Peyton. He and I will take this to Security in person. Shut down everything here, Captain. Have everyone report to my office, but not a word until I return."

"Yes, ma'am." Mark sent Connie to the opposite row of cubicles, cautioning him not to alert anyone. Mark took the opposite row. They notified the scientists to report to the colonel's office for a briefing. Mark had chosen the side with Désirée on purpose. Since the hospital had only released her hours ago, he worried the sudden order to stop the research might spook her. Mark knew about flashbacks. The vivid memories of being tortured and restrained by Beth Coulter still haunted him. He couldn't project how Désirée might handle the psychological trauma she'd suffered from the explosion, but he'd try to minimize it as much as possible.

When he appeared at her cubicle, she gave him a dazzling smile.

"Time to take a break," Mark said. "The colonel wants to brief everyone in her office."

She tensed, her smile fading. "Why? Has something happened?"

Unsure of what to say, he decided a half-truth was better than an outright lie. "We've been having these meetings to share updates." Mark held out an inviting hand.

"Very well." She swiped the cranial hologram closed and joined Mark, placing her hand on his arm.

Mark basked in the warmth of her touch, leaning in to catch a trace of her delicious scent. He matched her pace, giving him more time to stay by her side. "How's your wound?"

"I barely feel it. The nanites are amazing." She leaned against him in a casual yet intimate gesture. "I owe my life to you, Captain Mark Warren. Please, will you have dinner with me this evening? I must know more about what makes you act so fearless in such a deadly situation."

He squeezed her hand, excited by this sudden turn of events. "I'd love to have dinner with you." Before she got cold feet and backed out, he added, "Officer's Club, seven o'clock?"

She turned to give him a radiant smile just before they joined a stream of other scientists heading in the same direction. Everyone crowded in, standing side by side, due to the lack of chairs. They looked at Mark—as the only person in uniform—to explain the impromptu meeting.

Still elated over his impending dinner date with Désirée, he stepped up to address the group. "We have good news to report…" He stopped mid-sentence, drawing a sigh of relief when he saw Ongaru approach.

"Yes, I do," she said, taking command. "Our new location is ready. Please collect your holograms and personal items. Lieutenant Foster here," she said, pointing to the bright-eyed young officer, "will lead you to the reapportioned wing the

TMD has set up for us. The AI section will be following us shortly so the exercise starved troops can have their sweaty smelling gymnasium back." She finished on a light note by wrinkling her nose.

Energized by the news, they spilled out of the cramped space, chatting with their colleagues about settling into the new site. Ongaru drew Mark and Connie aside in the corridor. "Our Internal Security Division will be handling the search for additional bots. If they're determined to be the product of an outside entity, the Intelligence Division will take over." She thumbed up the Non-Disclosure Form on her tablet, then handed it to Mark. "You're both under orders not to share this classified intel."

Mark recognized it as the standard, nail-your-butt-to-the-cell-door document that promised to reward lawbreakers with lengthy stints in the choicest military penitentiary. He pressed his hand to the screen. Connie did likewise.

After trekking halfway across the base, Ongaru's group of white coats arrived at the newly designated AIRED Lab. Within the last twenty-four hours, it had undergone an extreme renovation from a small weapons/armor storage facility to an area large enough for forty-two scientists, with fresh gray paint and pale blue cubicles. The AI contingent was due to arrive in the next half hour. For now, Ongaru's people gathered in her new office, excited to share updates and settle into their new environment.

Mark stood back, moved beyond words, watching his fellow scientists engage in spirited discussions. After getting his degree, he'd volunteered for the TMD to contribute in the field of cybernetic research for the benefit of injured soldiers. The advancements he and others made were first tested on the military, then made available to the public. He wasn't ready to admit that getting shot—for the second time—might have been a good thing, but Mark had also been the recipient of cybernetic advancements. His new auditory canal had proven beneficial several times in the last four days.

Since witnessing the deaths of his colleagues, he vowed to become even more vigilant than before. Too many scientists had already died. He'd try his damnedest to see no one else did.

***

In the pre-dawn silence, Kamryn followed Axel along the narrow, winding streets half a block behind their three targets. She commed Ohashi to reposition drones as they turned right or left, but their targets had vanished.

"Where the hell are they?" Axel whispered.

Ohashi commed, "Go left. Drones showed them entering a large warehouse. Check your tablets."

"Well, there go our plans for an ambush." Kamryn's heart rate increased as she slid along the wall behind Axel.

"Ohashi, surround this area with drones. Send a schematic with dimensions of that building to our tablets." Axel added, "Mark the doors in green. If you can detect bio-signatures, mark them in red. We'll enter through the roof while it's still dark."

They backtracked to the nearest alley, climbing barehanded up the backside of the adjacent building. Between handholds, Kamryn groused, "This isn't a substitute...for the rock climbing...I had planned in Portland."

Reaching the top first, Axel bent over to pull her up. The rooftop was littered with cables, ductwork, pipes—a conglomeration of mechanical systems which provided plenty of hiding spots.

Axel stood on the corner, looked across the distance to the warehouse. "I think it's a good ten feet."

"Maybe a little more," Kamryn said. "Ohashi, got those specs yet?"

"Just sent them to your tablets. Only two doors—front and back. The three targets you were following went in, but we're reading a total of eight heat signatures now. I tweaked the drones. They're picking up traces of chemicals. We haven't had time to research it, but Petra thinks they're cooking drugs."

Axel spread his hands. "You want to call in the local cops?"

Kamryn responded with a mirthless laugh.

"Just asking," he said. "So that's five for me and four for you."

"Or four for you and five for me," she countered.

"Okay. We play this by ear. If we get separated—with no comms—we meet where the cab dropped us yesterday and haul ass back to the ship."

"Agreed."

They studied the schematic, watching the red dots mill around in the far corner.

Axel walked the perimeter of their rooftop. "Forty feet diagonal. Enough runway to sprint like hell before the jump. Picture where you want to land. I'll go first."

Although no longer soldiers, their skills in situational awareness were ingrained. As the brain encodes data, it records whether certain movements are right or wrong. Tasks like cleaning a weapon or tracking a target become second nature.

Kamryn's mindset focused on entering the warehouse undetected, neutralizing the enemy, and making it out alive. But first, she took a moment to gather all the emotions—hatred, fear, sadness in her heart—stuffed those feelings in a box, and locked it away. They had no place in what happened next. After she'd been shot, her armor had been taken away, because she'd played by the rules. Today, there were no rules. Her father's motto had always been, *"You're either part of the problem, or you're part of the solution."* Today, Kamryn Aurora Fleming was damn well going to be part of the solution.

After a final weapons check, they stretched, then jogged around the perimeter to loosen up. Suddenly, Axel exploded into a sprint, leaped up and out into the ten-foot expanse, raising his arms and knees as he sailed through the air. Near the opposite rooftop, Axel straightened his legs like a diver before hitting the water. He landed on the other building. Rolling head over heels into a somersault, he finished upright on his feet. He turned, motioning for Kamryn to jump.

Kamryn closed her eyes to envision making the jump in slow motion the same way Axel had, landing in the exact spot. She burst forth, gaining breakneck speed before the ledge, and sprang into thin air, putting her whole body into it. The time she was suspended in midair—with a ten-foot drop below—felt like forever until her feet touched a solid surface. She tucked into a ball and rolled into Axel, knocking him over.

"You're only getting a B-plus." He scrambled to his feet. "Since you assaulted the instructor."

"The instructor might want to move out of the way next time." Kamryn avoided the center of the rooftop, not knowing if it was stable, as they searched for an opening into the building. Two monstrous air conditioning units sat next to a generator, electrical access boxes, and a metal hatch cover.

He opened it, looked into the building. "Straight down. No stairs, no ladder."

"No problem. You first," Kamryn taunted.

Axel double-checked his tablet for the whereabouts of their targets before easing himself into the opening feet first, hanging onto the edges of the flashing. His shoulders were too broad. He let go with his right hand, slipped it under the roof, angled his shoulder under while holding on with just his augmented left hand until the last second, and finally dropped.

Kamryn heard a dull *whump* sound, then silence. She commed him. "You okay?"

"Need some NewSkin gloves."

"Didn't bring any. You ready?"

"Yeah."

She grabbed one side of the flashing with both hands, scooted her body over to the edge, slithered into the hole, and let gravity take over until she couldn't hold on any longer. When Axel's arms wrapped around her legs, she let go. He steadied her body as she slid into a standing position.

"We should be acrobats," Kamryn whispered, drawing her gun.

"I'm not wearing tights."

She clamped her hand over a muffled snort.

"We stay together as long as possible. When we split, I go right, you're left."

Kamryn nodded. "Ohashi, you reading our chips in here?"

"I am. Your colors are yellow. If you get separated, I'm monitoring you—Petra is on Axel. Targets haven't moved. Exits are north and south. Chemical analysis is complete. Elements are almost identical to the Gold Dust manufactured by Gérard in Canada before his arrest." Ohashi finished with, "You have nineteen minutes until sunrise."

In stealth mode, they maneuvered in tandem through sectors of the warehouse toward the opposite corner, scanning tablets as they cleared each area. The no-frills interior coupled with the overhead ductwork indicated the structure used to be a plant or some kind of shop.

Ohashi commed, "Stray bandit coming at you."

Kamryn broke left to position herself behind a support column. Axel backed up to the opposite wall, ready with a knife and stun baton.

A small beam of light preceded the straggler before he crossed their threshold.

Huge.

A three hundred-pound fat guy lumbered along, muttering to himself as he passed their hiding spots.

Axel whispered, "You want this one?"

"He's more your size."

Kamryn snapped her fingers.

The butterball stopped, turned ever so slowly in her direction. The light he held splashed across his wrinkled face. He had the features of a bulldog—drooping jowls, pug nose, and a bald head.

Axel blindsided him with a lefthanded powerhouse blow to the temple.

Nothing. The creature did not fall. An average human might have died, or at *least* suffered a concussion.

At 6 foot even, and certified in the martial arts, Kamryn delivered a roundhouse kick to his throat with ease.

He staggered backward, reached for his neck with one hand, for Kamryn with the other.

Surprised he was still standing, she twisted away while Axel circled behind to deliver several heavy stuns to the back of his neck, a particularly lethal spot.

At last, the beast collapsed into a mountain of lumpy meat.

"That's one down."

Kamryn shook her head. "He counts as two."

Chapter 12

Mark sat with Major Torance in the doctor's temporary office. Split images of Petra and Ohashi appeared on the vid screen. The young women took turns updating the men on their current situation while they monitored the movements of Axel and Kamryn.

Petra said, "We followed you to Norfolk, but after learning two AIs had been snooping around our ship, we left and hid for a while."

"Kamryn's revelations, plus a lot of cyber-sleuthing, led us to Panama in search of Gérard," Ohashi added.

"Are you okay now?" Petra asked. "Got all your old parts?"

"Yes, thanks to the Major," Mark said. "Everything's in turmoil here. There are spies, both human and bots, still trying to obstruct our research. Have you caught any webnews on the explosion? We're in a blackout."

"A little," Petra said, "but it's not good. A lot of speculation, not many facts—except for all the funerals making the headlines." She lowered her voice. "I've heard netchatter that Mars set up a blockade to intercept the last two ships before they reach Ganymede, with half the Terran Fleet burning like hell to seal off any escape."

Since Petra didn't engage in gossip, be it web or otherwise, he took her remarks as fact. It became the bright spot in his day. Mars was as heavy-handed as the TMD when it came to neutralizing their enemies. Months ago, Terra had worked with Mars to squelch a mercenary-led coup. Mark hoped this new alliance again ended in victory.

A thought struck him. The clones. Before the Indian manufacturer died, he'd admitted that Fulton had purchased clones. Mark's team had tried to save them, but now hundreds of innocent young people marked for a life of endless servitude were doomed. They hurtled toward celestial oblivion as their future played out on the frontier of space. The burden of guilt weighed heavy on him because he hadn't rescued them sooner. Mark hoped both militaries would take the clones' presence into consideration before "neutralizing" those two ships into subatomic particles.

Wade Fulton was in custody, given SP-27 and holo-interrogated until the TMD knew every lie he'd ever told. His fraudulent contract to supply electronics for the new Europa Mission—canceled. His plans to subvert the mission—destroyed. The Prime Council had confiscated Fulton's company along with the holdings of both his co-conspirators. Stepanov's laboratories were undergoing an extreme Red Level Scan by HazMat teams, every chemical being cataloged.

TMD had transferred Chang's cyborg and AI prototypes to Headquarters. In retrospect, a huge mistake, bringing the prototypes to the base. He'd give 100 to 1 odds in favor of Chang leaving them on purpose, using them as cunning decoys for the military. Although each had been scanned, inspected, and examined every way imaginable by experts with the best equipment available, clearly someone missed something. Unless...

Unless it had been added and triggered *afterward*, which implied the two Contract Management employees he'd overheard, plus the person controlling the spybot, topped the guilty list.

"Mark?"

Petra's voice snapped Mark out of his thoughts. "Yeah, how's Kamryn?"

"Good. One small hiccup. Axel took care of it."

"Where are they now?"

"Just entered the warehouse to take out Gérard," Petra said. "We have to go. Contact you when we leave."

Torance mulled over the news of Gérard's escape. "From the moment I learned of Kamryn's previous time with the DEA, I had a bad feeling it might follow her. The current situation doesn't surprise me one bit. She helped arrest some very bad people, and paid a high price for the last one."

Mark stopped himself from replying, "I know," because Kamryn had sworn him to secrecy. While she'd been in Portland's hospital from a gunshot wound, Kamryn had recounted her ordeal at the hands of Gérard. Mark's father had been attacked by a cyborg and was in the room next to hers. Kamryn had shared her story to give Mark hope that since she'd overcome her wounds, so could his father. Not only had it worked, but it had also been true. Since that time, he'd thought of Kamryn as one of the bravest people he'd ever met. Still, he worried what effect hunting for Gérard would have on her.

"Let's check your KorVu readings before you leave." Torance plugged a thin cable tethered to his screen into the monitor Mark wore around his wrist. The doctor analyzed his data as it downloaded the toxic gas vs. nanites levels. "Everything's in the acceptable range. More food and rest would go a long way toward moving your numbers into the good range. Improve your color, too. You look a little pale."

"Thanks, Major. I'll catch a quick lunch then head back to work."

Mark left for the elevator, saw a sign warning it was OUT OF ORDER, took the stairs instead. He descended one floor to find a pair of men in brown coveralls lounging against the stairwell door. Badges clipped to their collars identified the short one as Bill, the beefed-up one as Ted. "Is this floor closed off, too?"

They didn't move. Ted's face creased with a fake smile that didn't reach his eyes. "For you it is."

Oh shit.

A mental flash point erupted inside Mark's head. In a nanosecond, he went from *What the hell?* to kill or be killed. He coldcocked Bill with a ferocious blow under the chin, grabbed him by the shoulders and pitched him over the railing. Straight down. Three floors. Bill landed with a juicy thunk.

Mark's sudden first strike caught beefy Ted off guard. He reacted with a wild swing at Mark but missed. Mark wheeled around, slammed Ted into the corner—face first, before charging down the stairs four at a time.

A second later, Ted landed on Mark's back. The extra weight propelled them forward, throwing both down the steps. They rolled to the next landing, slamming against the wall, with Ted on top. He had Mark's right arm pinned underneath his knee. Ted landed a couple good blows to Mark's face, let up for half a second, reached back to grab something.

Mark pushed Ted sideways, freed his arm, smashed his fist straight up into Ted's nose. Cartlidge cracked. Blood Sprayed. Mark grabbed Ted's ears, pulled him into a head-butt. He meant to do it twice to knock Ted unconscious, then roll him off. Instead, Mark got zapped by a stun baton—over and over. Mark's reflexes were fried. His brain started to fade out, but his augmented ear heard Ted say, "Come get da bodies."

***

Natalya Stepanov paced in her quarters, furious at being detoured by the threat of Martian interference with her well-laid plans to reach Ganymede on time. She worried over the safety of her cargo, both chemical and clones, as the latter was integral to the successful outcome of the former.

Without human subjects to use in experiments, Natalya's research would come to a screeching halt. Organic humans were much too valuable to be used as guinea pigs for her advanced chemical warfare research. Clones, to the contrary, were perfect. She could replicate her arsenal of nerve agents and biological munitions without any measurable potency degradation, making them the ultimate cost-benefit weapons.

In his pitch to her and Lotus Chang, Wade Fulton had promised to split Ganymede in exchange for their collaboration in his Grand Plan—the first private companies staking a claim to any moon on the frontier. As the ninth largest object in the Solar System, Ganymede was three-quarters the size of Mars, with a confirmed ocean and a thin atmosphere. It made the perfect location for their joint venture. The rare metals recently discovered there amounted to mega-zillions, but Fulton couldn't accomplish this enormous project alone. He needed partners, yet had to be extremely choosy with whom he collaborated. Fulton needed two things: a disposable workforce and militarized security. That's when he began courting Lotus for her unethical advancements in artificial intelligence, and Natalya for her nefarious expertise in banned chemical warfare. He tempted them with the promise of wealth beyond anything imaginable on Terra if they joined him in a somewhat risky, but a once-in-a-lifetime opportunity. Ultimately, their conglomerate would import additional industries, thereby establishing themselves as the all-powerful, unfettered owners of Ganymede.

As she looked back over the past year, Natalya did not regret her decision to join forces with either Fulton or Chang.

After studying chemistry, physics and engineering in college, she'd worked beside her father to help him achieve a measure of success as a chemist. His untimely death in an explosion left her alone and broke. She ditched his lifelong mission of finding cures for diseases to a new goal of making money by producing specialized bioweapons—and worse.

She started out small, borrowed to purchase a bankrupt company, and expanded. It worked so well, she repeated the process multiple times. Word travels fast in the illicit pathogens trade, and it wasn't long until her name became recognized as one of the leading underground suppliers of chemical munitions. Natalya stopped just short of becoming the next face on a Global Wanted poster. Her only path forward meant one— into space. Ganymede would be her last home—if she could just make it there.

She opened a premium bottle of merlot, lounging on her bed to watch the bank of screens above her desk. It brought Natalya comfort to monitor the stability of her most precious cargo, the crates containing virulent pathogens and three nuclear warheads. In essence, she was penniless, having spent the fortune it had taken years to amass on what she couldn't beg, borrow, trade for or steal.

The clones were of secondary importance. Those who escaped her experiments would be turned into cheap, superhuman indentured slaves, courtesy of Chang's radical cyborg transmutation process. They would receive neural implants, thus enabling them to accept commands without hesitation. Metal limbs would replace human ones, much more suited for working underground in the mines dug by Fulton's equipment.

She dozed off, secure in the belief their spotty communications were due to CMEs—coronal mass ejections. If pointed at Terra, they triggered powerful geomagnetic storms. Strong ones disrupted communications. They'd also been known to light up Mars like a Christmas tree.

***

Major Torance left the Officer's Club after bidding three other trauma surgeons at his dinner table good evening. Before heading to his temporary quarters across base for a much needed catnap, Torance returned to his cubbyhole of an office to finish a few reports on recently discharged patients.

A flashing red light on his screen warned the doctor a patient had relapsed. He opened the file to find Mark Warren's KorVu levels had increased dramatically. Torance commed Warren—no answer. He sent a message to Warren's tablet—no answer. Next, he contacted Colonel Ongaru with his concerns about Warren's health.

"Colonel, I examined Captain Warren not two hours ago. His KorVu readings were at a healthy level. He needed to eat and sleep on a regular basis, but nevertheless was near a full recovery. Now his numbers are through the roof and he's not responding. I'm sure you're aware Warren has an embedded geolocator chip. We're on the clock here, Colonel. As his physician, I'm requesting you instruct the Internal Security Division to activate his chip. Warren's a pain in the ass, but I've become fond of him. We must find him within the hour while I can still reverse the damage done."

"Hold on, Major." Ongaru immediately connected them to the ISD in a 3-way vid. Addressing the Director, she said, "Captain Mark Warren of my Cyborg R&D Section is missing. First, I'm ordering you to activate his geolocator chip Next, I need a full review of security surveillance vids beginning with his last known whereabouts on the fourth floor of the hospital earlier today. But, most importantly, get a squad searching for Warren. *Now.*" Her voice was tight with worry when she added, "I should have sent Lieutenant Foster with Warren."

Torance shook his head. "Hindsight is 20/20, Colonel."

He signed off, stared at the black screen for several seconds, then jumped up and rushed to the nurses' station. The doctor questioned every nurse on duty whether they'd seen the handsome, blond captain. As he suspected, several nurses smiled, saying they'd seen Warren walk toward the lift, then backtrack to take the stairs.

Torance followed Mark's path into the well-lit stairwell, taking great care to search the stairwell as he descended one floor. When the doctor's educated eye noted small drops of blood near the door, his heart sank. Despite his growing alarm, Torance continued to the next landing, where a larger blood spray pattern marred the pale gray wall. He stooped to examine the trajectory, concluding it was evidence of a crime, not an accident. Torance continued inspecting every step down to the first floor, stopping in front of a smeared blood trail. He pulled out his tablet to contact Ongaru. In an eerily calm voice, he announced, "I've found fresh blood in the first-floor stairwell. Please have ISD send a Forensics team."

He rested on a step, waiting for the technicians, his energy gone. Elbows on his knees, Torance cupped his head in grim acceptance that the young scientist, whom he genuinely liked, had encountered an early demise. Thinking back over the years, Torance couldn't estimate the number of lives he'd saved, only to learn the same soldier had died during another battle in some godforsaken country. So many had died recently. Not soldiers, but scientists.

Faces of deceased patients crowded his memory like snapshots from an Old Earth photo album. Kamryn Fleming had almost died on his table, yet he'd saved her. Axel Von Radach had suffered three near-fatal wounds, and Torance had pulled him back from the jaws of death each time.

The doctor straightened, cleared his head, banishing the morbid memories. Torance hated how his mind always went to the worst place first, dragging him into a void from which he struggled to escape.

He replaced gruesome thoughts with positive ones about Warren's status. The young scientist was smart—sometimes too smart for his own good. Besides, Axel and Kamryn had put him through extreme physical and weapons training. Torance vowed not to entertain additional dire speculations concerning Warren until the forensics were proven.

The door opened a crack.

Torance stood, identifying himself before directing the five-member team to the primary testing locations. Dressed in white from head to foot, they used various equipment to scan for prints, then moved to the stairs and walls for radiation, gases, weapons fire, and bio-samples.

Colonel Ongaru joined Torance moments before Sergeant Claudia Chancellor reported from ISD. "My squad's waiting outside," Chancellor said. "We didn't want to contaminate the scene."

Lieutenant Emilio Voss, of the forensics team, drew them aside to issue his preliminary findings. "I'm pleased to report we found none of Captain Warren's blood, but did identify his bio-signature. We did, however, find blood plus bio-signatures from two others—William Boone and Theodore Finch. On cursory inspection, we believe there was an altercation, including evidence of numerous stun emissions.

"Boone and Finch are confirmed Maintenance employees. There's no current work order on record directing them to this area. I have *not* notified their Division or supervisor of our findings. The security data encoded in each ID badge has been red-flagged. The instant they're used—anywhere, ISD will know." The lieutenant looked at Ongaru. "Warren's security clearance is Code-3. It grants him access to almost every place on base. We red-flagged it when you reported him missing,

Colonel. I don't know if this is relevant, but Colonel Nash Harrington, the AI Director, has also been missing—since *before* the explosion."

Sergeant Chancellor, an athletic blonde dressed in ISD's intimidating black, ballistic-proof uniform, pointed to the large red area near her feet. "Whose blood is this?"

"Boone's," Voss said. "We found a bit more up on the third floor."

Torance said a silent prayer for Warren. Hopefully, he'd be found alive soon.

Chancellor rubbed her chin. "My guess is somebody chucked him over the edge."

Voss nodded. "We came to the same conclusion."

Chancellor looked from Voss to Torance. "You think Warren's still alive?"

Both men nodded in agreement.

Chancellor gazed upward. "Where's Finch's blood?"

"Landing between the second and third floors. Looks like facial spatter." Voss added, "That's where we picked up four or five stun emissions."

"Okay, so we're looking for Boone's dead body, Finch with probable facial injuries, Warren stunned unconscious," Chancellor summarized. "Does that sound about right, Major?"

"It does."

"If Warren's geolocator chip signal is not being received, it could mean he's in a shielded area. Any of you know of such a place?"

Alarmed at the insinuation, Torance asked, "You're not receiving his signal?"

"I said '*if*,' Major."

Ongaru broke her silence. "Sorry, I'm unfamiliar with this facility. I arrived from Luna just before the explosion."

"I'm stationed in North Dakota," Torance said, "Arrived on the first shuttle after the explosion. Been on the base many times, but only in certain areas."

Voss tugged on his ear. "I might've heard of...wait a minute." He walked back to join his team, conferred with them for a while, then brought another person back with him. "Couple years ago, they found a body near the Solid Waste disposal area. Corporal Bridges said his team couldn't get their equipment to work either because a weird shielding field interfered with the readings."

The young corporal offered his tablet, pinpointing the section where he'd encountered the problems.

Chancellor entered the GPS location on her tablet's map, just as it beeped. She studied a vid on her screen before speaking.

"We have surveillance vid. It seems Finch had help removing Warren from this location. Two unknown subjects wheeled a portable trash module in here and took it out within seconds. With three bodies stuffed inside, it was difficult to maneuver. They knew enough to keep their faces turned away from the camera locations."

Torance stepped inside Chancellor's personal space. His voice resonated with authority. "Sergeant, I'm going with you to the shielded site. Warren is my patient. His KorVu monitor shows he's suffered a relapse. We must stop at the Emergency Department for medications and put a retrieval team on standby. This is non-negotiable."

Unperturbed, Chancellor stood her ground. "Yes, sir, Major. Now that we have a head count on the perps, I'll have another ISD squad meet us there." As an afterthought, she asked, "Would you care to accompany us, too, Colonel?"

"No, I can't, but know this—General Dimitrios *personally* recommended Captain Warren. He's a trusted, high-value leader in my section. See to it you find him quickly, and *alive*. Let me know the minute you do. You are dismissed, Sergeant."

Chancellor snapped a salute.

Ongaru returned it, nodding to Torance before she walked out.

Chapter 13

Shrouded in darkness, Kamryn followed Axel across the warehouse. They stopped at the last archway before the section where the green images were gathered. Axel snaked around the corner for a visual of the group, then slid back to compare what he'd seen with the images on his tablet.

Several outdated lights hung from the ceiling. Their red target, Gérard, was flanked by two figures—likely guards, based on their dominant body language. One man along the perimeter held a weapon. A smaller figure milled about. The remaining two, dressed in face masks, aprons, and gloves, seemed preoccupied with tasks on a large, centrally located workstation where the drugs were being manufactured.

Axel used hand signals to tell Kamryn that he'd target the four on his right, giving her Gérard and his two bodyguards. After removing their light-colored shirts, which made them easy to spot, he commed Ohashi.

"Party starts in one minute. Get ready."

With mindsets of professional soldiers and guns drawn, they entered the large room, crouched low to blend into the shadows playing against the walls. Ten feet inside, Kamryn stopped when she had an unobstructed angle to her targets. Axel continued fifteen more feet before he located his most effective position. He glanced back over his shoulder to Kamryn. They each silently counted to three, rose in unison, and began firing.

Bursts of orange-red plasma hit their targets. One young man took a hit to his forehead, a burn searing down the length of his face as he toppled backward. Bodies fell, some dead. The injured sought cover. Confusion reigned. Men hurled curses in various languages. Threats of retaliation filled the air from those who still lived.

The enemy fought back; their weapon's fire shattered the air. Projectiles hit walls, pulse and flashing red plasma blasts seared through the darkness in every direction. Someone yelled out Axel's location. He rolled a few feet sideways then crept closer to deliver a barrage of fiery plasma to the survivors nearest him.

Pale sunlight filtered through the high-mounted row of industrial windows, chasing shadows into corners. A stillness settled on the room, broken by dying moans heard here and there.

Kamryn spotted a lone figure crawling toward the back door. As he crept along the wall, she rose to follow, arms outstretched, her gun gripped in both hands. She fired a shot in front of the form.

He flinched in terror and froze, whimpering.

Kamryn advanced on the man, now cowering in a fetal position. She knew who it was. "Cooo-perr," she murmured in a cooing, sing-song tone.

Moments passed before Donnie Cooper risked a peek, only to become slack-jawed in disbelief when he finally recognized the woman aiming a gun at him.

"Stand up," she coaxed sweetly, "or I'll shoot you where you lay."

"Nooo," he wailed, refusing to make eye contact again. "You're gonna' kill me anyway."

To motivate his compliance, she fired several bursts close to Cooper's feet.

He jerked, whining, "Okay, okay." Cooper inched his way upward. Plastered against the wall, he looked from side to side for a way out. "I didn't want to do this—they made me."

"Bullshit," Kamryn said mockingly. She grinned at him, unable to suppress an obscene giggle. "Take off your shirt."

Cooper had watched Gérard carve on her. Today, turnabout was fair play.

"Why? What're you gonna' do?"

"Just do it, you little pervert," she growled. The fire in her chest grew hotter and hotter, threatening to consume her from the inside out.

Cooper fumbled, but obeyed.

She seized her knife from a slot on her vest, and in one swift, lethal move, Kamryn Aurora Fleming gutted Donnie Cooper like a fish. She took a deep, cleansing breath. Years of hatred ceased to exist as the life drained out of her enemy.

Cooper's bulging eyes drifted downward while his hands tried to keep his blood from gushing onto the concrete floor. He muttered unintelligible nonsense while sinking to his knees, groaned before falling on his face.

With an unapologetic expression, Kamryn gazed at Axel. They shared a look of understanding. Her voice was cold as ice as she asked, "Where's Gérard?"

Axel pointed to the body pinned under his left foot.

"Is he dead?"

"Not yet."

"Why not?"

"He was wearing a vest."

"Let him up."

Axel slid his foot off Gérard. When he didn't move quick enough, Axel kicked him in the ass, prompting him to stand.

Blood of the other dead men stained his clothes, entangled in his wiry hair, matted his beard, and speckled his forehead. The signature piercing stare from his close-set black eyes changed to pure fear as Kamryn moved closer.

She stared brazenly at him. Her voice thick with emotion, Kamryn said, "Hello, Lucien."

Mimicking Cooper, he gaped at Kamryn. His dark features contorted first with recognition, then dread. He mouthed one silent word, *"How?"*

Her overwhelming hatred ignited. "Take. Off. The. Vest."

Again, Gérard responded too slowly. Axel grasped a handful of bloody shirt and yanked it off. Gérard fumbled with the vest's straps. It fell to the floor, exposing a torso of prison tattoos. His body was older, leaner than the images stored in Kamryn's memory.

She stepped to within an arm's length of Gérard. Their lives had come full circle. He had tortured her for days. She didn't have the same luxury. Kamryn intended to kill him, but instilling fear came first. She slashed his chest six times so fast he didn't know what had happened.

He looked down, gaping open-mouthed at the rivulets of blood running down his skin. Unexpectedly, Gérard lurched forward to the workstation and swiped his arms across the top. Glass decanters shattered, liquid flew in every direction, shards of glass spun through the air. He cleared the table by knocking powdered drugs onto the ground.

One nanosecond later a yellow haze mushroomed, filling the room. They lost sight of Gérard. The haze turned to a thick, acrid cloud, causing eyes to tear, airways to close, just as they escaped through the front door hacking and coughing.

***

Axel left Kamryn sitting on the ground, panting, tears streaming over her cheeks, while he returned inside to look for his tablet and Gérard. He found the tablet—smashed beyond repair, but not Gérard. When he went back outside, he couldn't find Kamryn, either. He commed her, but she didn't answer. He was worried, pissed, and confused. He wanted to shoot somebody. But everyone was already dead—except for the specific person they'd come to get.

Axel rubbed his watering eyes. "Ohashi, you copy?"

"Yes. Are you all right?"

"No, dammit," he sputtered, choked, spat out a lungful of phlegm. Catching his breath, he continued, "The lab blew up. Gérard's alive and missing. Kamryn's missing and not responding to my comms. My tablet's trashed. You'd better be picking up their locations."

"Her chip's on the move. Two blocks north, one west. She's not responding to our comms, either. His signal disappeared the minute Gérard left the warehouse."

"Keep feeding me her location. I'm ordering you, Petra and Malone to gear up—you're boots on the ground. We need to find them. A-*SAP!*"

"I'm tracking your chip. Wherever you go, we'll meet up with you in ten—or sooner."

Axel heard Petra let out a whoop in the background.

He jogged through the narrow, twisting streets, thankful only stray cats and dogs were out at this hour. Soon, though, the city would awaken. Throngs of people would crowd the streets, making his mission twice as difficult. He must figure out where Gérard was—a safe house, a doctor, or a ship for a quick getaway?

Axel cut through an alley, noticed a dog lapping water from a puddle. He searched for the source, saw a leaking pipe, and stuffed his head underneath to flush the drug residue from his face. Axel caught water in cupped hands to drink, clearing his raw throat before resuming his search. He could breathe and see better, his perception sharpened. In the early dawn light, he noticed dark red spots on the ground, equidistance apart. Blood. He'd spilled enough of other's and lost plenty of his own, knelt to look, touched it, took a whiff. Gratified, he commed Ohashi.

"I've picked up a blood trail. How's Kamryn's chip looking? Any problems?"

"None yet. She's moving at a steady pace."

"It's Gérard's. She sliced him up pretty good before things went sideways."

"Nguyen flew us to a small strip near your location," Ohashi said. "We'll be there in a few."

Petra asked, "You need anything?"

"Yeah, a new tablet, a shirt, and a bigger gun. Gérard could have more friends we don't know about." He moved quicker, tracking the blood left as breadcrumbs by his target. In retrospect, he wondered if Kamryn's tablet or comm had also been damaged. The bigger question: where was Gérard heading? Since he hadn't ducked into the first open doorway to seek refuge or aid, he had a destination in mind. Could he have more people waiting for him? Did he have access to a ship?

Every few minutes, the daylight increased, turning a smoky gray sky toward pale yellow. As shadows grew shorter, aromas of fresh coffee and grease frying wafted by on a lukewarm morning breeze. Any other day, Axel might have enjoyed a sunrise jog through the streets of an exotic tropical city.

Not today. Axel kicked himself in the ass for giving her time for revenge—something he'd told Kamryn he wouldn't do. If she'd taken care of business and neutralized her targets, they'd be finished and on their way out of Panama.

In his heart, he couldn't blame her for what had happened. Sometimes, no matter how well-laid your plans, even the best tactical strikes could go south. At least she'd followed Gérard. Kamryn could track a snake in the jungle. He trusted her skills, but he had reservations about her state of mind. Axel understood revenge firsthand. He'd try to make sure it didn't consume his friend.

Axel turned a corner to see Petra running at him. She screeched to a halt just short of smacking into him.

"I brought supplies," she said panting and breathless while she thrust things at him. "Shirt, water, holster, hand cannon, tablet—it's already set up same as your old one. Omigod, your hands are all cut up. Your eyes are red, too. Really red. Must've been the fumes. Here, I brought you jerky, your favorite kind. Ohashi and Malone are coming. I jumped out and ran ahead. Kamryn's a couple blocks to the left. We don't have a clue where she's going. When she stops, we'll recall the drones, then deploy them around the new perimeter."

Axel shrugged on an old sleeveless shirt with lots of pockets and a washed-out blue ship captain's hat with sweat stains. When the last two members of his team arrived, they looked the part of day laborers heading to work on a fishing vessel.

"We'll split up to flank Kamryn. No matter which way she turns, one team will be right behind her," Axel said. "Ohashi, you're with Malone." Axel squatted, pointing to blood stains on the street. "Gérard's been bleeding for the past three blocks. Not heavy, but I'm betting he's weak and looking for help. Maybe he's got friends, or a ship. If you get a clear shot, you have orders to take him out. Understood?"

***

Under a dark winter sky, a red hover trolley sped across open spaces of the TMD base. Floodlights shining from the corners of every building provided enough illumination to rival mid-day. Major Torance sat next to Sergeant Chancellor, who turned out to be a stickler for protocol. She stated it was SOP that everyone wore a vest and carried a weapon. He complied, but the new vest fit like a cast encircling his chest and forced him to sit erect while the small pulse handgun bulged in the pocket of his arctic white parka.

Torance griped his handrail as the trolley swerved around buildings. He glanced down at the medical case held firmly on the floor between his boots. It contained every life-saving tool he needed: a medical scanner, new KorVu monitor, military-grade nanites, pharmaceuticals for any contingency—even snake bite antivenom, a defibrillator, plus instruments to perform emergency surgery, if necessary. The closer they drew to the Solid Waste building, the tighter his gut twisted in knots with the uncertainty of what he might find.

Their driver, Corporal Saadir, made one last sharp turn before he parked beside other empty trolleys in front of a double metal door labeled: SOLID WASTE. The large, gray, two-story building occupied the northwest corner. Its new coat of paint failed to camouflage the architecture dated back seventy-five years or more, which made it one of the oldest structures on the base. As the primary waste facility, it disposed of paper, plastics, wood, food, glass, metals, and some hazardous wastes.

Saadir tapped his tablet to tell ISD they were on scene. "Sergeant Laughlin's squad got here first."

The rest of Chancellor's people arrived, dismounted, checked their gear, and waited for orders to enter. "Five minutes ago, Sergeant Laughlin's unit evacuated all Solid Waste employees. Her unit began searching for Captain Warren on the second floor. We have the ground floor. Everyone has a schematic of the building on their tablets. You will search every corner, cubbyhole, niche, nook, box, bin, and locker. We're looking for one of our own, an officer, alive or dead, in one piece—or parts. Understood?"

"Yes, Sergeant," they responded in unison.

"When you've completed a thorough search of each section, mark it off on your tablet. There's a sketchy diagram showing an old basement. If Warren is not found on either floor, both units will search the basement together. If you find something questionable, comm me right away." She opened the doors. "Let's get to it."

Torance grudgingly trudged after Chancellor, wishing she hadn't included "dead" or "parts" in her orders, despite knowing it might very well be true. Although Torance hadn't yet arrived at HQ when Colonel Harrington went missing, the doctor had accessed the colonel's medical records on the ride over. If the colonel was injured and required a transfusion or other emergency procedure, Torance could administer assistance. If found in an unrecognizable condition or deceased, the medical scanner could identify the remains within seconds. Admittedly, the same held true for Warren.

Over the next hour, the doctor responded to numerous requests for testing suspicious substances. He grew increasingly exasperated, however, when his scanner didn't work inside the building, which supported the accounts of shielding or interference with the use of electronic equipment. Over and over, he kept taking samples and running them outside to feed into his scanner for the biosignature tests. So far there'd been, seventeen positives for blood, but none belonging to Warren or Harrington. Teams searching every remote crevice on two floors of a large building full of hidden compartments took time. Lots of time. Torance wondered how much Warren had left.

An agitated Chancellor ran toward him shouting, "Doctor, to compactor number eight."

Torance rushed to meet her. They trotted in silence to the site. Two black-clad soldiers stood pointing at a questionable trail of dark spots. The doctor knelt to inspect the degraded substance, then took a sample outside for testing.

In seconds, his scanner identified it as belonging to Corporal Marla Dellucci, a clerk from DCM, the Defense Contract Management Division.

Chancellor brought him up to date. "Dellucci was reported AWOL three days before the explosion. We conducted a search but found no sign of foul play. She just…vanished."

"No, Sergeant, humans don't vanish. Since I cannot fathom any plausible explanation why her blood would be in proximity to a Solid Waste compactor—across the base from her office—I'm calling this a crime scene. Bring in a crew to dismantle that machine and haul it outside. I need to scan every part for biosignatures. Since there's evidence of one missing person in this facility, I've every reason to believe Warren is here, too." Feeling a cranky spell overtake him, he yelled at Chancellor as she walked away, "And find out why my equipment won't work in there!"

The doctor's scanner beeped again. The full spectrum analysis results on Dellucci's blood were complete. An addendum to the original report showed an overdose of VF-64, a fast-acting synthetic opioid in her system, incapacitating her within five minutes.

Without question, Torance saw this as another piece of the jigsaw puzzle incriminating Majors Ashley and Whitaker. Not only had they been colluding with the enemy for profit and implicated in treason, now their crimes included murder. The intel gathered by Warren and Foster must be shared. He scowled at the thought of having to run it up the chain of command again. Maybe he'd take his chances on going straight to the top. Not right then, but soon.

The Engineering team arrived. Their blue hover trolleys parked among the ISD red ones on the west side of the building.

In fifteen minutes the engineers had disassembled the compactor and spread the parts out on white hygienic tarps for Torance to scan.

When Sergeant Laughlin's unit finished searching the second floor, her team joined Chancellor's to complete the ground floor. Both sergeants moved outside to wait for the doctor's report. He passed the scanner over each piece with methodical precision, drawing red circles around the components registering even the slightest indication of a biosignature. Moments later, 97.5 percent came back belonging to Dellucci.

"Sergeant Chancellor, you may notify Forensics. I've found the remains of Corporal Marla Dellucci," his voice trailed off for a moment before adding, "such as they are." Torance took a knee, brought a fist to his chest, bowed his head in honor of a fallen soldier. A young, dark-eyed beauty with so much potential, drugged and callously thrown into a trash receptacle. An obscene waste of human life. Judging by the caliber of this crime, the odds of finding Warren alive plummeted.

Corporal Saadir appeared. "The first-floor search is finished. One of Sergeant Laughlin's people discovered an old blueprint. He might have located a basement door."

Torance stood, glared at everyone around him. "No engineer leaves until my equipment works inside that building. No one else leaves until Warren is found."

Chapter 14

Distorted thoughts. Broken memories. A galaxy of jumbled spaceships, guns, tunnels, and prisons. His mind disconnected. Lost in a nightmare that seemed all too real with ghosts of his enemies swirling close enough to touch.

Voices.

Neurons fired in his brain. They communicated across synapses, spiking a cascade of electricity until a jolt flipped the switch. His mind started to function on a sentient level. Something in his head screamed, *Think!*

Spurred by pain mixed with the frightening realization of being restrained, Mark awoke—bound and gagged.

That wasn't the worst part.

The stench of death turned his stomach. On the floor next to him lay a corpse. Not one dead from natural causes, either, as evidenced by the deep, razor-thin incision around his neck. From images circulated after his disappearance, Mark barely recognized Colonel Nash Harrington, TMD's missing Director of Artificial Intelligence. No longer in rigor, Mark estimated the body had been dead four or five days. The poor colonel smelled awful and looked worse—discolored, bloated, with dried blood trails from his mouth and nose.

Mark would join the colonel unless he devised an immediate escape plan. The last time Mark had been in a similar position, his friends had rescued him. Snowball's chance in hell of that happening today.

More voices, louder now, ranting, seething, furious. Not entirely in English. Russian.

Oh, shit.

Mark turned his head a few degrees to angle his augmented ear toward the noise. He heard the scuffle of feet, a door clanging shut, and one person muttering to himself. Mark peeked over the colonel.

Oh, boy. Another body. Bill. The unlucky maintenance worker Mark had tossed off the third-floor stairwell earlier. He looked worse than the colonel. Mark groaned internally. The bodies were piling up in this impromptu morgue. Mark feared he had a big number three on his forehead.

He tried to loosen whatever tied his wrists together. His increased activity brought back the same headache he'd had in the hospital. A real kick-your-ass-to-the-curb type of pain that came on in a flash camped for a while, then receded, returning later for an instant replay. Mark would rather get shot than experience more of these…uh-oh, something must be wrong with his KorVu monitor. He wouldn't have this headache if the nanites were doing their job.

"Hey, you." The voice came from behind him.

Oh, what now? Mark scrunched his eyes closed, held his breath.

"I saw you moving around over there."

An agonizing pain streaked through Mark's head. He flinched as footsteps approached. Rough hands rolled him over, ripped the tape off his face.

Ted. The alpha personality with the sociopathic, gray-eyed stare, not to mention the big knot in the middle of his forehead from the head-butting incident. And a busted nose.

Mark tried to speak, but gagged from a dry mouth.

Ted sneered as he threw water on Mark's face. "They might need you, so I have to keep you alive, or you'd already be like those two." Ted moved around, proud, dominant, giving his captive a malevolent glare. "Billy wasn't the sharpest tool in the shed, but he was useful."

Pleased to hear he might live a while longer, Mark renewed his efforts to undo the bindings around his hands while he kept Ted talking. "That's not my fault. I defended myself."

Ted gave him another look. "No, you killed him. I'm a witness."

Mark knew that look well. He'd received it from the female psychopath who'd tried to kill him. "Nooo, *you're* an accomplice. You and Billy set a trap to kill me. I'm the victim. You two are the criminals. No matter who gave the orders, you'll go down for it."

"Nah, I got juice." Ted pushed the sleeves up on his beefy arms before relaxing in the room's only chair.

Mark snorted. "You'll *get* juiced is more like it. A heavy dose of SP-27 with a halo interrogation until you're turned into a puddle of crap. They'll scoop you off the floor and fling you into a cell to rot."

Ted gave him that smile again, the one that didn't reach his eyes. "Billy did it. I killed nobody. I swear," he said, raising hands to the sky in a quasi-religious gesture.

Mark stopped short of laughing. Not a good idea to aggravate his captor while at Ted's mercy. Mark had a bad habit of thinking he could walk on water, but it wasn't happening this time.

Ted stared at Mark like a mountain lion eyeing a wounded deer. His pupils narrowed, one side more than the other, as if he were zeroing in on Mark through a long-range scope. Ted, the hunter. Mark, the prey.

Mark had to escape, especially before Ted's boss returned or they changed his orders. Spurred to action, Mark rolled to an upright position for better leverage to work on freeing his hands. Mark still had his vest, and the knives in his boots. Although he didn't see a weapon in the room, Ted weighed more, might have a knife, but wore no vest. With all the hours recently spent functioning on a scientific level, his brain reduced the components of the present situation to a basic formula: Sociopath + mass + knife vs. Intelligence + vest + knife (x2). Simple, yet doable.

Mark congratulated himself as his right thumb slipped free of its binding, whether aided by sweat or blood, he couldn't tell.

Faint whirring noises from Ted's tablet broke the silence. He checked it for messages, looked at Mark with lifeless gray eyes. To unnerve his captive, Ted stood and walked over to gaze down at Mark. "Plans have changed." He drew a knife from his boot, exactly where Mark kept his own, slit the tape between Mark's ankles. After pulling a gun from his brown coveralls pocket, Ted hoisted Mark up, opened the door and pushed him into a long, dark hallway. "Move."

Mark stumbled forward, only the dim light from Ted's tablet providing light. Mark realized how wrong he'd been about Ted's weapons. He wouldn't underestimate the man again.

Not knowing why or where they were going, much less what would happen to him when he arrived, triggered another headache. Mark's head pounded. He faltered, and fell.

***

Kamryn missed Gérard by seconds. She'd tracked him to a run-down sailor's bar where he'd disappeared. No one even remembered seeing a bloody man.

She walked outside, leaned against the wall, slid to the ground. and hugged her knees.

Kamryn faced it head-on. This was all her fault. Seeing Gérard in person had triggered so much more than she could handle. Her stomach churned, bile rose in her throat. She swallowed to keep from heaving. Without her tablet or comm, she sat alone, stricken with remorse for Gérard's escape. Defeated, and way past hungry or thirsty, Kamryn succumbed to exhaustion. She bowed her head as a mountain of guilt the size of Mt. Everest weighed on her.

Someone walked out of the bar. *"Qué tal una bebida, señorita?"*

"Step off, scumbag," she growled.

Paper money floated down between her ankles, a crisp Terran fifty. Ready to spout a string of obscenities, Kamryn shot a glance upward.

Axel smiled down at her. "You didn't wait for me." When he held out a hand, she reluctantly took it. He pulled her up.

They locked eyes.

Kamryn stood only an inch shorter than Axel, but at this moment, she felt small. "I knew you'd be okay." She hung her head in disgrace. "I lost him."

Petra approached cautiously from behind Axel, unsure how volatile Kamryn might still be. "It's okay. Ohashi and I found him."

Kamryn's face lit up. "Is he dead?"

"No." She handed Kamryn a comm unit and tablet. "But we have to hurry."

As the three jogged away, Kamryn inserted the new comm in her ear.

Ohashi's voice came over it immediately. "We redeployed the drones to search for Gérard. They spotted him getting into a car with two other men. It delivered them to a ship at a private spaceport minutes from where you are. Malone is with me. We're surveilling the location. Nguyen's ready to pick us up here as soon as they leave. We'll be ready to follow them wherever they go."

A feeling of absolution lifted the cloud over Kamryn. Running side by side with Axel, her spirits rose with the promise of catching Gérard. Fate was granting her one last chance to rectify a mistake she should never have made. Kamryn would take it, no matter what it cost her.

They advanced on the security barrier surrounding the site. Petra checked her tablet for Ohashi's position, then led them to an impromptu opening in the fence, courtesy of Malone, behind a maintenance shed. Gathered on the far side, Ohashi pointed to the craft perched on the edge of the tarmac. "Moments ago, two men almost had to carry Gérard onto that steel blue ship with G-38 on the tail. It's a Diplomat model, less than one third the size and speed of ours, maximum capacity of ten passengers. They're getting ready to depart. Don't have their destination yet, but I'm working on it."

"Look—look!" Petra exclaimed. "Landing gear's up—liftoff."

Malone commed Nguyen with an all-clear message. Within seconds, she descended on the very spot left by the other ship. *MAVREK* didn't land, just hovered as the hatch swung open. Nguyen motioned them in before running back to the pilot's cabin.

Kamryn sank into her chair to harness up, grateful to be back on their ship, no matter where they were headed. Interior lights dimmed to a soft blue as they lifted into the air. Both cybers worked their tablets to infiltrate the Diplomat's systems. Trained by the military, Petra and Ohashi were experts at long-range hacking, not only into ships systems, but communications, weapons, satellites, drones, and everything in between.

Except for a visual verification, *MAVREK* would remain hidden from the Diplomat because of an anti-surveillance program Ohashi had designed while on Mars. Once the TMD learned of its existence and capabilities, they had made her an offer she couldn't refuse. Ohashi sold her proprietary software, labeled SRVL, to the military and made a fortune. Without their knowledge, however, she'd kept the most advanced model under wraps—for her ship alone.

Malone announced over their comms, "The Diplomat wasn't built for interplanetary travel." He snorted. "It's nothing more than a fancy taxi cab, not even as space-worthy as a TMD shuttle—and those are tanks with wings."

Nguyen chimed in. "My cousin piloted a Diplomat. He ferried CEO's globally, to the Space Station, and Luna. But its size limits them to translunar flights." She chuckled. "We won't be going to Mars today."

"Hey," Petra chirped, "guess who owns that ship."

Everyone gave her their attention.

"*CenPharmica*, a Guatemalan pharmaceutical company." Petra became hyper, flapping her hands. "You will *not* believe this—guess who supplied Gérard with drugs in Canada!"

"Wait…I remember *CenPharmica* from his trial," Kamryn said. "The Canadian and American authorities put them on the International Watch List database for corporations involved in criminal enterprises. No wonder he headed straight for this area. They must be bankrolling his new location in Central America."

"Which is non-operational," Axel interjected. "Their lab is trashed. All the employees have been fired. The kingpin, if you can call him that, has been sliced and diced. What's left?"

"He's still alive. And he knows it was me," Kamryn said. "If I were financing an enormously lucrative illicit business that suffered a setback, I'd pick up my marbles, go down the street, and start over again."

Nguyen's soft voice came over their comms. "She's right, you know. The pilot who shot my ship full of holes turned away to take out another ship because he thought I was dead. Instead, I did something unexpected—rolled over and came up underneath him. Sent every torpedo I had left into his port side.

Four missed. The last two didn't. They blew right through the center of his ship. I gave him the finger on his way down. If you cripple an enemy, you finish him so he doesn't come back to bite you in the ass. I ended up losing both feet in the crash, but my new ones work just fine. Anyway, I'm here, and he isn't."

Kamryn had heard the story several times, but with each telling, a new little nugget of information came to light. Still, truer words were never spoken. Even as soldiers in the elite Armored Unit, she and Axel knew their job wasn't done until every enemy had been neutralized—a euphemism for killed. She suspected Axel didn't want to put the rest of the team in any more danger as his reason for accepting the status quo. So be it. She'd make her apologies, then go it alone.

***

On orders of Captain Dyllan Wexler of the Martian Military Command, Lotus Chang's ship, *Kailani*, had dropped their shields and powered down to drift in space. Captain Hector Torres paced on the raised dais platform in front of his command chair, hovering between the pilot and navigator.

To the left, Lotus Chang struck a pose, arms crossed, scowling at everyone on the bridge. She fumed, barely able to contain her wrath at coming up on the short end of a situation, much less acquiesce to a power greater than her own. With all her neurological enhancements, Chang had never failed to decrypt or infiltrate a system—until now. The Martian ship had proven un-hackable, as had every attempt to stall or waylay them. Time had run out. They were in a dead zone.

The lethal MMC warship advanced into their forward viewscreen, torpedoes, plasma cannons, and gun turrets trained directly at *Kailani's* bridge. It bristled with enough firepower to slag a planet, much less reduce Chang's ship to sub-atomic particles.

A voice barked orders over the commlink. "*Kailani*, be advised, *Armageddon* is coming alongside. Open your main outer airlock and prepare for boarding by order of the Martian Military Command. Any uncooperative, hostile, or *stupid* move by a Terran will be met with a terminal response."

While Torres remained on the bridge to oversee the docking maneuvers, Chang ran down three levels to await the Martian boarding party. Crew members flattened themselves against the bulkheads to avoid being trampled. She arrived moments before a shudder from the MMC's boarding shuttle clamped onto the hull to secure a seal over the outer hatch. Martians filed into *Kailani's* airlock, waited for it to pressurize, then opened the inner hatch. Sixteen giant soldiers in midnight blue armor flowed into Chang's ship, their humanity hidden behind mirrored faceplates, hands enclosed in metal gauntlets that aimed foreign rifles at every Terran assembled to greet them.

Captain Torres appeared beside Chang. Compared to his normal, jittery state, he seemed remarkably calm.

Martians moved aside to allow an armored officer from the rear through their ranks. They stopped in front of Torres, thumbed up their faceplate, revealing a dark-skinned man with blue eyes. "I am Captain Wexler of the MMC warship *Armageddon*."

Torres stepped forward to introduce himself, offering a tablet to Wexler. "We are not pirates, Captain, as you can see from our manifest."

"State your business in this quadrant," Wexler said, his tone both clipped and grumpy while he scanned the datapad.

"*Kailani* is a ship of explorers on their way to Ganymede to survey for the possibility of setting up an outpost."

"Personally, I don't care where you're from or where you're going. Owing to increased reports of piracy, my orders are to search every ship passing through this quadrant. We've found the wide majority of pirates are Terran. As a result, all crew and passengers will submit to a DNA check. I will hold anyone with an outstanding warrant in our brig and ship them back to Terra. We don't need Terran criminals in our space."

Chang froze. First, she'd forgotten about the old warrant from five or six years ago—an insignificant act of retaliation for someone who'd defaulted on payment. They'd received an explosive gift which had accidentally been fatal. Second, since Chang had transformed herself into a cyborg-artificial intelligence hybrid, her DNA had also changed. She took small steps backward, fading into a group of uniformed officers, trying not to draw attention to herself.

Wexler addressed Torres. "Captain, please have someone show Lieutenant Janek and his platoon to the cargo hold." Wexler half-turned, motioning additional armored troops forward. "Lieutenant Zocchi and her platoon will follow you to the bridge."

Chang paused at the unexpected doubling of Martians. She was torn between sneaking back into her quarters to remove the warrant from the Terran Criminal Justice database, or accompanying the Martian soldiers to ensure they disturbed none of her 112 prized possessions in the cargo bay.

The deck vibrated from heavily armored footsteps rushing through the corridors in opposite directions.

Chang's sense of self-preservation won out. Ready to make a break for her quarters, she eased away from the cluster of crew still gathered awaiting orders. Before she turned, Wexler looked her straight in the eyes.

"Who are you?"

Stopped in her tracks, she said, "Lotus Chang. *Kailani* is my ship."

He tapped the datapad. "Well, that's a problem. It says here Mingzhu Chang is the registered owner."

"That's my legal name. My father called me Lotus as a child. I use it to honor him."

Wexler waved a soldier forward who'd been behind him. "This conflicting information needs..." Wexler hesitated, listening to a message on his helmet's comm. "There's another problem. Miss Chang, please lead Sergeant Lassiter and myself to the cargo hold."

Chang eyed Lassiter, an armored 6-foot female with a deadpan expression, her gloved hand resting on a large sidearm. Chang had no choice but to obey, as it had been an order, not a request. The longer these Martians were on her ship, the more she felt they would never leave. Her entire plan was unraveling, and she didn't yet know what problem waited for her in the cargo bay.

Chang took the long way, compiling a list of every scenario the Martians might see as a negative while creating a plausible explanation for each one. She arrived in the main cargo compartment, confident she had the situation in hand.

Lieutenant Janek's raised face shield showed a look of disgust imbedded in his deep frown lines. "Captain, we've discovered 112 clones in cryopods. They are children, sir. Most are under the age of consent. According to documentation, no reason is given for their transport."

"Miss Chang," Wexler intoned, as though a teacher speaking to a troublemaker. "Mars has a zero-tolerance policy regarding trafficking of any kind." Wexler tapped his tablet as he spoke. "Under the Articles of Martian Constitutional Law, Statute 8, Chapter 12 recognizes clones as equals to natural born humans, having all the same rights and privileges.

"Section 714 prohibits interplanetary trafficking in persons, whether for commercial sex, forced labor, involuntary servitude, bondage, or slavery. Clones shall not be property. The penalty for each offense is nine years multiplied by 112. You're looking at 1,008 years, plus a fine of 50,000 credits per offense which equals 5,600,000 credits." He offered his tablet to Chang as proof of his claims.

Unnerved, Chang concealed an influx of stinging resentment while admitting this wasn't the only option she hadn't expected. She also hadn't foreseen losing communications with *Stellaria* or being stopped by a Martian warship, either. Too many coincidences to be an accident. She needed an excuse for the clones and decided to blame it on Stepanov, who'd gotten away so no one could refute her story. "But, I'm only transporting them for an associate who did not have sufficient space on their ship."

"You have claimed ownership of this vessel. Therefore, you are transporting them *illegally.* That decision will stand." Wexler motioned to Lassiter. "Sergeant, you may take the crew's DNA. Start with Miss Chang's."

Lassiter lifted the right forearm of her armor, slid back a plate covering the embedded scanner, and held it in front of Chang's mouth. "Open your mouth. Please exhale between the red lines."

Chang glanced around the room. From right to left, every Martian's weapon was trained on her. She had no place to run, no place to hide. Indignation mixed with fear rose to critical levels in Chang as she complied with the order.

In seconds, a disturbed expression replaced Lassiter's deadpan stare. She turned to Wexler, reporting in a clear voice, "Captain, this…*lifeform*…is less than 20 percent human. However, there's still enough DNA to match with an outstanding Terran Murder Warrant issued five years and seven months ago for Mingzhu Chang."

"Cuff her," Wexler barked.

Gloved hands pulled Chang's arms behind her. As the stun cuffs were slipped on, Chang panicked. She exploded in a flurry of unhinged rage, fists striking the soldiers who surrounded her, legs kicking the midnight blue armor in a vain attempt to lash out at her captors. The enhanced strength of Chang's cyborg limbs and the increased speed from her enhanced neural implant rendered her an overwhelming opponent to an average human. Nevertheless, she was no match for the professional Martian troops sheathed in armor from head to boot. They had her on the deck in no time, hands and feet cuffed, plus a gag to muffle the obscenities she spewed at them.

This morning, Lotus Chang had been the mistress of her own ship, giving orders, streaking across space toward the promise of riches beyond imagination. In an instant, all her dreams had disintegrated. She now lay restrained, with no choice but to watch and listen.

"Lassiter, where are our ships?"

"They've arrived, sir. *Marauder* to port, *Vindictus* to starboard. This ship isn't going anywhere."

"The Terrans?"

"The TMC warship *Achilles* is coming in hot, sir, with *Titan* right behind her. Two more, *Vengeance* and *Colossus,* broke off to follow *Stellaria.* They plan to cut off any escape while our *Hellindra* will join *Scorpius* to meet her head-on."

"Very well." Wexler turned to Janek. "Lieutenant, have Chang hauled to the main airlock. Keep her shackled to the deck, under armored guard for the Terrans." Wexler bent over a pod to look at the face of a young, dark-skinned girl. "Lassiter, let's open one of these. I want to know what—if anything—

these children were told about where they were being taken or why. And record it."

Chapter 15

"No," Axel said, his voice loud but steady. "You're not going by yourself. It isn't safe."

"Well I sure as hell can't ask anyone else to risk *their* lives!" Kamryn yelled back, face flushed with emotion. Back to being a brunette, she stood across the conference table from him with a belligerent set to her jaw, not about to give in.

From their seats at the table, the cybers and pilots had remained silent as they witnessed the two alphas verbally butt heads over how best to proceed.

"I'm volunteering. No need to ask," Axel said, equally unshakable.

Ohashi cast her vote. "Me too."

Just above a whisper, Petra said, "Me three."

"I love a good fight." Nguyen cracked a smile.

"We're all in." Malone made it unanimous.

A reluctant Kamryn slumped into her chair, acknowledging they had outvoted her.

With NewSkin gloves covering his raw hands, Axel gingerly pushed away from their conference table and adopted his sergeant persona. "The drones have been surveilling *CenPharmica* for hours. We know Gérard's inside, probably in their infirmary on the second floor. We'll breach the building from the top at night. Neutralize him. Torch the place like we did in India. Be out in no time. We leave no trace and bring down one of the biggest criminal drug enterprises in Central America."

"First, we need to get into their system." Ohashi tucked a wayward lock of hair behind her ear. "These people don't have cyborgs or armored guards, but there is plenty of high-grade tech."

In mock disbelief, Axel asked, "Are you saying you can't handle it?"

"No!" cried both cybers in unison.

Ohashi tapped the table to emphasize points as she spoke. "We need time to exploit vulnerabilities in their operating systems. Trojans, worms, viruses, locating backdoors, installing rootkits—they all take time. I'll start by sending them a very impressive resumé, which will get us into the system. Then the fun begins." She waggled her eyebrows.

Petra swung her vid screen around for everyone to see the building schematic. "I'll attach a stick of RD-81 to the drones, and program each one to attach itself to a specific load-bearing wall. When you give the command, they'll detonate in sequence to give you more time to clear the area."

"Since Mark's not here, I'll use his armor," Malone said. "It's too big for Nguyen, so she'll stay on the ship and monitor us from here."

"After we're finished in Guatemala," Nguyen advised, "our next destination will be the Arizona desert. It's the safest place I've seen in years—almost 100 percent free of electromagnetic interference. Without knowing how long we might have to stay, I suggest we stock up on supplies. Don't want people dying of starvation." She pushed a tablet toward Axel. "Took inventory of the Med Lab. We're also running low on a few of those things. They're on my list."

Axel looked straight at Kamryn. "We have a plan for getting in and getting out and where to go to lie low. You have anything to add?"

Kamryn shook her head. "Thank you all," she intoned in a small, soft voice, not meeting their eyes.

"Good. You can drill Malone in the finer points of using armor while Petra and I go pick up supplies."

"Oh boy, a field trip!" Petra said. "Can we stop for lunch?"

Axel chuckled as he draped an arm over her shoulder. Leaving the conference room, he bent over to whisper in her ear. "What have I taught you, Petra?"

"Keep my head on a swivel, check my six, keep my back to the wall, and never leave home without a gun." She rushed off toward her quarters, saying, "Meet you at the hatch."

He stopped off at the weapons locker to stow his vest and the large plasma hand canon, opting for a shoulder holster with the smaller pulse gun.

They had followed the Diplomat ship carrying Gérard to a substantial facility housing *CenPharmica* Laboratorios, fifty miles northwest of Guatemala City. On the surface it was an unusual location for a large pharmaceutical company, though, in retrospect, ideal considering its illegal pursuits. It sat on the edge of a decent-sized city with an up-scale suburban district populated by the well-paid drug company employees.

Wearing what might be mistaken for pilot's uniforms, they left *MAVREK* tucked away from view in a public spaceport. A quick cab ride through tree-lined streets dropped them at the nearest shopping complex. Inside, Axel gave in to Petra's pouty request for lunch at a trendy sidewalk café. Their young waiter kept sneaking appreciative glances at Petra.

"He keeps giving you the eye," Axel said. "I'm going to look around. Chat him up. See what he knows about *CenPharmica*."

Thrilled to assume the role of an undercover operative, Petra became secret agent Megan Lennox, a newly graduated astronavigator employed by Mavrek Air.

Axel left her chatting with the waiter in private while he searched for a bakery. He returned carrying a pale pink box of sweets in each hand. "Did you learn anything?"

"Boy, did I," she said, walking beside him to catch another cab. "The waiter, Carlos, makes good money—mainly because

CenPharmica is the largest employer in the region and pays their employees well. Carlos heard the local law enforcement has also been on their payroll for years with orders to bury anything negative affecting *CenPharmica*."

"Good to know. You can research that connection when we get back to the ship."

"Ohashi was monitoring my commlink and heard everything. She's already working on it." Petra stared at the boxes. "Whatcha' got there?"

"Bribes."

"What flavor are they?"

"Chocolate, mango, and coconut."

"I'll take three bribes."

"Not yet," Axel cautioned. "But I'll let you carry the boxes if you promise not to open them."

Petra nodded eagerly as she reached for the boxes.

After the cab made two more stops, they returned to the ship with a load of medical supplies and food stuffs.

***

Mark's head throbbed with every heartbeat. He lay on the floor. It felt ice cold against his face and hands, indicating he had a hellacious fever.

"Get up, smartass," Ted insisted, nudging Mark with his boot. "You're too big to carry. I'd just as soon leave you here and send someone else back to get you."

With his hands still bound, he struggled to stand, reaching out for the wall to steady himself. Despite his weakened condition, his mind created a mantra in case a miracle presented an opportunity to escape. Stumbling through the dark, dank hallway, he followed Ted's light, silently repeating, *Knife in boot, gun in pocket, take the tablet.*

A whirring noise echoed in the emptiness. "Jeez, what do they want now?" Ted stopped to fish the tablet out of his pocket. "Yeah?"

Mark rested his back against the wall, then bent over as if taking a breather. He paid no attention to the conversation. Instead he focused on Ted. The longer his captor spoke the more distracted he became. With slow, cautious movements, knowing this moment committed him to escaping, Mark slipped the knife from his boot.

No turning back now.

He slit the tape between his hands while trying to banish the drumbeat in his head and ignore the rivers of sweat running down his temples. Realizing he had neither the strength nor the stamina for a fight, Mark decided to aim for Ted's jugular. He'd killed a man there before, he could do it again.

A wave of dizziness washed over him, threatening to derail his plans. Without an iron will to slow his pulse or grant him temporary sanity, he would never be able to pull this off. Somehow, he found a measure of peace lurking in the darkness.

Mark repeated his mantra and waited—not for long. Intuition alerted him a nanosecond after Ted ended the call.

Faking a stumble, he bumped into Ted. Anxiety fueled adrenalin sped through Mark as he slashed across the jugular vein with such precision Ted gave no indication, he even felt the wound.

Until he saw the blood flowing down his coveralls onto the ground.

Mark staggered backward out of his captor's reach. The euphoria of success evaporated, as did his stamina.

"Wha…" Ted dropped his tablet, turned to Mark, bug-eyed, a strangled whimper escaping his open mouth. He clamped a hand over the cut, helpless to stem the blood pumping through his fingers. It ran down his sleeve like water out of a garden hose. His tablet lay on the ground, its light shining on dark, glistening pools forming around his boots. Ted clearly could not fathom what had happened. Gurgling, he sank to the ground, folded at the waist, and fell face forward.

"That's what you get for making me miss my date with Désirée."

For one fleeting millisecond, a twinge of regret passed over Mark about what he'd been forced to do. But it passed. He still wasn't used to killing and hoped he never would be. Regardless, he respected the hefty dose of self-preservation that Axel and Kamryn had beaten into him.

Mark took Ted's gun, retrieved the tablet, and tried to contact Torance. The message failed. He tried Ongaru. The message went through.

Seconds later she called him, a look of pure shock on her face. "Warren, where are you?"

"I don't know," he said, feeling so weary he sat on the floor, leaning back against the wall. "Underground, I think."

"Don't disconnect, whatever you do." Ongaru turned away, yelling, "Lieutenant Foster, have ISD trace this call immediately—it's Warren!"

Addressing Mark, she asked, "What do your surroundings look like?"

"I woke up in a room with two dead bodies. Then I was moved through a corridor without lighting." Mark's proximity to the pool of coppery-smelling blood triggered a wave of nausea, accompanied by the return of his splitting headache. He began to spiral downward. "Sorry, Colonel, I think I'm going to pass out soon."

"Negative, Warren. I'm ordering you to remain conscious until help arrives." She turned to bark at Foster again. "Lieutenant, I want that location *now!*"

"My KorVu isn't working…fever…headache…" Mark closed his eyes, sliding to the floor, grateful for the cold surface next to his cheek. It reminded him of damp, crusty snow. He suddenly wanted to go skiing. With his brother. And Maeve. No. They were dead. Weren't they? Well, maybe another time.

His mind wandered, trailing off on strange tangents, unable to concentrate on anything for longer than a second or two.

"Warren? Warren, answer me, dammit! We have people on the way. Hang on a little longer."

Mark's augmented ear heard the words, knew on some level they were spoken to him, although he couldn't focus on their meaning. The intense pounding in his head rose and fell with irregularity, making the pain impossible to anticipate or control. He fought it with all the willpower he had left, then surrendered to unconsciousness.

***

"Come on, son, wake up," said a familiar voice as hands patted his face—not in a gentle manner.

Lots of chatter from different people filled in the background noise.

Mark's eyes fluttered open to a well-lit corridor with uniformed personnel giving and responding to commands. His headache had faded to barely noticeable.

A rugged face with pale blue eyes and a full head of white hair came into view.

"Glad to see you, sir." Mark croaked.

Major Torance grinned at him. "Right about now, I'm sure you're glad to see anybody."

"Especially you, sir." Mark never meant anything more in his whole life. He tried to move, but his body didn't respond.

Torance passed a scanner over Mark's head and torso. "Had to work awhile to stabilize you. Not to worry—no irreversible harm done. You're half-naked and strapped to an emergency gurney. I came bearing gifts: nanites, battlefield drugs, and Sergeant Chancellor."

A pretty blond peeked around Torance's shoulder. "Hi there, Captain. You the one who took out Jumbo Jim over there?"

"'Fraid so."

"I'm impressed. You looked a little gray around the edges when we first got here. You've improved a lot since then. How did you end up down here, anyway?"

"No idea. I don't even know where *'here'* is. You find the other bodies?"

"Yes, sir. We've notified Colonel Harrington's family."

"Colonel Ongaru?"

Torance peeled the electrodes off Mark's chest. "She'll join us later. You gave her quite a scare. That woman wields a big stick. She had scores of people tracking you within seconds."

Chancellor signaled for three ISD soldiers. The male came to guide the hover gurney, while both females walked point in tandem with rifles cradled in their arms.

As the group moved out, Chancellor walked beside Mark to the left. On his right, Torance said, "We were close by in the Solid Waste facility, but an unusual dampening field interfered with our comms. We notified Dimitrios when Harrington was located. That's when everything came out. And I do mean *everything*. He's meeting with Ongaru and Foster now. They're waiting for us at the hospital."

Mark cringed, praying his part in Fulton's capture and release never came out. The slight rhythmic motion of being transported plus the euphoria from the combined drugs and nanites lulled Mark into a cozy, relaxed state. It vanished the moment they lifted him onto a bed.

"Major Torance, is Captain Warren lucid enough for debriefing?"

Mark recognized the general's voice immediately. He attempted to sit up, but several pairs of hands pushed him down as they attached wireless electrodes and monitoring equipment.

"Warren's coherent, sir," Torance replied. "Just be advised he's had emergency resuscitation, been oxygenated, received a double dose of MG-9 nanites, and a list of pharmaceuticals too numerous to mention."

Hospital personnel moved out of the general's way as he approached Mark's bed. "Are you up for this, Warren?"

Mark thought he saw genuine concern fixed in the deepening lines of Dimitrios' face. "I've had quite a day, sir, but I'll try to answer your questions."

Torance dismissed the nurses. Sergeant Eklund, the general's longtime aide and former light heavyweight boxer, brought a chair to Mark's bedside for Dimitrios. He parked himself, undid the top button of his tunic, and leaned forward with a very perplexed expression. "I want to know what started all this. Eklund's recording every word."

And so it went, beginning with Mark's overheard conversations between Majors Whitaker and Ashley. Lieutenant Foster stepped forward. He picked up the story with his orders to surveille the majors and his sitrep to Torance and Mark. Torance shared Axel's reporting of AIs hunting for their ship. Colonel Ongaru described how Mark detected the SIB-25 bot in the wall. Torance interjected the part about Mark's KorVu readings and the hunt for him. Chancellor added the segment where Marla Dellucci's DNA was found in the Solid Waste compactor and locating three corpses before they found Mark. He finished the narrative by glossing over the encounter with Bill and Ted, feigning a lapse of memory on exactly how Bill died. No need to dwell on irreversible technicalities. Besides, he'd already admitted to killing Ted—only because he had no one else to blame. In retrospect, he'd have some tales to tell when he returned to his ship.

During the discourse, the general remained quiet, although his expression changed a number of times, from engaged to alarmed, somber to indignant. At the end, all five of them waited for his reaction.

"That's the most convoluted story I've heard in a long time. Sounds like a tale some drunkard in a bar on Luna might spin." Dimitrios laughed. It carried a cynical ring and had a chilling effect on the room. "I'm certain each of you is 100 percent loyal to the TMD, or you'd all be decomposing in a stockade." He scrubbed his face with both hands, ran fingers through his silver temples, grabbed his knees. "Clear the room…please—and wait for me outside. Torance, Eklund, you two stay."

With only four people left, the pale green room seemed large and empty. Torance stood on the opposite side of his patient to monitor the machine's screen as it received data from the dozen electrodes scattered over Mark's face and chest. "Will this take long, sir? Warren's stimulants are tapering off."

"No, Major, I have a few more questions—of a personal nature. How is your father?"

"Dad's doing good, sir," Mark replied. "Back to seeing patients. We'd finished dinner and were getting ready to trim the tree when Major Brandt arrived. But I think mom was near tears as I left."

The general frowned. "And Sergeant Von Radach?"

"Just as hard-core as ever, sir. Chews nails for breakfast."

This brought a genuine smile to his face. "I've seen the vid he sent Torance of those two AIs who were looking for your ship. You have any idea how they're connected to this scenario?"

"I admit to being clueless on that one, sir. I haven't spoken to any of my team since I left Portland—due to the blackout. Colonel Ongaru did authorize a call to my family."

"These are perilous times, gentlemen. Again, I find myself having to deal with traitors who rained death and destruction down on the sacred ground of TMD Headquarters. The recent developments have unequivocally undermined the most prominent and fundamental of Terran institutions, corroding faith in our ability to defend the value of human life in the nations we've sworn to protect. The guilty have forsaken loyalty for greed in their attempt to destroy our way of life for the betterment of their own." High emotion edged his complexion toward an unhealthy shade of crimson. "I vow to purge every single disloyal soldier in uniform, regardless of rank," he pounded his knee with a meaty fist, "even if I have to administer the SP-27 myself."

TMD used the drug, a vastly upgraded form of Sodium Pentothal—or scopolamine—as a mainstay for every military interrogation. They made no assumptions of guilt or innocence until all parties were questioned under the influence of SP-27, used in conjunction with a medical halo attached to the subject's head like a crown. Thus, the phrase: Sitting in the Truth or Die Seat. Mark had received a dose during his debriefing after the attack on CAMRI, and definitely didn't want another.

"Before the day is out, I will have Majors Ashley and Whitaker confessing to every sin committed since Jesus was a corporal. Then have them both burned at the stake in front of the main entrance to Headquarters—on a Sunday." Dimitrios turned to his aide, Sergeant Eklund. "Get me Colonel Iverson in ISD. I want those two sonsabitches in my stockade yesterday."

Torance waved a scanner over Dimitrios. The doctor shook his head, scolding with a tsk-tsk. "Sir, we need to bring down your vitals if you intend to monitor their interrogation. It'd be a shame if you didn't live long enough to see their demise."

Eklund clamped a hand on the general's shoulder to prevent him from leaving.

"Very well," Dimitrios grumbled, "but make it quick."

After the doctor left, Dimitrios leaned forward, adopting a confidential tone. "Warren, report to me when Torance releases you. I have a plan, and it needs a scientist who can handle himself and is smarter than the people we're dealing with. I'll inform Ongaru of your reassignment." He held up a hand to halt any potential remarks from Mark. "You'll get your tablet and comm back. I also want to talk with Von Radach about that AI incident."

It would've been a lie to admit he wasn't interested in what the general had in mind, yet Mark had gotten comfortable being in charge of his Cybernetic unit and being near Désirée.

Torance breezed back in with an injector full of happy juice for the general. After a few moments, the beet red color in Dimitrios' face drained away.

"Thank you, Major. Now if you give me your word Warren will be released in the next six hours, I'll be on my way."

The doctor's shoulders sagged as he huffed in protest. "I'll have to pump him full of drugs."

"If it's good enough for me, it's damn well good enough for him, too."

Chapter 16

The drugs worked. Six hours and twenty-one minutes later, Captain Mark Warren sat in a conference room with seven other officers, all his senior by many years. On the surface, Mark did not look like everyone else. He wore the uniform, but in accordance with the general's orders, remained unshaven with long hair. The last to arrive was a man his age in civilian clothes who resembled Mark in build, yet with dark features. A face covered in rugged stubble made the newcomer look as shaggy as Mark.

Sitting at the head of the table, Dimitrios cleared his throat. "Everything said in this room is classified as Top Secret, contingent upon the loss of rank and pension including time in a military penitentiary." He slid a tablet to the gray-haired, three-star general at his right. They all pressed their palm print to the screen as a biometric signature before passing it on.

"Now I will share our latest news from the Martian authorities. Two Terran ships were tracked into Martian space. From our interrogation of Wade Fulton, we knew their names and payloads. The first one, *Kailani*, has been stopped by the MMC *Armageddon*. All crew and passengers taken into custody without causality. She carried 112 underage clones, a veritable cache of cyborg and AI prototypes, fifty-seven crew—including Lotus Chang, the person we deem responsible for the explosions and loss of life here at Headquarters. As a bonus, Chang had an open murder warrant, which means she'll never see the light of day again. She's warming a bench in the Titan's stockade while they and the *Achilles* escort *Kailani* back to Terra."

This intel was met with guarded smiles and murmurs of approval, Mark's included. However, the reason for his presence remained a mystery. Across the table, his counterpart wore a poker face, giving no hint if he knew any more or less than Mark.

"The sister ship, *Stellaria*, may have gotten spooked. She veered off around the far side of Mars. We have two TMD ships, *Vengeance* and *Colossus*, coming up behind her to cut off any escape while the MMC *Hellindra* and *Scorpius* will confront her. *Stellaria* is carrying the apocalyptic payload: three doomsday viruses, and enough components to produce nuclear and/or thermonuclear warheads to obliterate a moon."

Dimitrios closed his eyes before assuming a calm, almost weary expression.

"From a preliminary interrogation of Chang, we've learned *Stellaria* was fitted with black-market weapons and is carrying 117 clones in cryopods. These are *children*, for God's sake, purchased for the sole purpose of being used as slaves on Ganymede." With elbows on the table, Dimitrios cupped his head in two beefy hands. Seconds stretched into an uncomfortable gulf of silence. He scanned the faces at the table. "I'd prefer to save the lives of those children, but…we all know *Stellaria* must be stopped—one way or another. The firepower brought to bear by four warships against her would obliterate all evidence of that ship from the galaxy."

The left side of his mouth twitched with a smile, showing the first signs of an upswing in his attitude. "We do have a Hail Mary left open to us—the RAM-XT. General Krieger has a final update for you." Dimitrios waved an open palm at the officer to his left.

As one of those men who'd developed a shiny bald head with a crown-like fringe of white hair, Krieger looked more like a monk than a four-star general. "Under normal conditions, it would still be in the experimental phase, although tests have proven 98 percent positive. However, due to the unprecedented circumstances, all four Terran warships left carrying the weapon. Our new microwave pulse, or RAM-XT, is capable of destroying every type of power, including electrical, computers, and electronics, thereby crippling all civilian and most military systems. The two TMD ships encountering *Kailani* didn't need to use it, so it remains untested in actual combat." Krieger waggled his finger in the air. "We have to make sure not to aim it at the Martians. They've been real short on humor since the attempted coup." His comment brought head bobs and snide chuckles from the others. "Our ships are under orders to use this on *Stellaria* as soon as they come within range in an effort to save lives, but only if warships are not already being fired upon. Then we do what we must."

Dimitrios dismissed everyone except Mark and the new guy. "Warren, this is my nephew, Dr. Brett Russell, Nuclear Science and Engineering. Brett, this is Dr. Mark Warren, Xenobiology and Cybernetics."

Something clicked in Mark's head as they shook hands. "Scarlett McDonnell?" Mark said under his breath.

"Oh, don't mention that name to me," replied Russell, turning away with the frown of a bad memory.

"You're the other officer she used to gain a promotion." Mark remembered the general mentioning how McDonnell had used relationships with his nephew and Mark to gain favors as she climbed her way up the ranking ladder.

"You, too?" Russell asked.

"Yup."

No longer strangers, they were joined by the dubious distinction of having been played by the same conniving, scheming, auburn-haired beauty.

"Well, now that you two have established a rapport, we can get down to business. I have a special assignment for you. What I didn't share in the meeting was that Chang has turned herself into a cyborg-AI hybrid. The medical scans indicate she's less than 20 percent human with a neural interface. She's not responding to SP-27 as a normal human would. We don't yet know if her co-conspirator, Natalya Stepanov, has been altered in a similar fashion. When Chang arrives on Terra, she'll be housed in a special holding facility. You will both be waiting for her."

"As guards, sir?" Brett sounded incredulous.

With an odd look, the general responded, "Not exactly."

Oh, holy shit.

It hit Mark like a 10-ton meteor. "Excuse me, sir, you can't mean...as *inmates?*"

"As a matter of fact, yes. We need people with your expertise in proximity to Chang who can converse with her on the same level. Pick her brain. Find out every criminal, immoral, confidential, or proprietary secret in her bag of tricks. Do the same with Stepanov if she's brought back alive. We will get every scrap of that information one way or the other. Your disguises are ready, along with your legends and all the intel we have on Chang. Commit it to memory on your way."

Brett finally found his voice. "Way...to *where*, sir?"

"Rheinholdt Military Penitentiary outside Fort Yukon, Alaska, north of the Arctic Circle."

Mark knew the answer before he asked the question. "Isn't that where all the mercenaries were imprisoned after the failed Martian coup because there weren't enough jails on Mars to hold them?"

"It is."

"I can't go, sir," Mark said. "Some of them have seen me. They'd be able to identify me."

"You'll be in a different wing."

"But sir, I can't do undercover. I'm not good at it. In fact, I'm piss poor, begging your pardon. I really am a nervous wreck—almost passed out once. I sweat profusely."

The general ignored Mark's protests. "You'll do fine." Dimitrios commed his aide. Sergeant Eklund cracked the door and poked his head inside. "Sergeant, see to it these two get on the shuttle to Rheinholdt in the next fifteen minutes."

Eklund placed a hand in the middle of their backs and pushed them out of the general's office, where he turned them over to a couple of female ISD soldiers. Sergeant Claudia Chancellor, the pretty blonde who'd been with Torance, greeted him. "Fancy meeting you again, Captain Warren."

He shuffled alongside her, the despair in his voice palpable. "Are you escorting us to make sure we get on the ship?"

"No, sir, we're going with."

"To Rheinholdt?" Brett asked, giving Chancellor a lingering glance.

"Yes, sir, all the way. Sergeant Laughlin and I will be your handlers under the guise of prison employees."

Brett looked at her wide-eyed. "You're acting as our guards?"

"I believe the accepted terminology is 'Correctional Officers' sir." Chancellor added, "The general said he had a plan but didn't want to bring in any new people, so we volunteered."

Mark had to ask. "Did you know Rheinholdt was the destination?"

Sergeant Laughlin, shorter than Chancellor and built like an Olympic discus thrower, grinned as if she'd just won an all-expense paid vacation to an exotic island. "Oh, yes, sir."

"Unbelievable."

***

Natalya Stepanov clenched her teeth. She stood on the bridge, eyes glued to a pair of red blips on the tactical officer's screen. The two bright red dots crept closer, presenting an unmistakable threat. Mars had *Stellaria* in its sights. Their warships were infamous for firing first and asking questions later—*if* there were any survivors left to ask.

"Captain Rylak, are we within communication range?"

"Unknown," Rylak said, brushing a wayward lock of white hair off her brow. "Although their systems are certainly more robust than ours."

"How long to intercept?"

"Best estimate is a day, maybe more. No one has hard data on Martian systems, so it's impossible to say."

Stellaria had weapons, but could never match a pair of military warmongers laden with weapons capable of reducing her ship to rubble in a matter of seconds. "Options?"

"We could plot a course change over the pole. Keep in mind, however, Mars has many ships other than the two we've identified."

"Change course, Captain. I'm not going to make it easy for them."

Rylak held her position, arms crossed, feet spread wide, barking orders at the bridge personnel. "Mister DeSilva, set new course and speed. Mister Boone, expand your tactical sensors to max range. Report any new ships the instant you spot them. Helm?"

Mister Kinkade answered, "Course laid in, Captain."

Since no one had offered an update on their sister ship for hours, Stepanov asked, "Captain, have we still heard nothing from *Kailani*?"

Rylak clamped a hand on Mister Yancy's shoulder.

"Not a peep, Captain. No comms, no transponders, zero. They've disappeared."

As the four men worked at their consoles, Stepanov's anger mounted, now mixed with a healthy dose of dread that Chang had met with adversity, either lethal or judicial. Mars, much like Terra, employed a justice system whereby the accused was guilty until proven innocent. The red planet had little room set aside for prison facilities. Instead, they relied on Terra to house long-term offenders in the most severe penal institutions. If such were the case, Chang would be sent back to Terra and housed in a draconian military prison until her death sentence was imposed. Stepanov knew of the booby-trapped AI prototypes left precisely for the military, which prompted her to create a similar failsafe plan should she encounter any unforeseen menace along the way.

Before leaving Terra, Stepanov had given her crew the standard off-world inoculations. Unbeknownst to any, she had also infected her entire crew with Sorak-2, a new strain of an old and particularly viral bioweapon. The virus would become active a month after their projected date of arrival on Ganymede. If they landed at the destination without incident, everyone would receive the antidote, with none the wiser.

On the way to her cabin, Stepanov felt compelled to concoct another backup plan. One could never be too prepared. Before leaving Terra, she'd experimented with a genetically engineered airborne or aerosolized version of Zdeth, one of the ten worst bioweapons. The strategic advantage to aiming a warhead with the deadly toxin at an enemy was no less intimidating than one with a nuclear device. If the unthinkable happened, however, and the enemy boarded *Stellaria*, an undetectable airborne weapon would be required to quell a takeover—collateral damage be damned. She'd shed no tears if every Martian fell dead on her ship.

She changed direction, descending three levels to her temporary lab, a small area next to the main cryopod chamber. Stepanov smiled, climbing into a hazmat suit and helmet to experiment with the formula. The Martians might try to stop her ship, but there would be hell to pay if they did.

***

The impact of their mission became evident as preparations advanced. The burden of responsibility weighed on Kamryn as she made the rounds checking on people. In the conference room, Ohashi's hands blurred over multiple screens while she hacked past *CenPharmica's* firewalls to plant stealthy malware codes. In the lab, Petra studied the structural blueprints, then programmed 12 drones with specific locations. Each drone got a name (Bruce, Monty, Caesar, and so on) before she carefully attached the sticks of RD-81. Axel spent time drilling Malone on how to use the HUD inside the armor's helmet, which could be very disconcerting to a newbie. Nguyen monitored *CenPharmica's* spacecraft activity, employee shift changes, patterns, and any anomalies. Kamryn settled down to clean rifles, double-and triple-check the onboard weapons in the armor: mini flame throwers, razor-edged boomerangs, hand cannons, stun guns, smoke bombs, laser cutters, even the emergency triage drug dispensers.

Nguyen commed the team from the pilot's cabin, "Looks like early morning hours are best for breaching the building. They run three shifts. Fewest number of employees are on the premises from 2300 to 0700. Also, two of the three spacecraft are gone."

Kamryn entered the conference room, eyed the pastries, chose a mango flavored one.

Sitting at the table in front of three screens, Ohashi replied, "Ships went to Paraguay. Won't be back until tomorrow afternoon—I checked. Pilot for the third one has a drinking problem. I hacked into his apartment. Disabled the power. Nothing's gonna wake him up." She giggled. "He'll be sleeping it off until the plant's been demolished and he's unemployed." Now she snickered twice as hard.

Petra finished her drone project in the lab and waltzed into the conference room. She grabbed two more chocolate pastries from the tray before plopping down next to Ohashi. "Do you think any of the clones on those ships can be saved?"

Ohashi frowned. "I don't know. I don't like thinking about what might happen to them. If any are recovered, I hope Mark can find out if they're returned to Terra."

"I feel bad we didn't find them before—"

"Don't go there, Petra," Kamryn warned. "We did what we could, which is a hell of a lot more than anybody else. The convent in New Zealand is overflowing with teenage clones rescued from Mars, including the last bunch we delivered from Fulton. When this Gérard business is over and Mark is back, we can resume our search for clone slave traders. Truthfully, nothing would give me more pleasure."

Axel appeared in the doorway. "Everything's set for 0130. Get some shut eye. I want everybody fresh and ready for action. There's no room for screw ups here, and I have no intention of winding up in a Guatemalan prison. Got it?" He waited for a nod from each one before turning toward the onboard gym.

Kamryn followed him. She needed a release for her anxiety. Good idea to work it off.

Axel didn't seem surprised she'd joined him. They pulled on sparring gloves, circled one another, and traded a few punches. "I'll follow your lead," she said.

"Okay." He delivered a lightning double tap to her left shoulder, bobbed away from her return jabs.

"You can take the killshot." She ducked in close to pummel his midsection. It didn't faze him.

He rotated clockwise, threw a hook around to her left kidney. "You sure?"

"Yeah." Kamryn thrust upward clipping his chin. "I screwed up, just like you said."

Axel bobbed outside her reach, then delivered a quick jab to her torso. "That wasn't meant for you."

"Doesn't matter." She threw a body-head-body combination with plenty of power to knock a normal man down. "I concede the right. It's yours."

"Fine by me." He grinned and punched her in the jaw, knocking her off balance. She fell on her ass and slid off the mat.

Kamryn rubbed her cheek, tossing him an evil look. "A simple 'okay' would have been enough."

"Not this time." He extended his hand to help her up—for the second time in the last two days.

Face to face, with errors in judgement set aside, they clasped arms in a warrior's agreement.

Kamryn gave him a crooked smile. "I get to give the order to blow up the place."

"No problem."

Good soldiers to the core, they headed for the armor locker to do a visual on their weapons.

Petra met them in the corridor. "I've programmed your HUDs with *CenPharmica's* schematic. The quickest route to the Infirmary is in red. Drones will follow you in and find their targets. On your orders, I'll trip the timers. You'll have three minutes to clear the building."

"Got it. Now you and Ohashi hit the sack." As she turned to leave, Axel called after her, "And no more chocolate."

By the time Kamryn stretched out on her bunk, she'd done thirty-five push-ups, sixty sit-ups, and had a steamy shower to relax, both physically and mentally. She felt peaceful. At last things could be set right. The past would be dead and buried under tons of rubble. Taking down the corrupt drug company was a bonus.

With hands behind her head, she slipped into dreams of skiing down pristine slopes of fine, powder-white snow. Afterward, she'd go sit by the fire in the lodge to drink hot buttered rums.

Chapter 17

The atmosphere throughout *MAVREK* was heightened, but restrained. Three suits of armor stood open like clamshells waiting for their human partners. Set to non-reflective matte black for their initial assault segment of *CenPharmica*, the armor adopted colors or patterns depending on its surroundings and ambient lighting.

Axel wore only a mesh athletic support to allow for maximum internal sensor readings of his pulse, respiratory function, temperature, and blood pressure. He stepped in backward, snapped his heels down to close the boots, and pressed the back of his knee against a plate to lock the leg sections closed. With his spinal column in place, the torso unit sealed on its own, followed by the arms as he locked in his elbows. After snapping the helmet in place, his gauntlets were the last pieces attached with resounding double clicks.

Malone was next. Kamryn watched, ready to help if needed.

Petra moved the mini-drones to the hatch.

At her screens in the conference room, Ohashi verified everyone's internal sensors as they came online, also testing the HUD readouts and commlinks. "Base to Axel. Do you copy?"

"Roger, loud and clear."

"Do you have schematics?"

Axel used his chin to work the menu until a file displayed blueprints across his faceplate, showing their path to the Infirmary. "Roger on visual."

Nguyen commed them from the pilot's cabin. "Liftoff in ten...nine...eight..."

Interior lights dimmed to steel blue. Petra harnessed up.

Three mighty figures in black armor stood unflinching as the ship took flight. In two minutes, it hovered inches above

CenPharmica's roof. Axel opened the hatch, and jumped free of the ship, landing with a solid *thud* inches from their entry point. Malone landed next, Kamryn right behind him, functioning as rear guard. Petra unleashed the drones before closing the hatch.

A new moon shed meagre light, but the displays inside their helmets provided ample illumination. In single file, the three dark forms opened the roof's access panel, descended the service stairs, drew their guns, and proceeded to the second floor's emergency door. Kamryn checked all drones were tracking them.

Axel paused, letting the HUD display an update to show their designated path in red.

Petra's voice streamed into their helmets. "I've synced the drone feeds. Open the door—they'll find their targets. Copy?"

Kamryn cracked the door. All the little drones floated to the ceiling and silently zipped into the softly lit beige hallway one right after the other. "Roger, drones away."

They stood for a moment to get their bearings while the armor transitioned to a vapor white before Axel led the trio forward. Thermal imaging showed no one in the hallway, but did indicate a few bodies in rooms farther down the L-shaped corridor.

The trio moved quickly—until a green image in a side room walked toward a door. They flattened themselves against the wall.

The door opened. A sizable woman stepped into the hall. Axel zapped her with a heavy stun from the gun built into his right arm. Her knees buckled.

"I got her," Malone said. He caught the woman, dragging her back inside, closing the door as he left. Their destination was another fifty feet down the corridor. Although most night shift employees worked on the ground floor, a few more people might be on this one. The intruders constantly scanned back and forth, looking for the odd figure who might enter the hallway and alert others.

They made it to the Infirmary without incident. Thermal images indicated two bodies inside—one horizontal, one sitting nearby.

Axel turned the door knob an inch at a time, pushed it in millimeter by millimeter, exercising extreme patience under pressure.

A young man in canary yellow scrubs dozed in a chair next to the bed which held their target. Hair slicked back, Lucien Gérard, the "Ghost," lay propped up on pillows with a peaceful expression, hooked up to a monitoring machine on the opposite side. His torso was bandaged from breastbone to abdomen.

Axel pointed at Kamryn, then gestured to the sleeping nurse with a flip of his hand, as if offering her a present. "This one's for you."

She curtsied and blasted the guy with a heavy stun. He slipped out of the chair and it fell over as he crumpled to the floor.

The noise woke Gérard. It took him several long seconds to grasp the gravity of the situation. His eyes grew enormous, darting from one giant armored figure to the next.

Kamryn thumbed up her faceplate, sending him an *I-am-your-worst-nightmare* look.

"Oh, no-no, not again." He held out both palms to keep them at a distance. "I can pay—anything." His voice trembled as he bargained. "Just name it…anything…"

Before either Malone or Kamryn realized what had happened, Axel pulled his plasma hand cannon and shot Gérard in the shoulder. The stench of roasted flesh made Kamryn's eyes water.

Gérard's howl came as a delayed reaction.

"You can have what's left," Axel said. "Make it quick."

Kamryn rushed to the bed, jerking the sheet off Gérard's lower body. She grabbed the knife from the casing on her thigh.

Axel suspected what was coming. He and Malone turned to leave when they heard thrashing, followed by a smothered gurgle.

Kamryn uttered a primal scream. It grew into a roar that lasted forever, until it finally faded, becoming a distant whisper.

After, Kamryn joined them in the hallway. Fresh blood covered her gauntlets. "Light 'em up, Petra," she said. "The party's over."

"Roger that."

No longer in stealth mode, the trio ran for the exit. Their heavy footfalls sounded like rolling thunder echoing in the corridor. Before they mounted the service stairs, Axel flipped the fire alarm, giving the workers a minute to clear the building. "Nguyen, we're on the roof in five seconds. Copy?"

Her chuckle filled their helmets. "Roger. Waiting for you up top."

True to her word, the ship hovered yards away as they climbed out of the access panel.

Ohashi stood by the open hatch, her dark silhouette backlit by a warm glow from the interior. "We had a message from Mark and one from General Dimitrios, too."

They harnessed up for Nguyen's express getaway, everyone savoring the knowledge Kamryn's nemesis was no longer a threat—to her or anyone else.

Axel removed his helmet. "Congratulations on a job well done. I'm buying the first round."

His comment brought lots of thumbs up with a celebratory round of applause. When they leveled off, he changed to black exercise togs, stopping in the galley for beer before joining the team in the conference room.

Ohashi swore under her breath as she experienced unusual problems establishing a vid link with Mark. Finally, a fuzzy image appeared.

"You working hard, or hardly working?" Axel asked. When the image stabilized, he realized Mark was harnessed to the interior of a TMD shuttle. "Where are you?"

"You are not going to believe the shit that's been happening," Mark grumbled. "Everything's gone to hell. I'm on my way to Rheinholdt."

"What?" Axel bolted forward in his chair, ready to give the pilots an order to change course. "Tell me," he ordered.

Mark's image kept flickering while he recounted the entire saga nonstop, going into great detail during the Bill and Ted incident, much to their enjoyment. He finished with meeting Scarlett's other amorous victim, Dr. Brett Russell, the general's nephew. Dimitrios had drafted them into his whacky, clandestine intelligence operation, which involved being sent to the worst military prison on the planet. Their mission: to spy on the newly captured Lotus Chang, reported to be only 20 percent human. Dimitrios feared Chang had left other booby-trapped sites just waiting for TMD to stumble upon them and die in the process. Brett and Mark would pick her brain for any intel the TMD could use. Their backgrounds made them his most trusted assets, able to converse with her on a scientific level.

I didn't think you liked spy work," Petra said once Mark had finished.

"I did *not* volunteer. I *hate* spooks and undercover work."

Kamryn changed the subject. "What does he want to talk to Axel about?"

"The two AIs that were looking for the ship in Norfolk."

"I don't know anything," Axel replied. "When they showed up asking questions about our ship, we were already gone. We didn't see them, only the surveillance vid taken by the flight school."

"Lucky you," Mark countered, "otherwise Dimitrios might try to press you into some weird plot to hunt them down. I'm betting he wants to find them in the worst way."

"You think?" Axel's inner voice said maybe this wouldn't be such a bad idea. He'd kick it around now that the Gérard problem was off the board.

From Mark's left, Brett poked his face into the image. "Hiya. Sorry about uncle Eli commandeering your friend. The general asked if I could help, but didn't say with what. So, we've both been shanghaied. It's not the first time for me, either. I should've known better."

"How long will you be there?"

"Probably until he gets the intel he wants," Mark groused. "Gotta go, we're about to land. I'd give anything to fight with cyborgs again rather than this. Mark out."

"Poor Mark." Kamryn shook her head with a chuckle which turned into an infectious belly laugh that had everyone in tears.

When the laughter settled down, Axel looked at Kamryn. "How about it? Want to hunt for AIs?"

***

They arrived at 0230. Jumping out of the shuttle into the coldest temperatures he'd ever experienced made Mark's private parts shrivel up to the size of walnuts. He cursed General Dimitrios with every four-letter word he'd ever used on another human being, then was plagued by a pang of guilt when he remembered they were here to save lives.

Sergeant Chancellor first lead them to a temporary, no-frills detention room where he and Brett stripped, donning bright orange, numbered coveralls while the two ISD sergeants changed into olive green guard uniforms behind a partition. A stern Major Peerce, built like a bulldozer with hair and beard the color of arctic tundra, led the group through miles of yellow corridors to Rheinholdt's sparsely populated D Block. They were ushered into adjacent cells—cramped, oblong boxes with vid screens mounted on the back wall. The only amenities, if you could call them that, were a bunk, stall shower/sink combination, a toilet along one side, and nothing on the other. Each cell was encased by a transparent force field fortified with enough electromagnetic energy to knock a prisoner out cold for hours. The metal bars were obsolete, but still in place for psychological effect.

The legends—or backgrounds—prepared for Mark and Brett branded them as stepbrothers, who operated a spybot enterprise catering to corporations who sought to steal proprietary secrets from their rivals. When one of their bots went rouge and killed a human, they were arrested, tried and convicted, now waiting for an appeal that might not ever happen. Once best friends, now they were constantly at each other's throats, and in all likelihood might try to kill one another if they got the chance.

As their presence pertained to Lotus Chang, however, they were to seduce, cajole, or trick her by any means necessary into giving them as much intelligence as possible, even by promising to include her in their escape plans—should they devise one.

Mark had an advantage that Brett didn't. Mark had been the middle child of three, with an older brother and a younger sister. For the last year and a half, Axel had filled the gap left by Eric's death, not to mention Mark lived on a ship with six other alpha personalities—all of them highly skilled, lethal in their own way, thrill-seeking heroes who had learned to work as a team.

Mark kibitzed, argued, fought, laughed, cried and bled with his adopted family, whereas Brett was an only child.

Mark cautioned his new cohort, "I don't know how badass you can be, but two sergeants of TMD's elite armored unit trained me. If you don't know how to respond to something—just cuss. Growing up, mom didn't allow profanity in the house, but my brother got away with saying 'up yours' all the time. It works in almost every situation."

Employing one-upmanship, Brett said, "I went to boarding school, university, then Star Command Academy. I've had six years of martial arts training and my father is an admiral who can swear in three languages. I gotcha covered."

Mark snorted. "Great. Glad I don't have to babysit you."

While Major Peerce disabled the energy fields of each cell, Laughlin and Chancellor unlocked the metal doors. "Okay boys—uh…sirs, in you go."

"They're not Sirs here," Peerce snapped. "Address them as prisoner D165 and D166, or scumbag, sleazeball, vermin, or any anything else you can think of but *never* by name or rank. I don't relish telling Dimitrios this mission was blown before it ever started."

Both women snapped to attention with smart salutes. "Yes, sir, Major Peerce," they chorused.

Chancellor added, "It will not happen again, Major."

Peerce tilted his head sideways for a moment, listening to his commlink. "Our star prisoner is due shortly. You two," he waved at the men, "make those cells looked lived in." Peerce turned toward the women. "And you two—follow me for some last-minute instructions." As he walked away Peerce bellowed, "I want to chalk this one up as a success and get you people out of my house A-*SAP*."

Mark flopped down on his bunk. He could do without the overbearing major, along with the my-father's-an-admiral vibe he'd gotten from Brett. Mark would size up Lotus Chang, determine the best course of action, and pry the intel out of her one way or another.

He and Brett had been given commlinks, which were being monitored by the two ISD sergeants and recorded as well. Mark knew he had to think twice before saying certain things out loud for fear of incriminating himself on a myriad of subjects. His team had functioned outside the law on numerous occasions...

Oh *shit*. Who was he trying to kid? They had done *sooo* many things—mayhem, arson, murder, theft, kidnapping, and cyberhacking the military, no less. If the TMD knew the truth, they'd keep him here for the rest of his life.

Paranoid.

He'd turned into a paranoid schizophrenic.

"D165," someone hollered.

The sound jolted Mark out of his mental nightmare. "Huh?"

Sergeant Chancellor stood in front of his cell. "We brought food," she whispered. "Eat it quick before they finish processing Chang."

A tray sat on the floor inside his cell door. He went over, took a knee, tasted a couple things. "Nope. Not eating this crap. I'll pass."

"You'll starve in here. This is the best they have—believe me." Chancellor looked distressed, her tone urgent.

"Is this what Major Peerce eats?"

She made an exasperated sound, pulled out the tray, and walked off in a huff.

"I thought so." Mark returned to his bunk. He needed a stiff drink, or three. He started a mental list of things to do when he got out of Rheinholdt. Number one was get good and drunk. The second was eat a steak the size of a turkey platter.

Satisfied his paranoia had passed, he worked on a plan to ensnare Chang. A game of chess: anticipate a dozen tactical moves ahead and never underestimate this opponent. After all, she'd played a deadly game until now and almost succeeded. Thank the gods for Martian warships patrolling the frontier.

He settled down to create his mental chessboard. Mark planned to use the experiences from his nefarious exploits to authenticate his criminal past. And he had an ace in the hole—his cybernetic hearing. Going in, he could keep it a secret, or reveal his cyborg part to establish a rapport with the cyborg woman. He'd play it by ear.

Mark chuckled to himself. Yeah, he could do this—if he kept the paranoia from resurfacing long enough to pull it off.

***

The deck plates shifted under Natalya Stepanov's feet. Moments later, a yellow light flashed on her tablet. The message read: *Course Change.*

After locking down all the chemicals in her lab, she discarded the hazmat outfit and proceeded to the bridge. "What's going on?"

"Ship approaching astern," Rylak replied. "It appears to be tracking us. Can't identify it yet. I ordered a slight course change to determine if it's part of the Martian posse or a civilian ship."

Stepanov peered over Mister Boone's shoulder at his console. The blinking pinprick barely registered on the screen. "When you have updates, Captain, I'll be in my cabin."

Sitting at her desk with a fresh tumbler of coffee, she worked at a screen to further refine the Zdeth formula's airborne version, still half-finished in her lab. Being ready for a Martian boarding party would go a long way toward ensuring she arrived at the chosen destination. Given a choice, she'd dose every damned Martian if it meant not ending up behind bars on Terra.

A beep sounded as Captain Rylak's face appeared in the upper left corner of her screen. "Stepanov to the bridge."

She made it in record time. Her anger, now a constant state, was mixed with good old-fashioned anxiety. Stepanov slowed, entered the bridge poised, fully self-controlled. "Have you news, Captain?"

Rylak's mood matched the black uniform she wore. Her sharp features seemed more hawkish than ever. She pointed straight as an arrow to the tactical console. "Report, Mister Boone."

"We've identified the ship." With reluctance, he added, "TMD *Colossus*—a warship."

She *knew* it! *Chert bi tebya podral*. In the back of her mind, she'd known the saber-rattlers were working together to ruin her plans.

Well, let them try. She'd kill them all. Every. Last. One.

Rylak stirred the air with two fingers, signaling Boone to complete his report.

"The Terrans and Martians simultaneously matched our course…their speeds also continue to increase at an exponential rate."

Stepanov's mind raced to consider an endless number of possible alternatives as she asked the obvious question. "Suggestions, Captain?"

The older woman rose, turning toward Stepanov to speak in an undertone. "The laws of physics dictate this ship is incapable of outrunning them. Even if we jettisoned everything not absolutely necessary to keep us from crashing—including the cryopods—they *will* overtake us."

"I have a plan, Captain. It's almost ready. Just keep us ahead of those ships and let me know the minute anyone contacts us."

Only after leaving the bridge did Stepanov unclench her fists; there were nail marks in her palms. There was no time to waste on anger—she *must* finish the aerosol. A quick sprint to her lab and several hours of intense preparation would put the final touch on the new weapon.

Working at a fever pitch, she recalculated the original formula. Theoretically, the original compound was designed to bring down an average Martian with a minimum dosage. Now she bumped it up to maximum. She rechecked the inhalation flow rate, body weight, and breathing rate according to the particle structure. Tweaking it a bit allowed the particles to travel the maximum distance. The formula showed a one-minute exposure caused symptoms of dizziness followed by unconsciousness. Antidotes were her specialty, and this one seemed surprisingly uncomplicated—*if* it worked. The trial required a few more hours to feed results into the computer.

When—not if—those ships caught *Stellaria*, she'd dose the boarding parties, then coerce both Terran and Martian captains by threatening to kill their crews unless they released her. These dimwitted military types were all about honor, duty, and trying to bring their people back alive. Playing on their worst fears would either gain her freedom, or they'd all die together. Under no circumstances was she going back to Terra in chains to spend the rest of what promised be a short existence behind bars followed by a death sentence. Not Natalya Stepanov.

Two hours later and *fait accompli*. The lab smelled of burnt plastic, but all diagnostics showed the weaponized biocompounds were complete. She'd contained the aerosol—odorless and colorless, with the dispersal rate and range set at maximum—in a cylinder resembling a fire extinguisher. No one would suspect anything abnormal. Pull the pin, aim the nozzle, squeeze the trigger into an airlock or ventilation shaft—*done*.

A triumphant Stepanov changed from the protective suit to a long jacket capable of hiding two things she needed: a small, self-contained breathing apparatus, and a pulse gun from a secret compartment under the desk. Her sense of accomplishment demanded a reward. She headed for her quarters with thoughts of a long, hot shower and a delicious bottle of wine.

A muffled beep escaped Stepanov's pocket. The message read: *Stepanov to bridge.*

Thoughts of the shower and wine faded with every hurried footstep to the one place she'd had too much of over the last few days.

The bridge was a hive of activity. She could see it, feel it—the air heavy, the tension palpable. Captain Rylak paced on her dais behind the front four animated officers at their consoles. Three others she barely noticed—the engineer, operations, and security officers—also worked at a hectic pace.

Stepanov moved up beside Rylak.

The captain spoke in a monotone. "They're gaining on us by the minute. We picked up chatter. Intentional, I'm sure, since it wasn't encrypted. Somebody has a new weapon. No mention of what it is or does."

The tactical officer muttered, "The minute they get close enough, they'll shoot us to pieces."

Stepanov heard the fear in his voice, as did Rylak. The captain stepped down, squeezing his shoulder in an uncharacteristic display of sentiment. "Keep it together, Mister Boone. They haven't fired yet."

Chapter 18

Kamryn sat with the crew, minus the pilots, watching an update from General Dimitrios on the vid screen.

His tunic was unbuttoned at the neck, feet up on the desk, an exquisite cut crystal glass with golden liquid in his hand.

"We've had no other reports of additional AIs or similar individuals—whatever they are—lurking around anywhere. Their images are loaded into our facial recognition software and broadcast to every military installation in the event there were duplicate models. So far—no hits. Could these be the last two? Where did they come from? But, more importantly, where did they *go?*"

Acting as spokesman, Axel said, "Sir, we have no idea. However, we're returning to the same location in Norfolk, hoping if we show up again, they will, too. It's Sky King's Flight School owned by Donovan King, a retired Space Command officer who's a friend of our pilot. Considering what happened at Headquarters, maybe you could provide some disguised security to make sure things don't go sideways."

"Consider it done. A squad of ground crew and mechanics will report there first thing tomorrow morning. Watch your six. Keep me posted. Dimitrios out."

Most everyone left to grab some much needed shut eye. Kamryn stayed for a while trying to figure out why these AIs were searching for them. She looked at it from every angle but got no answers. At last, she, too, went to bed. Sometimes you had to sleep on a problem to see the solution.

***

In the morning, *MAVREK* sat on the edge of the flight school's eastern boundary. Over breakfast, Malone warned them Donovan was none too happy with the TMD invasion of his business, but understood the precautions were necessary to keep his clients and ships protected. Malone handed out bluish-gray coveralls Donovan had left for the crew to ensure everyone looked like they worked there.

After their first landing in Norfolk, it had only taken the AIs less than twenty-four hours to hone in on this location, asking questions about *MAVREK*. Using the only logic available, Kamryn hoped it would happen again.

Ohashi released a dozen drones to surveil the surrounding fence, gated entrance, and client parking area. Their tablets were synced to several drones flanking the office and machine shop. She was perched on the flight school's roof, hidden under a quilted mylar blanket. Axel peeked out of the rank trash module on the corner of the building—he'd drawn the short straw. They waited in the cold, damp air of an overcast morning for the AIs to return. Inside the ship, both cybers monitored multiple screens on the conference table. Facial recognition programs tied into the super processor, Hercules, scanned for the uploaded images of the identical, light and dark pair of AIs.

Clients came and went. Donovan took students up and brought them down. Nothing unusual happened. They waited all day.

Kamryn came in to eat and get warm. She sat between the cybers in the conference room, glancing at the images while finishing her coffee.

At six thirty, something finally happened. It couldn't have been more unexpected.

An expensive red sports car pulled up to the main building. A gull-wing door lifted on the driver's side. Out stepped a tall, slender female with straight black hair, wearing an eggplant colored long coat. She entered the office.

Ohashi touched the screen, spreading her fingers wide to enlarge the image projected by the surveillance camera mounted on the wall behind the counter. Rotating the facial image for optimum scan, she tapped it twice to initiate the program. In the back of her mind, something clicked. She squinted at the female's face.

The computer emitted a sharp chirping signal at the same time Ohashi yelled, "WholeLeeShit!" A half-second later, Petra's system mimicked the chirping sound. The name *Mingzhu (a/k/a Lotus) Chang* flashed across the top of both screens, followed by the letters ASB, for All Systems Bulletin. A long list of civil, criminal and federal charges scrolled down the right side.

"Alert," Ohashi commed. "Lotus Chang is in Donovan's office. Axel—you copy?"

"Can't be. She's at Rheinholdt. You heard Mark."

"Don't tell me 'can't be' I'm looking *right* at her. Uh…unless…oh boy…you think—"

"—she made an AI of herself?" Petra blurted out, finishing Ohashi's sentence.

"Stay in the dumpster, Axel," Kamryn hollered, running flat out for the hatch. "I've got this."

Kamryn grabbed her parka and sprinted to the office in record time.

Stopping by the door, she slipped the gun in the left pocket of her jacket before walking inside.

"Hey Donny, Boris needs you in the shop."

Donovan looked up, frowned, started to say something.

Kamryn shook her head, drew a finger across her throat, jabbed a thumb toward the door.

He heaved a sigh, rolled his eyes, grumbled, "Sorry Miss Emeryx. Maude, here, will take care of you."

Kamryn traded places with Donovan behind the counter. "What can I help you with today, Miss Emeryx? Lessons? Or a nice pre-owned ship—they all come with a thirty-day guarantee and a discount on parking, if you need to leave it here." Kamryn made up the sales pitch on the fly. Good thing she hadn't lost the art of lying with a straight face.

"I require lessons in a particular model of ship. A Mixx-Reid Starcruiser 75."

"Hey," Kamryn said, "we have one on the property. But it's not ours. I think Donny and the pilot were in the service together. It belongs to some business out west, or maybe not. I can't remember."

"How do I get lessons on that ship?"

"I don't know if that's possible. It's not *our* ship," Kamryn repeated.

Standing her ground, the woman asked, "Can you contact the owner?"

"I don't know who they are." Kamryn made a mental note of how single-minded this person was. "I'll have Donny send a message to the pilot."

The woman didn't move.

"When Donny gets *back*."

Still, the woman didn't move.

"He may be awhile." Kamryn's exasperation meter was on a fast track to the top floor. She'd talked to computers that were more intuitive. Changing her approach, she said, "How can Donny reach you?"

"I'll be back tomorrow."

Kamryn walked around the counter toward to the door, opened it, extended her hand to the woman. "Thank you for stopping by, Miss Emeryx. We have to close up now."

Emeryx, ignoring Kamryn's outstretched hand, walked out in silence.

A flash of movement on the edge of Kamryn's peripheral vision caught her attention. She saw Axel rolling out from under the red sports car. He rolled left several yards, directly under the giant yellow tug unit used to haul spacecraft. "Uh, Miss Emeryx?"

The woman swiveled her head around to face Kamryn.

"Have a nice evening." Kamryn waved a cheery goodbye.

Emeryx got in the car and sped away into the night.

Axel crawled out from underneath the tug, dirt clinging to his sweaty face.

Kamryn ran over to punch him in the shoulder. "What the hell were you doing?"

"Putting a tracker on her car." He brushed gravel off himself. "If she spotted drones, she might've taken them out—*and* know we sent them. Petra raced up with a tracker so I could install it before she left."

Petra came out of the shadows from behind the tug. "Wait until you see the vid we got of Emeryx." She threaded both of her arms through theirs as they returned to the ship. They gathered in front of the screens with coffee to take the chill off.

First, Ohashi put up an image of the human Chang, then slid an image of Emeryx beside it. "There are subtle differences. Side by side, they're almost identical, even the hair, but Emeryx doesn't have a single imperfection. Poreless skin, absolutely straight nose, eyes on the same exact angle." She hit 'play' but muted the sound. "Now, as you can see when they're talking, the real Chang is more animated. Her face and head move. Not so with Emeryx." She added in a derisive tone, "Kinda freaks me out that she can blink and swallow, though."

"Okay, this is impressive." Kamryn sensed more unexpected news was about to surface. "But I want to know why she shows up instead of Tweedledee and Tweedledum, and what about the tracker? You have a location on it yet?"

Ohashi checked another screen. "Hmm...the car turned into a business called U-Stor-It. Why does that name sound familiar?"

"Mars," Petra said. "It's where Valerie Parker hid her weapons. They have U-Stor-It's everywhere."

After tapping on her screen, Ohashi added, "The car's in unit 97."

"They have security vid?" Kamryn asked,

"I'm working on it." Ohashi leaned in, tilting her head. "Oh, look. The car drove in. The door shut. No one came out."

"Well," Kamryn spread her hands, "if you're an AI you don't need a hotel room or a nice dinner and drinks before bed. You don't even need a bed. If she's there, maybe Tweedledee and Tweedledum are too."

Petra screwed up her face. "Eww, an AI ménage à trois? That's just too weird."

Kamryn started to get up. "Let's go take a peek."

***

"Negative." The expression on Axel's face said don't even bother trying to change his mind. "Someone sent three AIs to find our ship. It can't fall into that person's hands. I will go alone to take a peek. You—*all of you*—will stay here and guard the ship. That's an order." He walked to the doorway. "Ohashi, you'd better crank up your security system while I'm gone. Wait...," his brows pinched together, "we have the same SRVL system you designed for the TMD—right?"

"Yes, with a few upgrades they don't have."

"Maybe…it isn't our ship they want…but the surveillance system. Since they can't hijack a TMD warship, the next best thing is trying to get their hands on our ship."

This turned into a true lightbulb moment for everyone at the table.

Wide-eyed, Ohashi said, "Omigod, yes! But Emeryx is a mirror image of Chang, and Mark told us she's supposed to be in Rheinholdt. So, what's the angle?"

"I don't know yet." Axel hated admitting it. A wild guess was that someone planned on breaking her out and needed the anti-surveillance system for their ship. Just thinking about it put a knot in his stomach. First, he'd track down the Emeryx AI. Figuring out the answers would no doubt be more involved.

He left Kamryn in charge of keeping everyone safe, Ohashi responsible for the ship's security, the pilots on alert if things went south. Since the weather report predicted rain, Petra scrounged up a waterproof jumpsuit with lots of goodies tucked in the pockets. Monroe wrangled permission for Axel to borrow Donovan's electric motorbike, a cobalt blue, high-powered version of an Old Earth dirt bike. The matching helmet came with a HUD display, making it easy to sync the self-storage unit's GPS from his tablet. He sped down darkened streets, enjoying the freedom of the open air, all his senses hyper aware of the new surroundings.

The forecast came true. It started misting, which turned into a light drizzle as he streaked past vehicles. The helmet's green-tinted night vision helped him maneuver through traffic while a special glaze on the faceplate repelled raindrops. In retrospect, he relished spending time alone, even in the rain. It gave him time to think about Chang. She'd turned out to be one deadly, calculating, sneaky bitch. The look on Mark's face said it all; he wanted to strangle her for booby-trapping the prototypes that killed all those scientists. Judging by how Beth Coulter had died, Mark was certainly capable and smart enough to figure out a way.

Emeryx, on the other hand, presented an unknown. These new AIs were impersonating humans, a feat not attempted before. Under normal conditions, AIs were used on the front lines in dangerous environments or embedded in high-tech operating systems. But these three were *different*. They'd gone unrecognized as AIs by the humans interacting with them. If it hadn't been for Axel's super cybers, no one would know.

He'd seen vids showing the enormous strength AIs possessed. Even with his cyborg limbs, he was no match. His brain couldn't compete with the speed of their processors, either, but he did have a lifetime of experience. He hoped it would be enough.

The destination address blinked yellow in his HUD display. He turned right, rode two blocks farther, then turned left. Behind the gated entrance, the U-Stor-It office sat closed. It anchored the front corner, with ten rows of units spread out over the property. The street looked vacant. One light threw a dim mist that glistened on the wet surface. Axel hid the bike and helmet in bushes across the street, then checked his comm.

"Axel to Base."

Petra's voice flowed into his ear. "We're tracking your chip and have disabled U-Stor-It's surveillance system. Two drones are flanking the storage unit. A third one will follow you there. Go down the second row in back of the office. Number 97 is near the end."

"Roger that."

Axel kept to the shadows as he broke into a run along the six-foot tall chain-link fence. Reaching maximum velocity, he pushed off with his left augmented leg for a high vault sideways over the barrier and nailed an Olympic ten-pointer. A quick jog down the dark aisle put him at a rollup door painted in the neon red numbers of 97. If all three AIs were inside, he doubted they verbally communicated. Instead, he suspected they shared data through a linked neural network. Whatever the Tweedles knew, so did Emeryx, and vice versa.

He pulled a device out of his pocket called a Chewy, a listening device the size of Old Earth bubble gum, to stick on the door. It could detect the sound of a pin dropping and was synced to his comm. He listened for any noise coming from behind the door and hear the faint, intermittent sound of rapid-fire tapping.

Axel reached for the second piece of tech—a pair of goggles that functioned the same as HUD optics. Any object producing heat, even computers, robots, or AIs presented as green-hued.

Gotcha. The goggles picked up five heat signatures: the vehicle's warm glow, a large one, plus a small one still inside the car, with two faint sparks in the far corner. He suspected they were the Tweedles, powered down in sleep-mode.

Axel whispered, "Ohashi, trace any comms originating from this unit."

"On it."

Several moments passed while he stood motionless, only the soft white noise of raindrops on the pavement keeping him company.

"I got it—Rheinholdt!"

Dammit. His wild guess had been right on the mark.

"Emeryx sent a message there," Ohashi continued. "Don't know to who yet. It's heavily encrypted—might take a while."

The car started. Metal screeched as the rollup door lifted off the ground, a shaft of light from the interior reflecting off the wet pavement.

Axel sprinted backward a few paces, sank into a low crouch, then power jumped up to the roof. He spotted the shiny red vehicle nosing out of the unit. "The car's leaving. Track it. We can find it later. If the Tweedles are still inside, I'll neutralize them first."

"Roger."

The door lowered with softer squeaks as the car exited through the gate, disappearing down the dark street.

Axel emptied the usual trinkets from his pockets onto the roof: mini stun baton, a twenty-function multi-tool, MedKit, zip ties, duct tape, two grenades, and a pair of nano-explosives dubbed 'Buster Bombs.' He tucked everything away except the explosives. With extra special care, he peeled the thumbnail sized disk-shaped devices off their backing and stuck each one to the inside of his wrists. Buster Bombs only worked after being placed on inorganic objects, then set off by a super-heated plasma charge. *Usually.*

His objective was simple. Enter the unit and disable two AIs with hair-trigger responses. This called for a really sneaky plan. Distraction.

"Ohashi, can you open the unit's door on my command?"

"Sure…gimme a minute…"

Axel moved to the corner above where the two faint heat signatures had been. He used the goggles to confirm their location. With a grenade in each hand, he stood waiting for her response.

"Yes. We can now open or shut any door, including the security gate."

A wide grin broke across his face. "Standby." Axel shook his body like a wet dog shaking off water to loosen his muscles and prepare for action. He knew what he had to do. The stakes were too high and he might not get another chance. Some might say taking on two AIs was a no-win scenario. Well, maybe for a normal human. Good thing he was a super human—that, and his skills honed in the military and law enforcement would have to be enough.

He backed up twenty feet.

"On my mark…three…two…one…GO!"

The door rolled up inch by inch, grinding and creaking, as light spilled onto the driveway.

Axel hurled the grenades against the roof with such force its corner exploded.

A jagged six-foot wide hole opened. Shrapnel of all sizes rained into the unit.

In one swift action, Axel dropped through the hole, landed between two AIs, smashed both his wrists on their clothes, transferring the Buster Bombs. Another half second passed as he fell to the floor and rolled away, reaching for his gun.

The darker AI lashed out first, kicking Axel in the kidney.

It knocked the wind out of him. Pain seared up his spine. He saw stars, but still managed to hold on to his gun.

The lighter AI snatched Axel's leg in a vice grip, lifted him off the ground and flung him into the wall like a rag doll.

Axel slid to the ground, numb, but the stars had cleared. He fired off a couple of wild plasma shots at the lighter one, amputating its hand purely by accident.

The dark one bent over to snag Axel's left arm.

Fear gripped Axel. He'd already lost that arm once. He held down the trigger, spraying a stream across the AI's center mass.

It exploded like fireworks. Large pieces spun away, clattering against the walls. Fiery shrapnel peppered Axel's skin. He choked on the acrid smell of burnt circuits.

From another direction, the one-handed AI came after him—again.

Axel fired at its midsection, hoping to hit the Buster Bomb.

The bolt of plasma missed the sweet spot. No explosion, but flames set a tangle of circuitry on fire—meaning the bomb was lost. The AI stumbled back a couple steps, jerked to the left, exposing a hole in its side section.

Axel tried to stand, couldn't, rolled farther away, and took aim at the AI's face.

It lurched forward, both arms outstretched, one hand missing.

Plasma beams pelted its face, missed the left eye, hit the right eye. The AI faltered, steadied itself, advanced. Its skull was pockmarked by melted holes, yet it still kept coming.

Axel did the unexpected. He scrambled on all fours behind the AI and released a stream of plasma across its legs at the knees.

It fell.

He waited.

The AI moved, pushing its torso up from the ground, rising up on its knees. It turned to face Axel.

As he zeroed in on the left eye, Axel spotted the Buster Bomb disk stuck to the AI's neck. He shot the eye first, then the disk.

Metal exploded.

The detonation threw him against the wall. Fragments zinged through the air in every direction.

When things quieted down, Petra's worried voice filtered into his ear. "Can you hear me? *Axel?* Your chip says you're alive, but please tell me you're okay."

After a moment he grunted, "I'm fine." He couldn't get up. "Maybe not. Think my foot's broken. Maybe my arm. Some ribs, too." He noticed a liberal amount of blood smeared over his jumpsuit, knew it had to be his. Every bone, muscle, and nerve ending screamed out in agony until he jammed the MedKit's syringe of painkillers into his thigh. Seconds later, relief.

"Should we pick you up?" Petra's voice was thick with concern.

Kamryn said, "I'll come get you."

"No." He forced the word out. Breathing was difficult. He crawled to the wall, leaned against it as he stood. "I made enough noise to bring at least several divisions of law enforcement. They'll be here soon. I'm leaving now." Axel took images of the decimated AIs. "Send these to Dimitrios. If he doesn't want the locals poking their noses in this, the TMD needs to get here A-*SAP*. And have Ohashi close the door—no need to advertise."

Axel grimaced with each movement. He wasn't going out the same way he'd come in. Between limping and shuffling, he made it to the hidden bike. Knowing the drugs wouldn't last forever, he took the quickest route back. He couldn't help notice a TMD shuttle pass by overhead. To alleviate jurisdiction disagreements, he hoped they got there first.

Rain hammered the helmet's HUD as it kept a trip countdown of time and distance elapsed. He had twelve miles left when the drugs began to wear off. Bumps in the road caused stabs of pain. Pins and needles came from wind and water buffeting his jumpsuit. Axel held onto the handle bars with a death grip the last few miles, swerving in and out of traffic on a wet surface at twice the speed limit. The cybers pleaded with him to slow down so he didn't have an accident. Axel damn near missed the final turn, almost laid the bike down swerving through the gate, but managed to ride up to the ship, get off the bike and drop to one knee. Searing agony riddled his body.

Tears running down Petra's face were the last thing he saw.

Chapter 19

Everyone ran to pick up Axel—not an easy thing to do, since he was unconscious and big and heavy and wet and slippery. They got him inside to the medpod. Nguyen eased off the helmet. Kamryn jabbed a syringe of painkiller into his thigh. Petra continued to cry as she removed his boots. Ohashi and Malone cut through the jumpsuit. Peeling it away in strips revealed blood everywhere from cuts, abrasions, and contusions, with swelling and discoloration around the ribs, forearm, and ankle.

Petra took his hand, tears streaming down her face. "I've never seen him like this. What can we do?"

Kamryn took charge, reverting to her former status of Sergeant Fleming. "Get a grip, Petra. Go contact Major Torance. Tell him what's happened." She pointed at Ohashi. "You—find a MedScanner. Cover every centimeter of skin looking for broken bones, organ damage, internal bleeding." Kamryn tossed rolls of tape to Malone and Nguyen, knowing they were EMT certified. "Wrap what's broken."

The MedLab's atmosphere had never been graver. The smell of blood, sweat, and fear was overpowering.

With antiseptic and surgical glue, Kamryn started on his face. Her hands trembled caring for a particularly severe wound. She hoped no one noticed. If she'd been alone, she would have wept, too. Her heart ached to see the indomitable Axel so badly beaten. She cleaned lacerations, closed them, and applied bandages when necessary all the way to his feet.

They worked on their patient like a battlefield surgical team, intent on keeping their friend alive and putting him back together. Nguyen sniffled, Malone kept clearing his throat. No one made eye contact.

Ohashi read the scanner's report. "His left kidney's bruised. Three fractures: right ankle, right radius, left number seven rib. No major organ damage or internal bleeding. He could use a double dose of nanites, but it doesn't indicate he needs any blood."

"Concussion?"

"Unknown—it requires a hospital CT scan."

Petra rushed in with a face still puffy from crying. She stopped short to stare at her bandaged hero.

Kamryn caught her attention. "What did you learn from Torance?"

"Lockdown's still in place. He can't leave Headquarters. Promised to send a care package." She crept toward Axel's wounded body, making an enormous effort to keep the tears at bay. "Hey," she brightened, "we have saline. Got it when we picked up med supplies in Guatemala." She rummaged in a cabinet, pulled out a set including bag, tube, needle, everything. "Saline will keep him hydrated. I know how. Let me do it. Please…"

Kamryn nodded. Everyone moved back, gave her space to work.

Petra scrubbed up, donned gloves, and without a hitch she had the IV inserted, taped down the tube, and attached it to both ends. "Malone, can you raise the hook?"

He unsnapped a lever at the head of the medpod to pull up an extendable metal rod, then flipped out brackets on each side at the top.

Petra hung the bag of saline from the hook, then watched the drip for a moment before she looked up, smiling.

"Torance would be proud." Kamryn checked the supply of drugs. Twelve painkillers. Would it be enough?

Ohashi brought the scanner. "I'll monitor his vitals." As an act of love, both cybers stayed by Axel's side for the next hour.

The lights started flashing. Loud pinging noises in sets of three followed.

"What the hell's happening?" Kamryn yelled.

"It's the SRVL system," Ohashi shouted back. "Axel said to crank it up."

Both pilots ran to their stations, preparing for an immediate takeoff.

Kamryn darted to the main hatch where piles of weapons were ready for war. She seized a GK-91 'Giantkiller' plasma rifle, ready to annihilate whoever or whatever tried to breach their ship.

"Wait!" Petra yelled from behind her. "Maybe it's the care package from Torance."

"Ohashi!" Kamryn screamed. "I want to know what's out there. And shut off that damned racket!"

On cue, Ohashi appeared with her tablet in hand, tapping at the screen like a demon. "It's a drone. Nothing else."

Silence reigned. No pinging. Lights quit flashing.

Kamryn signaled for Petra to open the hatch while she aimed the monster rifle at the entrance.

Petra cautiously unlatched the doors, peeked out. "Big drone…with a box attached."

The box held more than Axel needed, plus a vid on how to administer the military-grade nanites and apply temporary casts. An hour after Petra administered the saline and nanite injections, Axel's pasty color had returned to normal. Torance could now monitor Axel's progress through an 'unauthorized' link established between Ohashi's scanner and the doctor's system at HQ. Axel remained unconscious, yet his vitals showed he was recovering.

Atmosphere in the ship settled down as the team breathed a collective sigh of relief. Ohashi played the recordings from the three drones sent to the storage facility. Everyone watched with rapt attention as Axel accomplished the death-defying feat of dismantling not one, but *two* AIs, then getting away. The drones had followed him back, recording everything. Near the end, Petra wept or covered her eyes when Axel raced through traffic at suicidal speeds in the rain. Kamryn admitted to herself she could never have done what he did. Not one for showing much affection, she hugged Petra for support. Ohashi, no doubt, cared as deeply, but, like Kamryn, seldom advertised it. Had Mark been here, he would have fought side by side with the only man he called friend and 'brother.' Axel was the glue—no, the *fist* that held them together.

Kamryn's thoughts switched to Emeryx. "There's one AI left. Where is it?"

"Omigod, I forgot about it." Ohashi changed screens, tapped double-time for several seconds, then pointed to a spot on the screen. "It's in Williamsburg at a…Village Bed & Breakfast. It doesn't need to eat or sleep, so what's it doing?"

"Delivering something would be my guess," Kamryn muttered. "How far?"

"Fifty miles north."

In the pilot's cabin, Kamryn addressed Nguyen. "We need to get to Williamsburg. You know anywhere to hide our ship up there?"

"It's not like I haven't mentioned it forty or fifty times before. A shiny bronze ship ain't easy to hide. How 'bout trading it in on a nice black one?"

Kamryn scrunched up her face. "Maybe later. Williamsburg, now."

Resigned to the status quo, Nguyen nodded at Malone, giving him the go ahead to prepare for liftoff. She began searching through her database of old Space Command cronies for a contact in the designated area. Retired military preferred to settle near bases for easy access to healthcare and other perks.

"How do you guys feel about going undercover?"

Nguyen perked up. "Yeah," she paused, "doing *what*, exactly?"

"Emeryx has seen me, but not you two."

"I'll do it," Malone said. "One of us should stay with the ship."

Nguyen countered, "No, we'll flip for it."

When neither pilot found a coin to toss, Kamryn used a 50-dollar Martian credit squirreled deep in her pocket. She'd kept it as a lucky souvenir for getting off that planet alive—and in one piece. Reminiscent of a casino chip, it was red over black on the heads side, black over red on the tails side.

Nguyen chose heads, Kamryn flipped, Malone won with tails. Nguyen pouted, mumbling, "Friggin' tall people. *Thbbft*."

Kamryn left in a hurry, trying not to laugh out loud at the sound of Nguyen's raspberry. She headed for the MedLab to check on Axel's progress. The scene took her back to when Axel had visited her in the Portland hospital. A triage blanket with the TMD emblem covered his body, no doubt part of Torance's care package.

Petra sat beside him, dozing. Ohashi had rigged a platform for the scanner next to the medpod. Wireless electrodes scattered over his body supplied data to Torance via Ohashi's link.

Kamryn eased up to clasp his cyborg arm in their familiar warrior greeting. The arm looked human, the skin soft and warm to the touch, but that's where normal ended. She'd seen Axel inflict incredible damage no human could produce, not only with his cyborg arm, but leg as well. In her mind, she awarded the Medal of Valor to Axel for going up against two AIs and making it back to the ship alive.

A lump formed in her throat. Kamryn dismissed it, preferring to concentrate on his wounds. The nanites were speedy little healers. They shrank lacerations, reduced swelling inside the translucent casts, and made bruises less noticeable, even around the ribs.

The sudden pressure of Axel's thumb on her arm startled Kamryn.

She stared at his face, waiting, hoping for his eyes to open. Nothing. She bent over to whisper in his ear, "We gotcha. You're full of nanites. Torance is monitoring your progress. Rest easy."

He repeated the gesture.

Tears welled in her eyes. She beamed at him, now certain Axel's brain, as well as his body would recover.

His hold on her arm relaxed, the pressure fading away.

She stood at his side for a while, watching his chest rise and fall with regular breaths.

Malone commed her with a five-minute warning before liftoff. She swung the transparent medpod cover over Axel and locked it to keep him secure, then touched Petra's shoulder to wake her.

"Harness up. We're leaving."

***

With their comms restored, Mark and Brett conversed with each other from inside their respective cells in normal tones without fear of being overheard. Segregated in D Block, with no prisoners in the adjacent cells and video monitored directly by TMD Headquarters in Virginia, it was a perfect setup. They'd become comfortable addressing each other by their aliases—Brett played John Holt and Mark played Bob Dawson. They worked through various scenarios on how to approach Chang for the intel Dimitrios needed.

Mark heard the jangle of chains. "Wait…"

"What?"

Sounds of rattling metal echoed down the walkway, signaling Chang's arrival.

Mark had wondered about the reasoning for housing both genders in the same wing until he recalled something Axel had said about prisons. Male criminals received injections of P-3-11, a form of chemical castration. The equivalent for females, V-7-11, purportedly suppressed even the most ardent libidos. Regardless, prisons still relied on constant vid surveillance, metal bars, blackout force fields, sensory deprivation cells, plus a host of painful inducements to encourage criminals to follow the rules.

The two undercover ISD sergeants in olive drab guard uniforms perp walked the prisoner, shackled at hands and feet, past Mark's cell. He pretended not to notice as Claudia Chancellor, the cute, athletic blonde opened Chang's cell door. Terri Laughlin, the discus thrower, shoved the prisoner inside. The cuffs unlocked and fell to the floor as Chang crossed the threshold.

Laughlin retrieved them. "You missed dinner," she snapped. "Breakfast is at 0600."

The cell door shut with a reverberating *clang*. It activated the flash of a transparent force field amplified by a destructive level of electromagnetic energy. The guards left Chang standing alone in the middle of her new residence. The tall, model-thin Asian wore baggy orange coveralls identifying her as prisoner D180. She remained stationary for so long after the guards had disappeared Mark thought she might be ill or drugged—until she erupted. Chang shrieked with rage as she pulled the bunk off the wall, ripped the shower apart, wrenched the toilet off the floor and heaved it at the metal bars.

Mark flinched involuntarily as the toilet flew toward him. When it crashed into her cell's force field, the blackout feature activated. Her cell turned dark as night—and soundproof. Mark only managed a single comment under his breath. "Wow."

"Yeah," Brett said. "She's definitely not my type."

"Mine either," Mark agreed. "At 20 percent human, with a neural interface, she's closer to an AI classification. Anyway, her little demonstration showed us what she's capable of now."

"And to stay the hell out of her way."

"That goes without saying. After her temper tantrum I bet she's in time out until breakfast."

Brett chuckled. "Time out—temper tantrum?"

"I have a younger sister. Gina was a…free spirit."

"Well, this bitch is dangerous."

"It does change a few of my theories on how to deal with her."

"So how do you want to play this?"

"From the way Dimitrios explained things," Mark said, "this level of emotion is astonishing. I assumed she'd be more machinelike—computerized, unfeeling."

"Her body may be," Brett countered, "but what I saw was raw emotion in the form of unadulterated anger."

"Exactly. So we use it to our advantage, play on those emotions." Mark began to outline new scenarios he believed might stimulate a trigger, making her susceptible to sharing information.

"Yes, but there has to be a quid pro quo. To get her to share with us, we have to offer something in return."

"We let it slip we're planning a way out of here."

"Okay, Bob," Brett said, "I'll play devil's advocate. What if she's already planning one?"

"Then *you* think of something, John."

"Entice her with a list of disreputable military contacts that would offer her a means for retaliation. From the reaction we witnessed, I bet she'd jump at the chance. Once I share my background in Nuclear Science and Engineering, she'll see the logic of joining forces."

"Oh, fine, *John*," Mark said, taking their one-upmanship to the next level. "Then I'll mention my four ships, a secure lab, and closets full of money—icing on the cake, right?"

"Sure, *Bob*. And your attitude sucks," Brett mumbled.

A stress headache grew behind Mark's temples. "Look, we're supposed to be friends who got caught in a scam and hate each other. Well, we've got that part down. Now let's focus on the job, or we'll be here a lot longer than I want to be."

***

Natalya Stepanov fumed as she watched the red blips of her enemy inch closer to *Stellaria*. The warmonger's paltry efforts to instill fear with the deliberate slip of a "new weapon" might scare Rylak and her crew, but not Stepanov. They'd have to up their game tenfold to intimidate her. Little did they know she had shipboard weapons plus the ultimate surprise—Zdeth, something they could neither see nor smell.

Let them come and try to take her ship. They'd learn the hard way not to underestimate Natalya Stepanov.

"Captain?" Mister Boone motioned for Rylak.

She bent over his shoulder, watching as he pointed to his console.

Stepanov moved left, leaning in for a better view.

"*Two* Terrans?"

"Yes, ma'am. The second was shadowing the first so closely we detected a single TMD warship. They separated enough for our system to pick up two distinct transponder signals. We've identified them as *Colossus* and *Vengeance*. Both are at maximum burn on our portside. The Martian *Scorpius* and *Hellindra* are still closing in to starboard."

Rylak repeated, "*Vengeance*?"

Boone double-checked. "Confirmed."

"I know the captain, Rane Thorson." A pained expression crossed her face. "Very…aggressive."

Her remark made Boone wince. "At their speed, we'll have four warships flanking us before long."

Rylak spun on her heel, grabbed Stepanov by the arm, and dragged her to an alcove away from the Bridge personnel. "No matter what you told the crew, this was never an exploration mission," the captain snapped. "I don't know why four military warships are chasing us, but I do know what's in our hold: clones, bioweapons, and warheads. At this point, I'm certain you and Chang did something that pissed off the TMD so badly, they'll chase you to the outer reaches, and then kill you. Which incidentally, includes me and my crew." Rylak slammed her open palm against the bulkhead mere inches from Stepanov's face.

Natalya darted out of reach, unnerved by the captain's sudden outburst.

Rylak moved in, her cheeks flushed, eyes full of hostility. "Because we happen to be in Martian space, this has turned into an interplanetary version of war games. The Martian fleet is smaller, but just as lethal as Terra's. We're in a lose-lose situation now—outnumbered, outgunned, and will be overtaken shortly. They will offer surrender, or death and destruction. We are left with Hobson's Choice: take what is available, or nothing at all. There is no other solution. I know one of the captains. If he's in charge of the outcome, we will be space dust as soon as his ship is within range. Your blackmail threats are a moot point now. We will *not* die for you."

Stepanov continued to backstep as she considered whether to share the particulars of her Zdeth plan or keep them secret. "Trust me, Captain, we do have options," she said, trying to sound self-confident. "I'm certain they will contact us. Until they do, continue to our destination."

Stepanov dashed off to her Lab, Rylak staring daggers at her backside.

Six feverish hours later, after what she admitted was a manic episode, Stepanov had finished the second cylinder of her prized formula. She suspected the Terran military also knew *Stellaria's* payload consisted of clones, lethal bioweapons, and the likelihood of nuclear warheads. If the Terrans knew, so did the Martians.

Rylak had been correct; *Stellaria* was a moving target. A well-aimed missile from any one of the four ships and...*boom!* Subatomic particles scattered from Mars to Jupiter. Stepanov feared the war dogs had either hijacked or destroyed Chang's ship. There could be no other explanation. She vowed not to suffer the same fate, no matter what it took.

Chapter 20

Axel smelled coffee.

"Sergeant...Sergeant Von Radach."

The voice sounded familiar. Axel tried to open his eyes. They were glued shut. He tried to sit up. Couldn't.

"Sergeant Von Radach."

"Sir." His eyes fluttered open. Everything was fuzzy. Slowly, a tablet came into view with the smiling image of Major Torance.

"Welcome back, son."

In the next three seconds, visions of his fight with the AIs and harrowing bike ride in the rain flooded his brain. "Glad to be back, sir." Axel moved his hands and legs, relieved to find he still had two human and two cyborg limbs.

Nearby equipment emitted rapid, high-pitched beeps.

"Calm down, you're fine," Torance said. "Don't worry, no new parts were added. You were a little banged up—no worse than the Peruvian Rebellion, though."

Axel grunted, recalling the near-death escape that cost him a week in the hospital. "How bad this time?"

"The normal stuff. A few fractures, bruised kidney, bumps and cuts."

"Can I get up?"

"Yes, but go easy on the ankle or it won't heal properly." Torance turned away, then back again. "I've got to go. You're on a heavy nanite protocol, so no drinking. And don't cheat—I'm monitoring your vital signs. Torance out." The screen faded to black.

Petra whisked the tablet away and her smiling face came into view. "Hi. Want some coffee?"

"I'd kill for coffee." He'd also kill for food. He was starving.

She snipped through tape holding his limbs in place and helped him sit up. "Here." She held out a giant tumbler of his favorite brew.

He reached for it, saw the translucent cast on his right arm, felt a catch in his ribs, and a twinge in his kidney. The longer he was awake, the more he realized how lucky he'd been.

Petra pointed to his arm. "Torance said if you're good, that one can come off in two days."

He downed the steaming espresso while she gave him a sitrep. "We arrived in Williamsburg thirty-six hours ago. Malone's surveilling Emeryx. He says the AI's acting weird. Ohashi and I think there's something wrong with its neural matrix."

Kamryn appeared in the doorway. "I'm glad to see you've finished napping. Hungry?"

He salivated as visions of steak and eggs danced in front of his eyes. "I could eat a herd of buffalo."

"They're not on the menu. Torance sent meals for you. It's that or nothing."

He groaned at the thought of hospital food. Axel swung his legs off the medpod, saw the cast on his ankle. When the sheet covering him slipped, he glanced underneath. "Why am I naked?"

"We had to cut off your clothes." Petra blushed, but her eyes sparkled.

"Nobody thought to put more on?"

Kamryn smirked. "Why? You weren't going anywhere."

"Well I am now." He tied the sheet in a knot at his waist.

Petra brought crutches and followed him into the galley for Torance's version of "get well" food. Water mixed with the first packet of powder made a green vitamin drink, the second packet made a brown pudding substance, which became a soy steak after ninety seconds in the magwave oven. Axel had eaten worse, though not lately.

After a shower and fresh clothes, he hobbled on crutches into the conference room for an update from Ohashi.

"I heard you were awake."

"Awake, beat-up, and hungry for real food."

"So…cranky?"

"Pretty much."

"Sit there." She motioned to the captain's chair inside the door. Ohashi scooted around closer to him, moved her screen between them to point at a vague figure. "Malone's not bad at tracking. He stays in the background, doesn't draw attention to himself, wears different hats and a reversible jacket. Yesterday, Emeryx checked into the Holly Tree Inn. She—it—met with two men for dinner, both human. We ID'd them. One worked for Wade Fulton as a pilot, the other a pilot for Lotus Chang. Can't get close enough to record any conversations yet."

"Could the AIs in the storage unit have contacted Emeryx before I destroyed them?"

"Already considered the possibility, and my answer is: I don't know. Even if we had their neural matrices to analyze, I'm not an expert. Mark's much better, but it's not his specialty, either."

Her statement reminded Axel they hadn't been a full team since the TMD shanghaied Mark in Oregon. He'd never had a friend like Mark. For a scientist, he could shoot and take a punch and was game for almost anything. He wouldn't admit it to anyone else, but he missed the kid.

"They're planning something."

"I agree, but what?"

Axel tried to concentrate, but the painkillers were wearing off. The pins and needles of nanites working throughout his system made his skin itch in the very places he couldn't scratch—under the casts. Everywhere else twinges and throbs riddled his body. Still, something jogged his memory from his days on the police force in Phoenix. "Do these people have access to ships? If so, how many, and where are they?"

"Umm… good idea." Ohashi tapped at the screen, searching for the data.

Instead of embarrassing himself by passing out at the table, Axel exerted superhuman effort to stand. He hobbled back to the MedLab with one thing on his mind. Rummaging in the cabinet for painkillers, he caught sight of Kamryn and Petra in the doorway.

"You following me?"

"Kinda. Just in case." Kamryn grabbed his augmented arm and brought it over her shoulder to guide him to the pod. Petra gave him a dose of painkillers after he stretched out.

Looking worried, Petra squeezed his hand. "I think you got up too soon. We're going to close the lid to oxygenate you. In three hours, I'll be back to administer another dose of nanites. You should feel much better by then."

The drugs sped welcomed relief to every nerve ending in his body and dulled his mind. Axel desperately wanted to stay awake to figure out what the AI and its two human cohorts were planning, but he'd have to wait.

Petra stayed by his side until he drifted off into a drugged slumber.

***

Mark awoke to find Chang's cell no longer dark, yet still in shambles. She was sitting on the floor cross-legged, staring at him; a killer look if he'd ever received one. It creeped him out—

especially recalling her unhinged tantrum upon her arrival. He gave her a no-teeth smile paired with a timid "hey" wave.

She flipped him the universal finger and turned to face the far wall.

Shit. He *hated* undercover work.

Brett's voice floated into his comm. "You really have a way with women." He chuckled softly. "Watch and learn, Hot Shot."

Mark heard Brett shuffling around, then saw Chang tilt her head to give a sidelong glance at Brett's cell.

"Whatcha in for, Doll Face?"

After an eerie silence she said, "None of your friggin' business."

"Ha! I won." Brett chortled. "Bob and I had a bet who could get you to talk first."

Mark hung his head for fear Chang would see his smirk.

"He didn't even try, so you won by default." She moved closer to Mark's cell. "Why are you here?"

Okay, here goes nothing. "Johnny boy, over there," Mark tossed a thumb toward Brett's cell, "miswired a spybot we sold to a double-dealing corporate CFO. It went rogue and killed a woman, so we're both in for murder."

"It's not my fault," Brett said forcefully.

"Was too." Mark thumped his chest. "My cybernetics were spot on—perfecto. You can jump up and down and set your hair on fire, John, but it all comes down to the fact that you screwed up—big time."

"For the hundredth time, Bob, it's not my fault," he repeated. "I have a master's degree in nuclear science and engineering. I haven't made a mistake wiring anything since I was four years old. That forensic specialist—and I use the term loosely—was dumb as dirt. A wiring error did not make that bot go rouge." Brett became silent, until he whispered into Mark's comm, "It's up to you now Hot Shot. Reel her in."

Oh, no pressure.

As a gambler, Mark had faced many professional card sharks, and knew he must play the right card at the right time. He gave her a hangdog look, finger combed his hair, trying for a passive approach to Brett's aggressive style. "I'm Bob Dawson. That's John Holt, my stepbrother. We were partners in a lucrative spybot business before this happened. We're waiting for word from our attorneys about an appeal. Word is the authorities haven't found our assets yet, but they're bound to sooner or later."

"You have resources?"

Mark rolled his eyes and gave her the kind of cocky grin a person makes after getting away with something. "*Mega* resources." He winked—boldly.

Bingo. He detected tiny tells in Chang's facial expression which indicated her interest level had risen exponentially. Seizing the momentum, he played one card after another, first easing her into conversations about how he and stepbrother John started a legitimate business, but went underground for the big bucks of corporate espionage.

"What's your specialty?" she asked.

"PhD in Xenobiology—Cybernetics."

"Really…" Her eyes sparkled.

If Mark were sitting at a table playing cards, he'd be drinking scotch. A double shot of O'Bannon's Special Reserve would certainly steady his nerves, yet Mark pressed on without it. "May I ask what brings you to this out-of-the-way establishment?"

"A difference of opinion with the TMD."

"Ah, yes. It happens to the best of us." He began sharing truthful tidbits about his resources to pique her interest. Mark had indeed broken the ice, though drenched in sweat by the time their guards delivered breakfast trays. He gave Chancellor a covert thumbs up and was so hungry he devoured the dreadful prison food.

Chang ate nothing.

After breakfast, Brett eased into the conversation. Chang remained guarded but more relaxed, even hinting she didn't expect to be at Rheinholdt long. Neither he nor Brett pressed her as to why.

Mark's augmented hearing detected heavy footsteps approaching. He turned away to whisper, "Heads up Brett, someone's coming."

Major Peerce appeared like a bearded, white haired monster from a bad dream to hover in front of Chang's cell. "Prisoner D180, you've destroyed Rheinholdt property. Punishment for the first offense is forty-eight hours of sensory deprivation. A second offense will draw ninety-six hours. Beginning now."

Her cell went black and silent.

Mark jumped up. "Colonel Peerce, sir, we'd just begun to make some headway. This punishment will delay our stay by two days—at least."

"Rules are rules. It can't be helped." Peerce left without another word.

Mark flopped on his bed, disillusioned and disgusted, but also secretly thankful for a breather. The stress of trying to gain Chang's trust overwhelmed him. Getting her to open up about her plans would take a lot more time than General Dimitrios projected. His plan had been flawed from the beginning. It could take months—or longer—to get the information Dimitrios wanted. Mark had no intention of remaining in this prison another forty-eight hours waiting for her 'solitary' to end.

***

Axel smelled coffee. This time it was Kamryn who held out a tumbler. Since the last infusion of nanites, painkillers, and another nap, he almost felt like his old self.

"If you don't want to miss anything, get up and follow me."

"Lead the way." He slid off the medpod and hobbled on the crutches after her to the conference room. They joined Petra, who munched on cookies while she stared at Ohashi's screen. Axel downed the coffee and snagged a handful of cookies off the tray, the breakfast of champions.

Ohashi pointed to the AI. "Malone's two tables away."

From Malone's lapel camera, they watched Emeryx sitting alone in the dining room of the Holly Tree Inn. Less than a minute later, the two humans she'd spoken with last night entered.

Malone waited for the distraction of the men seating themselves at her table. He bent over to retrieve his dropped napkin, then covertly lobbed a Chewy across the floor. It rolled underneath their table, smack up against the pedestal to rest between one of the four legs.

The small listening device transmitted every word spoken at their table. The taller, blue-collar type named Randall, worked for Fulton. The shorter, muscular one called Gunther worked for Chang. Both were unhappy Emeryx had not acquired *MAVREK*.

The AI sat frozen, hands folded, fingers laced together. Her eyes moved from Randall to Gunther as the men ate dinner, drank expensive booze, and argued about everything, giving no reason why they wanted the ship.

Until Randall unloaded the bombshell. "This morning I got news Wade's being moved from TMD Headquarters to Rheinholdt in two days. We have to have that ship. It's the only one the military can't track, and we need it to rescue him the minute he gets there. Once he's inside, it'll be impossible to get them both out at the same time."

A wide-eyed Petra clapped a hand to her mouth.

Gunther promptly offered another jarring surprise. "I've paid off a technician and some guards to release Chang and get her outside the minute Wade arrives. You've got to get us that ship, Emeryx, or the whole thing falls apart and it'll be your fault."

His guilt-trip was wasted on the AI.

Emeryx stood. "The ship in question will be in my possession by tomorrow evening." The AI pivoted and abandoned the men, who finally left after racking up charges like VIPs with unlimited expense accounts.

"If Emeryx were human," Ohashi observed, "a shrink would've diagnosed her as a sociopath—even a psychopath by the antisocial behavior she's exhibited. Assuming Chang programmed the AI, its personality matrix is likely similar or a duplicate of her own."

Kamryn added, "Which makes Chang more of a challenge than any of us expected."

They all traded looks, then turned to Axel.

The fingers of his right hand drummed on the table while his other hand smoothed the stubble on his jawline. "Contact Dimitrios."

Ohashi established a link and sent Malone's recordings on the movements of the three targets. Petra ran for more coffee. Kamryn propped Axel's leg up on a chair.

Dimitrios remained tight-lipped as he viewed the vid. Afterward, Axel didn't mince words delivering the report on his encounter with the two AIs.

"General, sir, we're not prepared to continue without support from the TMD. My casts come off today. Even in armor, I wouldn't be 100 percent. And we're down a man because Mark's on the inside. If we go along with their plan and allow them to use *MAVREK*—which I have strong reservations about—we'll need plenty of high-powered backup." Axel folded his arms across his chest, lowered his chin to look straight at Dimitrios. "Sir, I chose to go up against those two AIs and got my ass kicked for it, and I'm half cyborg. But I won't put any of my friends in harm's way."

A pained expression passed across the general's face. "Fulton, Chang, and Stepanov are collectively responsible for the deaths of twety-two scientists, plus Colonel Nash Harrington and Corporal Marla Dellucci, whose funerals I attended this week. Not to mention the destruction of military property and years of research. If it were up to me, all three would be flayed and buried alive in a mound of African army ants. Of course, that's not on the list of current sentences, but a word to the right people and I might be able to swing it."

Dimitrios steepled his fingers, contemplating for a moment before he continued.

"You'll get two warships, Von Radach, each with a platoon of armor—more if you need them. We must know who their contacts are and what other plans they have in the works. I won't be caught with my pants down again. All your systems will be linked to ours in a coordinated effort. It's the only way I'll approve this mission." With a smirk, he added, "And don't worry about Warren. I plan on getting him and my nephew out of Rheinholdt as quickly as possible, or I'll be answering to my sister."

Chapter 21

Nightmares plagued Stepanov with visions of firefights, hordes of armored soldiers overrunning her ship shooting everyone in sight, her corpse drifting in the vastness of space for millions of years. She awoke gasping for air, soaked in sweat, enraged her well-laid plans had withered to nothing more than a memory in the last few days.

After a cool shower, and still troubled by the bad dreams, Stepanov needed a pick-me-up. She donned the new red exosuit set aside for landing day on Ganymede, piled her hair high, and grabbed a silver long coat as she left for the bridge.

A skeleton crew manned the bridge in the early hours before the regular shift started. Rylak was conspicuously absent. Stepanov tiptoed down the passageway, pausing at every door until she heard sounds behind the Captain's Ready Room, a place she'd never been invited. A steady stream of angry men's voices traveled through steel faster than light speed. They railed against taking any aggressive action on the Terran or Martian warships, fearing reprisal—which would cause their collective annihilation. Over time, Rylak's calm voice pacified the arguing, but her pitch dropped too low for Stepanov to make out the words.

When chairs scraped across the deck, Stepanov sensed the meeting had ended and scurried away before the door opened. She also sensed a mutiny brewing among the bridge officers.

What had Rylak said to appease them? If Stepanov ordered Rylak to fire on the warships, what response could she expect from the Captain—or the crew? Stepanov hadn't even had coffee yet, and her day was going from bad to worse.

"You're up early," Rylak said, catching up with Stepanov. "Headed to the galley?"

Stepanov forced a smile and a chatty response. "Thought I'd get an early start this morning, but not before I've had my fill of coffee."

The two women shared a table. Rylak lowered her voice to a confidential level. "Some officers had become…anxious about engaging in a firefight with four military warships. I called a meeting this morning to let them vent their concerns. It's never good to let tensions rise on a ship without a mechanism to let off steam."

Stepanov relaxed, reasoning Rylak had volunteered the truth, otherwise she would have remained silent. "So, everything's fine now?"

"They voiced their opinions, then cooled down. Before their shift's over they'll be back to normal."

"Glad to hear it."

Stepanov left the captain nursing her second cup of cinnamon java espresso. Jogging all the way aft to her cozy lab, she mulled over the men's harsh words. Dissention led to mutiny on a ship. What would happen if the crew turned on her? Stepanov couldn't kill all the officers—she needed some to pilot the ship. Rylak was an excellent pilot, but even she couldn't do it alone.

Stepanov spent hours searching her lab for mind-bending drugs she could use to control the officers, should problems arise. She found plenty of chemicals for bioweapons, but not one synthetic hallucinogen suitable for concocting a psychoactive drug.

Her frustration reached a boiling point. She snatched a beaker and hurled it against the wall. It hit the bulkhead, exploding into shards. They pinged off every metal surface—except Stepanov. Her face stung where tiny slivers pierced her skin. The hard sections of her exosuit repelled the shrapnel, although the soft parts looked like a pincushion full of crystal splinters. She grabbed another beaker, but stopped herself from repeating the foolish move. Stepanov's rage simmered while she removed the facial shavings and dotted on surgical glue to close the cuts. She spent another half hour tweezing the glass out of her new exosuit.

More inclined to anger than tears, today she felt much closer to the latter than she had in years. Too many setbacks and unexpected obstacles had derailed her plans. She saw her entire fortune and months of preparation being jettisoned out a waste tube.

The captain's terse voice interrupted Stepanov's thoughts. "Stepanov to the bridge."

Stepanov sneaked into the bridge from the rear entrance, staying in the background to avoid calling attention to her presence. Cool blue light filled the area. It chilled the atmosphere and turned human faces into ethereal apparitions.

Rylak remained seated, watching the crew with a hawkish expression that was second nature.

After a flurry of screen taps, Mister Boone said, "Uh…Captain, we may have another problem." He pointed to a new oncoming red dot, enlarging it between his fingers.

"Could it be a civilian ship?"

"Not at that speed," he replied, glancing at Rylak over his shoulder.

Silence engulfed the bridge.

When Boone's console beeped twice, he glanced at the screen. "Martian warship number three verified. Transponder signal belongs to the *Phantom*. It's five against one now."

A sickening feeling rose in Stepanov's throat. The arsenal of traditional weapons on her ship should defend against the unlikely scenario of pirates. Even a torpedo armed with bioweapons might threaten one adversary, not five military warships. It was time she accepted the inevitable: the warmongers would board *Stellaria*.

But…she still had the aerosol, and vowed to infect every single soldier who stepped foot on her ship. Terrans and Martians be damned, she would not give up the goal of claiming her share of riches on Ganymede.

Mister DeSilva signaled for Rylak to approach. They spoke in hushed tones before she moved around to the next officer, conversing with each one at their stations.

Finally, the captain stepped in front of Stepanov. "There is no escape," Rylak said, her tone clipped and menacing. "We are quickly approaching a dead zone—one of our own making. As captain of *Stellaria*, they will order me to drop shields and power down. I will not refuse because if any of those ships fire on us, we disappear without a trace. Look around, Stepanov. The news media isn't covering this event with cameras and reporters. The only witnesses are the ones pulling the trigger, so—who will know?"

Rylak's eyes were inky shadows in a pale blue face. "When they board us, they will take everyone into custody for interrogation. I don't know what they think you've done, but now I'm certain it includes the death of military personnel. It's the only reason for the size of this posse," she hissed. "If I die for my crime, that's one thing. I will not allow my crew to die for yours." Rylak spat the words out before returning to her chair on the dais behind Boone.

Stepanov was certain Rylak would have struck her if they'd been alone. She remained paralyzed as new versions of her dreams blossomed into waking nightmares.

Evidence! *Chort poberi!*

She spun around and raced back to her cabin to get rid of all the incriminating evidence. If the Terrans had Chang, they at least suspected Stepanov knew of the booby-trapped prototypes left for the military, making her an accomplice in any deaths. Rylak had guessed correctly. Scrubbing her files of everything even remotely related to Chang moved to the top of her To-Do List.

No sooner had she slid into her chair and tapped the screen than the unthinkable happened—everything went dark: a black screen, no lights…but most catastrophic—no sounds of life support.

She commed Rylak, "Captain?"

Her commlink was dead.

The earlier sickening feeling dropped to the pit of her stomach.

***

On board the TMD warship *Vengeance*, eight bridge officers, including the captain, sat holding their collective breath awaiting confirmation of a successful strike.

"Direct hit with the RAM-XT, sir. *Stellaria* is dead in space. All systems inoperable."

"Yes!" Captain Rane Thorson slapped the arm of his chair, delighted the new microwave pulse weapon had crippled the civilian ship. His officers reveled in the celebratory atmosphere spreading around the bridge. "Well done, Mister Riley. Still, it's a shame we didn't get to blow a few holes in that piece of scrap metal."

"Sir, it's not over yet. They might resist," Riley said, only half joking.

"Let's hope so, Mister Riley. I'd relish the opportunity to put a few dents in their hull." Thorson turned to the comm officer. "Mister Loomis, notify Captain Tham on *Colossus* and let the three Martians know we've deactivated our target.

Extend my invitation to join us as we encircle and swarm *Stellaria*."

Thorson stood, tugged at his gray tunic and smoothed the black goatee that made him look devilish. "According to our Chief Engineer's precise calculations, by the time we get there all crew members should be unconscious due to the lack of life support."

Personally, he didn't care if they were alive or dead. Thorson had cultivated his mean bastard reputation by always winning—everything—no matter what it took. He'd inherited his father's intellect, but not his towering stature. As a youngster, the dumber, larger Neanderthals bullied him until he'd learned the deadly martial art known as Krav Maga. Then things changed, and he became known as that *mean little bastard*. After a latent growth spurt in his teens, the word *little* no longer applied. Since becoming captain, the term *mean* had become interchangeable with *sneaky*, which he also savored.

"Mister Riley, who arrives first?"

"The Martian *Phantom*, sir. Captained by Vera Sheridan."

"Is there any way we can beat her?"

Riley rubbed the back of his neck for a moment, stalling his negative response. "Not possible, sir."

Thorson snapped, "Then send this emergency alert: 'Do Not Board—Level 5 Bioweapons Onboard.' Put it on a repeat loop every ten minutes. I'm certain she's been warned, but let's make it clear Sheridan knows *not* to board that ship. Send the list of bioweapons they're carrying. I sure as hell don't need a Martian dying because they boarded a Terran vessel carrying deadly pathogens. We'd never hear the end of it."

More to the point, he'd be damned if another captain would steal his thunder by boarding *Stellaria* first. "Are we still ahead of the other three?"

Riley grinned. "Yes, sir. We should arrive twenty-nine minutes before they do."

"Notify me the instant anything changes. I'm meeting with Lieutenant Burnett in my Ready Room."

Thorson left, thinking about the previous discussions he'd had with Burnett on how best to deploy his armored unit once they boarded *Stellaria*. The most expedient method might not be the safest. Thorson was twice as adamant about none of his crew falling victim to Zdeth—not to mention the full complement of twenty-five Terran scientists and doctors who would accompany his crew.

Between the two Terran ships they carried epidemiologists, microbiologists, chemists, and nuclear engineers to inspect *Stellaria's* lethal payload and safeguard its contents. The human cargo required a team of medical geneticists to examine the cloned youngsters purchased to use as slaves on Ganymede, ensuring they hadn't been altered or mistreated. That aspect of *Stellaria's* mission appalled even a mean bastard like Thorson.

***

The Mavrek crew spent hours hashing out the fine points of a dangerous and potentially disastrous plan to go along with Emeryx's scheme. Using their ship to transport the two people they most wanted behind bars away from prison seemed ironic, to say the least.

"We're agreed then?" Axel said, scratching his right arm where the cast had been. Nanite protocol always generated an itching sensation like pins and needles once the cast came off.

Petra snorted. "It's so *wrong*."

"I don't like it." Ohashi dropped her face into cupped hands.

"This sucks," Kamryn said, summing up the unanimous, albeit awful, decision.

Axel hammered away at the pros of the argument. "We have weapons and armor on board and will have two warships armed to the teeth at our backs."

"Yeah, and they'll be aimed at us," Kamryn said, pointing to herself with both hands.

"You can stay here."

"Oh, like hell I will," she scoffed. "Who's going to make sure you don't get your ass kicked again?"

The cybers looked from Axel to Kamryn to see if the remark had been in jest. It wasn't. They leaned away from the table, giving the two alphas plenty of space.

Axel's dark eyes bore holes through Kamryn before he pressed on. "In the beginning, our plan had been to take all three down for clone trafficking. That didn't work out because two had already left Terra. Now we have a second chance to finish the job. I'll meet with Emeryx and agree to rent the ship—no questions asked. We go to Rheinholdt, pick up Chang and Fulton. When their destination is entered into our linked nav system, the TMD will have plenty of time to get there first and set up an ambush. The minute we land and open the hatch, the TMD arrests them. Easy-peasy."

Both cybers rolled their eyes.

"Nothing is ever easy," Ohashi said under her breath.

"Never," Petra agreed.

Nguyen poked her head into the room. "I've disabled Ohashi's SRVL system. Our Nav is part of the TMD's network. The next time we take off, they'll be able to track us all the way to Saturn." She made a disgruntled face at Axel before leaving.

"Okay, I get it," he said. "*Nobody* likes the plan. But none of you came up with a better one, so this is the one in play."

He needed to get away from the women, and left for the gym favoring his right leg. Axel eased into a workout routine to limber up his ankle and arm, careful not to abuse his ribs or kidney. In less than twenty-four hours his physical status must be as near perfect as possible. The nanites continued to repair bone and tissue while the painkillers kept the uncomfortable side effects at bay, but the itching drove him crazy. He attached the KorVu monitor Torance had included with the med supplies to track his nanite protocol and cardio. Axel worked the heavy bag, then pounded the speed bag until sweat splattered the bags and stung his eyes. After checking the monitor, he smiled before moving to the weight bench. Half an hour later, he stopped. No sense in overdoing it. He'd take a shower, eat, and return for another round in the gym this evening.

Ten minutes later, Kamryn burst into his shower. "Emeryx is here. The AI can't see me on the ship in these clothes. Hurry and get dressed," she said, dropping a pile of leathers on the floor. "It's waiting for you." She tossed a gun on the heap and scooted out the door.

Oh crap. Axel hopped out, barely dried off, tugged leather pants up over damp skin. Catching sight of himself in the mirror, it looked like he hadn't shaved for a month. Axel was certain the AI hadn't seen him on its first trip to the Flight School. However, it saw Kamryn—even interacted with her as "Maude" in the office. Damn. He'd gotten out of one nasty situation only to be thrust into another.

He missed Mark. With his polished, articulate nature, the kid could charm people into swallowing a line of pure bullshit and believe it was the absolute truth. By comparison, Axel's technique involved issuing orders to comply versus the threat of bodily harm—which hadn't worked on the first two AIs and wouldn't work this time, either. It galled Axel to admit he'd miscalculated not once, but twice now.

Inserting the comm in his ear, he set it to broadcast so everyone could hear the conversation before walking out to strike a bargain with the devil.

Ohashi stopped him right away. "The AI is waiting for you in the passenger cabin. This is too freakin' spooky. It's blinking and breathing like a real human. Kamryn and Petra are armed if you need backup. They're hiding in the starboard Lav."

Good to know. He hoped they wouldn't miss and shoot him instead.

Axel walked down the passageway to the rear cabin as Ohashi disappeared into the galley.

Okay, here goes.

He entered to see the AI sitting in Kamryn's favorite blue chair, legs crossed at the ankles, hands folded in its lap. Axel held out his hand. "Sorry to keep you waiting. I'm Axel Von Radach. And you are…?"

"Ms. Emeryx." The AI neither stood nor offered to shake hands. Simple human courtesies went unacknowledged.

He sank into a chair opposite the AI. "What can I do for you, Ms. Emeryx?"

"I wish to hire your ship for a delicate business merger that can't take place on the planet's surface due to threat of corporate spies and espionage. I will need it for twenty-four hours beginning tomorrow evening at eight o'clock. You can name your price, but no additional information will be forthcoming."

Axel paused for a moment, not wanting to seem eager. "Why my ship?"

"It's a business class Mixx-Reid Starcruiser 75. This model came recommended by a mutual acquaintance."

He wanted to ask what *mutual acquaintance*, yet continued with caution. "I need assurances no harm will come to my crew and nothing illegal will transpire aboard my ship."

"You have my solemn word." Emeryx looked him straight in the eye. "I wouldn't be involved in such dealings."

Axel now knew two facts about these AIs: not only did they use deadly force against humans—contrary to the Terran Code of Ethics—but they also lied convincingly.

Let's see how badly they want my ship. He tapped out a figure on his tablet, and handed it to Emeryx.

The AI nodded.

"In advance."

"Of course." Emeryx handed it back for Axel to enter his account data, after which the funds were transferred. The AI stood, dropping the tablet on the chair, before walking to the hatch. Emeryx opened the heavy door as if it were tissue paper, then faced Axel. "Be prepared to leave when I return at seven forty-five tomorrow evening." Again, the AI engaged in no human pleasantries.

After the hatch clanged shut, Kamryn and Petra burst out of the Lav. As Ohashi ran in from the galley, Axel gave the tablet to her. "Transfer those funds somewhere untraceable, A-*SAP*."

Ohashi looked at the figure, wide-eyed. "Omigod..." She perched on the edge of a chair, her fingers a blur as the exorbitant figure traveled through a dizzying number of financial institutions around the planet.

Malone joined the group. "Since we don't have the final destination yet, Nguyen's making preparations for a lengthy trip."

Kamryn's wary nature was aroused. "How lengthy?"

Malone pointed skyward.

She smacked her forehead, groaning, "This is a terrible idea."

"Oh, suck it up, Fleming," Axel snapped. He walked to the galley for a beer, missing Mark more than ever. Kamryn was getting on his nerves. Over his shoulder he added, "If we make it out of this alive, everybody gets a bonus."

Chapter 22

Mark couldn't take his eyes off the darkened cell across the aisle. It laid in wait; a black hole, ready to swallow anything venturing too close. His agitation grew as he practiced his speech for the better part of an hour. His emotions had reached a boiling point and were ready to spill over at the slightest opportunity.

When Chancellor brought his meal, he couldn't restrain himself. "I'm finished. The woman in that cell is insane. She wasn't here sixty seconds before she ripped everything off the wall. She'll do it again in a heartbeat. If she's only 20 percent human, she doesn't give a crap about sensory deprivation. It could take us *months* to get the intel Dimitrios wants and I'll be damned if I'm sitting here another hour. I want out—*now*."

He almost reached through the bars to grab her arm, but knew the instant his hand touched the invisible electromagnetic force field a super shock would send him to his knees. "They picked me up from my parent's house in Portland. We were getting ready to decorate the Christmas tree when a TMD major and two MPs shanghaied me. Since then I've been blown up, stunned unconscious, and kidnapped. If there's anywhere I do not want to be during Christmas, it's sitting in a military penitentiary below the Arctic circle when I've done nothing wrong. I don't care if they court martial me. I don't need the commission. Just send me home." He was breathing heavy, and hot, clammy sweat clung to his palms.

She pushed the tray along the floor inside his cell door. The corners of her mouth turned up. "Are you through?"

"Umm...maybe?"

"I'm here to grant your wish."

"Which part—court martial or sent home?"

"You're being released."

"When?" Skepticism in his voice.

"In the next twenty-four hours."

"Russell?"

"Him too."

"I'm tickled pink," Mark said with a sardonic grin. "But why?"

"Can't explain now." She waggled her finger at the tray of food. "You need to eat. It may be awhile before you get another meal," Chancellor said, walking away.

"Wait...what?" He glanced at the food. Hot dogs and beans with some kind of green goo for desert. A nibble of the hot dog proved satisfactory. He finished it in three bites, then hoped it didn't cause an acute abdominal catastrophe.

Brett's voice filtered into his ear. "You get the news?"

"Yup," Mark said around a mouthful of beans. He stopped. "I only saw Chancellor, not Laughlin."

"She was here."

Mark shoveled in another spoonful of beans while he pondered the arrival of both women from opposite directions. They'd always arrived together until today. He grew suspicious. A tingling sensation crawled up his spine. "Something's wrong. There's a catch." He tossed the spoon onto the now empty tray. One horrible scenario after another flashed through his mind.

Damn.

"I think Dimitrios is going to stick it to us again."

"You're paranoid."

"I have good reason to be," Mark countered. "What did Laughlin say, exactly?"

"First she said, 'Arrangements have been made to get you out of here within twenty-four hours,' then she winked at me."

"Winked?"

"Uh-huh."

Sergeant Laughlin, the discus thrower, was not the winking type. He now believed a terrible surprise awaited them on this trip.

Oh no.

They were getting out of here—but a specific destination hadn't been named. The tingling sensation squirmed up between his shoulders. Now he doubted whether they were being sent home, or even back to HQ.

***

Lotus Chang sat in total blackness, drifting in and out of a dissociative state, completely detached from a world of her own making. She observed her past from a distance as though watching excerpts of an Old Earth movie, neither feeling nor relating to any part of it.

After an indefinite period, she roused from the trancelike stupor, awakening to her one driving force: a consuming hatred for the Terran military. They were the reason she sat in this frozen hellhole. Her freedom now rested solely with Wade Fulton. If the worst-case scenario materialized, he'd sworn to set a failsafe plan in place. The last remnant of hope for her escape would come soon—or not at all.

As full consciousness returned, Chang fine-tuned her neural matrix to pick up every mechanical ping, scrape, and creak within 100 yards. That's when she detected the vibration of footsteps—running footsteps. She remained immobile, her external faculties sharpened to the highest pitch.

The vibration halted in front of her cell.

She waited, as motionless as a bronze statue, for something to happen.

Dim light flooded her cell.

A blonde female guard swiped a key card to open her door. "Come with me," she said. "We have ninety seconds."

She followed the guard's orders without question while observing a stocky female guard opening doors for two men across the aisle.

Chang's guard quickly led them past sleeping prisoners toward the exit door. They ran at breakneck speed down the stairwell, bursting through a second door into a dark underground tube tunnel, steps from where a small, bullet-shaped hover car waited.

The blonde guard shoved Chang and both men inside. She flung her arm around Bob Dawson's neck and kissed him. "Be quick changing into those clothes. There's a ship waiting at the end. Good luck, Bobby."

The door slid closed, sending the car off at an unexpected velocity. The men scrambled to grab pieces of clothing,

Chang put the leftovers on top her orange coveralls. She did not like how things were unfolding. Fulton's escape plan hadn't included strangers—likely a spur-of-the-moment addition by the female guard at the last minute. She'd as soon kill the men and leave them buried under a snowdrift…except for the money Dawson had bragged about. It might be worth keeping him alive for a while.

Their ride came to an abrupt stop. The door slid open to a blue-tinged panorama of frozen wasteland lit only by a billion faraway stars. Chang's internal sensors gauged the temperature at 58 degrees below zero. Arctic winds whipped into the car. Both men jumped out to search for a ship.

The mouth of the tunnel suddenly spit out another hover car, startling Chang.

A single passenger stepped out.

Wade Fulton was bundled in high-end snow gear from head to boot. "Lotus, glad to see you made it," he said, approaching with an outstretched gloved hand.

She smiled in spite of herself, gratified by his presence. "I didn't know you'd been sent here. Where's the ship? When are we leaving?"

"I've just arrived. I timed this to the split second. Everything's been arranged…"

Dawson and his brother came running toward them shouting, and pointing to the sky.

A loud whooshing sound drowned them out.

Everyone looked up as a large object with six red lights flashing on its underside blotted out the stars. It floated past them to land thirty yards away. Within seconds, the hatch opened, spilling a cone of golden light on the icy surface.

Four figures sprinted toward their salvation.

***

Mark and Brett had seconds to digest what Terri Laughlin whispered to them about the faux escape as she opened their cells. She barely had time to cover the high points, but none of the details before they arrived in the transport tunnel. Mark concentrated on her parting words: "Play dumb, but stand your ground. You're criminals—act like it."

The next alarming surprise happened when he encountered Wade Fulton. Although Fulton hadn't seen Mark during their first meeting, it galled him to act clueless knowing Fulton's crimes. Particularly when he considered Fulton one of the poorest excuses for a human he'd ever met, and was close enough to punch his lights out.

But the biggest shock came as he ran for the ship—he *recognized* it.

What the hell? It was *his* ship.

Every weird reason for *MAVREK* being there zipped through his mind.

Then it hit him.

The SRVL system—it couldn't be tracked. Dimitrios must have 'drafted' Axel into getting involved. Mark grudgingly admitted it bordered on genius, but also put his friends in a huge amount of jeopardy.

This couldn't get any crazier. Mark had no idea if he could play it straight enough to convince Fulton or Chang the people on the ship were complete strangers. Regardless, he had no choice. If he didn't pull it off, someone would get hurt—or worse.

Fulton and Chang led as they jogged toward the ship. Mark's breathing became painful as shards of ice stung his lungs, numbness claimed his feet and hands, exertion slowed him to a crawl.

An unknown woman stood to the left of the airlock. "Fulton…Chang," she said acknowledging the first pair to board. She stepped in front of the opening to block Mark's entrance. "Who are you?" she asked in the voice of a headmistress.

"We're two last minute passengers," Mark said as Brett pushed him inside.

"This flight is restricted," the woman said. "No additional passengers allowed."

Ignoring her, Brett pulled Mark farther into the cabin. "We paid. We have tickets."

"Emeryx," Chang said, "they're okay—for now."

Over the ship's PA system, Nguyen's familiar voice announced, "Liftoff in five…four…"

Interior lights dimmed to a deep blue. Everyone grabbed a seat to harness themselves in.

Mark relaxed a bit, rubbing his frostbitten fingers together. Nguyen would never be navigating if Malone wasn't piloting. They might bicker like an old married couple, but they were a duo no matter what happened. His thoughts gravitated to Axel, Kamryn, Petra, and Ohashi. Where were they? Could Dimitrios have replaced them with undercover operatives? After the unnerving surprises he'd experienced, it would be a great relief to know his friends were safe.

As he considered the welfare of his adopted family, an uncomfortable feeling came over him; the creepy sensation you get when someone is staring at you. He looked up into the soulless eyes of the woman Chang had called Emeryx. For an unknown reason, he couldn't look away. Instead, his detail-oriented brain logged every millimeter of her entire appearance. Something…was *off.* Not quite right. Not quite hu—

Holy shit. She's—it's—an AI.

If his background hadn't included years of cybernetic research and development, he wouldn't have recognized the miniscule tells of artificial intelligence. Surprised, yes, but not astonished. Given Chang's history, the pieces fit together. She'd created the two AIs hunting for his ship and this third one who sat staring at him like an undertaker waiting on a man to exhale his last breath. No great leap to theorize there were more AIs, considering the scope of Fulton's plan. Mark suspected many more were hidden in a plant or inconspicuous building anyplace on the globe.

Uh-oh.

He'd bet a fistful of uranium they were heading to that place right now with the Terran military's two Most Wanted fugitives, and an AI ready to toss him out the airlock any minute.

Times such as these made Mark long for the days when he gambled, drank, and chased pretty women without a care in the world. Those days were long gone. Since the morning his lab had been attacked in Canada, he'd been on a roller coaster ride, either as the hunted, or the hunter of the planet's most detestable criminals. His brother had been killed, his father and Axel barely escaped death, and a colonel had shot off his ear! From where he stood, things were already so far downhill, they couldn't get much worse.

Mark swore this would be his last foray into the criminal underworld. He could quote odds like a veteran bookmaker and knew the law of averages was what most people called Luck. Well, their luck had run out. Somebody was going to die.

After the blue interior lights reverted to a warm glow, a young blonde woman appeared wearing an unusual uniform. Mark had memories of seeing an Old Earth vid with stewards—no, stewardesses—dressed in similar attire.

Whoa.

Petra—as a full-fledged blonde in a short skirt and knee boots. He kept thinking this couldn't get any worse, and every few minutes it did. Axel would never have allowed her to be here alone, so the whole crew must be aboard. Just what he didn't want.

"Miss Emeryx," Petra said, courteous but businesslike, "we've prepared the conference room for your meeting. If you and your associates would kindly follow me, please."

As they filed out, Chang tossed withering looks at Mark and Brett. "You two stay right there. We'll deal with you later."

Her behavior no longer intimidated Mark. He knew where all the weapons were hidden. He also decided if Petra ever left the cyber warrior ranks, she had a promising future in acting.

When a firm hand gripped his shoulder, Mark nearly wet his pants. He whipped around to see Kamryn's smiling face.

She leaned down between the men to stuff a tiny commlink in Mark's hand. "Axel says he's glad you're home," she whispered. "He's barricaded himself in the pilot's cabin after the epic disagreement with Emeryx about her renting *MAVREK* unmanned—she wanted her own crew. He won, of course, but it got hairy. I'm playing the engineer, Ohashi's the galley tech. Indonesia is our destination. Two warships are shadowing us."

Kamryn winked at Brett, then slipped away.

Brett watched her leave with a wolfish gleam in his eye. "Who's that?"

"A kickass sergeant who can cut your throat before you blink." Mark tucked the comm inside his organic ear, giving him instant access to the whole crew again.

Brett shrugged. "Pretty."

"Deadly," Mark insisted. "Pretty deadly."

Emeryx walked toward them.

Mark involuntarily stiffened.

With a magician's sleight of hand, Emeryx produced a pair of stun cuffs. In a heartbeat, the AI had Mark's right hand shackled to Brett's left hand—through the arms of their chairs, with no opportunity for escape.

Heavy on the sarcasm, Brett asked, "Are you afraid we're going to run off somewhere?" When Emeryx didn't respond, he added, "What if I have to pee?"

After Emeryx disappeared, Mark said under his breath, "It's an AI."

Brett shook his head as he mouthed the word, *No.*

Mark nodded.

A few minutes later Chang returned wearing an aubergine colored exosuit and settled into a chair across from them. "I don't know how much you paid the guards to smuggle you out, but I didn't get my cut, so you still owe me. Where are the funds you spoke of, Bob?"

Mark chose a location on the opposite side of the planet. "European Union."

She offered a tablet to him.

"Impossible," Mark said, as he decided the best way to thwart her demand.

"What do you mean?"

"John, does this sound like extortion to you?"

Brett joined in the charade. "Yep, it does. Look, Doll Face, our attorney paid for our release. *And* a ride. If you didn't get a cut, that's not our problem. Drop us off in any big city, we'll find a way home."

Chang's demeanor hardened. She took a different tack. "You may have paid to get out of Rheinholdt, but to get off this ship it will cost you the balance of your funds," she persisted, again thrusting the tablet at Mark.

"Like I said, impossible. It's a 5PWP." Mark quoted an Old Earth banking practice, "Five Point Withdrawal Protocol: in person, iris scan, DNA, faceprint, fingerprint. *Everything*—times two."

"It takes both of us." Brett flashed a toothy smile, enjoying the momentary banter. "We set it up that way on purpose, in case Bob tried to take the money and run."

"Or John," Mark joked, as he and Brett elbowed each other.

Chang shot them icy looks before she stalked back to the conference room.

"Whew, we squeaked by that one, huh?" Brett wilted in the aftermath of their close encounter with the female cyborg. "I was afraid she might rip my arm off and beat me to death with it."

Chapter 23

Dressed in commercial royal blue uniforms, Malone, Nguyen, and Kamryn occupied the pilot's cabin. Axel perched on the jump seat behind Malone. Kamryn sat to the far right of Nguyen, at the seldom-used spare console. After a quick course in elementary astronautics, Kamryn had learned enough to make a few simple calculations. To everyone's relief, however, Nguyen was still in charge of the automated guidance and propulsion systems. The criminal nature of their passengers made locking the cabin's door mandatory. The biometric keypad would allow those with the code to enter. Those without were shit out of luck.

Since Emeryx had already interacted with Kamryn as Maude at the Sky King Flight School, Kamryn became Maude Loomis, *MAVREK's* engineer. Petra and Ohashi assumed new roles as service crew members to warrant their presence on the ship.

Despite all their preparations, the deal almost fell apart when Emeryx arrived with the two pilots she'd met at the Holly Tree Inn. Axel refused to allow them aboard and a serious argument erupted. When Kamryn feared they would come to blows, she stepped in to defuse the situation. Thus, the general's mission was salvaged, yet tensions on the ship remained elevated. As a bonus—or drawback—the general failed to inform them his nephew and Mark had been thrown into the mix. Now they were also responsible for Brett's welfare, which significantly raised the stakes.

Once plans changed, so did the outcome.

Before liftoff, Emeryx had ordered them to set a course for Indonesia. Six minutes into the trip, a buzzer sounded in the pilot's cabin. An orange light blinked on Kamryn's console.

She glanced at Nguyen, who nodded permission. Kamryn pushed a corresponding button to the conference room. "This is Engineer Loomis."

A female voice said, "We have an exact destination."

Kamryn recognized the voice as Chang's. "Go ahead."

"West Kalimantan, Indonesia, 5.6 miles northwest of Sintang."

Nguyen gave a thumbs up, accompanied by hand signals.

"Noted. Is there a landing pad?"

"Yes. It's adjacent to a 60,000 square foot manufacturing plant. Can't miss it."

"We'll let you know five minutes prior to touchdown. Loomis out."

Kamryn broadcast the destination to everyone's comm. The instant Nguyen tapped the additional data on her NAV screen, it fed into the TMD's system. The military now had the exact location of Chang's destination, and as planned, would send one of their escorts ahead to secure or neutralize the facility.

Twenty minutes later, Petra commed Kamryn. "Something's wrong. I'm coming in. Don't shoot me."

In one fluid motion, the cabin door slid open, Petra slithered inside, and it shut behind her.

"I delivered food to the conference room and saw a tablet on the table. It showed a map. Definitely not Indonesia."

"I knew it," Kamryn growled, stabbing a finger in the air.

Axel asked, "Where?"

"China. I'm sure."

"Indonesia was a detour," Axel said. "A wild-goose chase."

"A snipe hunt's more like it," Nguyen grumbled.

Malone turned toward Axel. "The SRVL system will mask all our transponder signatures to get us over the border, but the Chinese have backup systems, long-range spotters, and a host of other means to identify infiltrators."

"The Chinese are still not our friends," Nguyen reminded them. "Once we cross their border, we're *persona non grata* and could be jailed or expelled—*without* our ship."

Kamryn laid a hand on Petra's shoulder. "Where in China? Inland or on the coast?"

"Dunno. Only saw a place called Jixi."

Nguyen searched for the city, then groaned. "It's in northern China, 1,450 miles south of the Arctic Circle and less than thirty miles from the border with Russia—the other unfriendly nation."

"Wait," Kamryn muttered. "How do we know this is a real location? Maybe it's another trick."

"We *don't* know," Malone said. "Have to wait and see."

Nguyen added, "I've relayed the intel and coordinates to TMD."

***

Military satellite images streamed into Nguyen's console. They confirmed the plant's location as described, plus the presence of a massive ship half-hidden in shadows under a thick canopy of rainforest trees.

Axel leaned over Malone's shoulder to watch red blips on the screen. One TMD warship broke away and raced ahead to secure the Indonesian site. "I get the feeling there's more going on between these two than we suspected. It's why Fulton included her in his escape plan. He doesn't have a charitable bone in his body. They're an odd pair. This is her plant, probably full of her AIs."

"Agreed," Malone said. "And the ship? It's a Titan-class hauler, couple sizes smaller than the Goliath he sent to Ganymede. Perfect for transporting equipment, people, lots of food, water, and supplies."

"So…you think they're going to make another run for Ganymede?"

Malone nodded. "That would be my guess, with one last stop in China before leaving."

"Why?" Axel rubbed the stubble on his jaw. "What's there that isn't here?"

"Wish I knew."

Axel's mind raced through a process of elimination. Fulton's ship of mining equipment, personnel, and supplies had made it to Ganymede. Chang's ship of clones and supplies didn't. Fulton remained on Terra to chaperon the last payload of everything these people trafficked in: weapons, clones, and AIs—Chang's specialty. She could have outsourced manufacturing a large number to an obscure location far away from the prying eyes of the military.

Which leaves clones. If Fulton determined more were needed, he had time to cultivate many resources to acquire them.

"We need an interior scan of the plant to know if they were making AIs or clones."

Nguyen's fingers blurred over her screen. "I'm on it." Seconds later an image popped up on her screen. "The building's empty. Completely empty. Nothing's left but the four walls. Its contents might already be in the *Titan*."

Axel studied the surrounding terrain for anything out of the ordinary. He pointed to a small glow moving through the shaded tree line. "What's that?"

She zoomed in until part of a humanoid outline became visible. "Android. Not human."

"Well, now we need to find out how many."

Kamryn couldn't resist a pithy reminder. "There's never just one."

"I know." Axel patted his ribs. "Believe me, I know."

Nguyen tapped her screen to access a digital report while she talked. "We're too far away for a comprehensive site scan, but the lead TMD ship touched down. Their preliminary survey of the property reports considerable amounts of silicon, metallic glass, ceramics, synthetic polymers and various metalloids."

"AIs then, not a medical facility with cryopods."

She nodded. "From these concentrations we're talking an *army* of androids."

"That could mean twenty or thirty—they're cyborgs on steroids."

"More like 100," Nguyen muttered. "And most likely hidden in the trees waiting to ambush us the minute we touch down."

Axel uttered a guttural sound followed by a string of virulent profanity he seldom used in front of women. Picking a fight with two AIs was bad enough. Now he'd compounded it by allowing prisoners aboard *MAVREK*. In retrospect, hijacking one bad guy for interrogation might be overlooked, considering the circumstances. He'd never live down volunteering to be a getaway ship for criminals. They were nothing more than garbage stinking up the ship.

It wasn't a slam dunk mission anymore. He couldn't afford to make another mistake.

"When we deliver the prisoners, our job's done. *Period.* We are *not* going to China. All TMD ships have the SRVL System. They can track the *Titan* and blow it out of the sky to keep it from reaching Ganymede. I don't give a shit." He looked at Nguyen. "How long until we reach the coordinates?"

"Twelve minutes, or…however long you want. Why?"

"Make it ten." Axel bolted upright, motioning to Petra tucked away in a corner. "Come with me." He went straight to the weapon locker with Petra in tow. "Take these." He thrust guns and ammo at her. "Split them with Ohashi. The second you kick those people out the door, we lift off. Change into exosuits and vests. I don't know what else they might have hidden in the trees. This isn't a warship, so it could get nasty. Now go!"

He visually checked the three suits of armor, poised like lethal warriors ready for action. After jamming guns into every pocket, he crept around blue passenger chairs to where Mark sat.

"Jailbirds," he whispered, crouching next to his friend.

Mark's head spun around with a huge smile plastered on his face. "Man, am I glad to see you."

Axel couldn't help but return the smile, happier than he thought possible at seeing Mark back aboard their ship. Knowing Mark's fondness for showing affection to those he considered family, Axel warned, "If you try to kiss me, I'll slug ya."

"Break these off and I promise not to." Mark rattled the chain holding his cuff to Russell's.

Axel reached over, snapping the titanium chain apart with his augmented hand.

Russell's eyes bulged. "Wow, how'd you do that?"

"Ask him." Axel jerked a thumb at Mark as he passed a gun to each man. "Don't let them know you're not cuffed, and try not to shoot anybody until we're on the ground. Nguyen thinks we're going to be ambushed. I think they've wanted to steal our ship for weeks for the SRVL system—to reverse engineer it. This last trick of being involved in a jailbreak 'so-the-bad-guys-will-show-you-where-the-loot-is-buried' even fooled the general."

"I heard." Mark tapped the comm in his ear. "I think you're both right. There's something else, too. From their tone, Fulton and Chang started arguing half an hour ago. Sounds like there's trouble in paradise. It's getting pretty heated, but I can only pick up a word now and then."

"Suit up the minute our three passengers are gone." As an afterthought Axel added, "And stuff Russell somewhere he won't get shot."

He returned to the pilot's cabin, barking orders like a sergeant. "After we unload the garbage, raise shields. Depending on the number of androids, the TMD might need some help until reinforcements arrive. Take us a mile away and land again. Be ready to liftoff on my command."

"Copy that," Nguyen said. The cabin's atmosphere suddenly changed. Both pilots adopted battle modes, donned combat flight helmets, cinched their harnesses tight.

Axel turned to Kamryn. "I'm not looking for a fight, but we're here, right?"

They locked eyes, a shared emotion passed between them. With a lopsided smirk, she said, "We're just backup. Gotcha."

"Intel," Nguyen said, her voice feeding straight from her helmet into Axel's commlink. "Got a close-up of the tree line. Remember the one android we saw earlier? Picking up lots more now."

***

"Arrival in two minutes," Nguyen announced over the ship's PA system. The interior lights dimmed to blue.

Mark and Brett secured their weapons within easy reach, ready for the slightest hint of trouble. The ship vibrated under foot for several seconds as Nguyen adjusted thrusters for a smooth touchdown. Once stationary, the dark blue lights returned to a normal golden glow.

Petra hurried forward, leading Fulton first, Chang second…but no Emeryx. She cranked the hatch open. A dusky, humid Indonesian evening greeted them. Metal stairs unfolded as she stepped aside. Still in costume, she positioned herself against the hull to bid them farewell. "Thank you for flying Mavrek Air."

Mark heard someone running before he saw an odd-shaped form racing from the rear of the ship toward the hatch. In a blur, it sped through the passenger cabin, brushed past Fulton and Chang then took an enormous jump outside, landing fifteen feet away.

Mark realized too late it was Emeryx—with Ohashi slung over its shoulder.

All hell broke loose in the chaos of the moment.

Mark jumped over chairs, gun in hand, shooting rapid-fire at Fulton and Chang. "The AI captured Ohashi!" he yelled. "And it's running away!"

Fulton plunged to the tarmac, howling in agony while he crawled away. Chang fared much better. Imitating the AIs jump and speed, she broke away at a 90-degree angle, racing toward the far edge of the clearing.

Mark charged after Emeryx, who swung to the right heading straight for the ship concealed in the trees. Afraid of hitting an unconscious Ohashi, he concentrated on shooting at the AIs legs— impossible to hit at a dead run.

Petra joined the fracas. She veered left after Chang, firing nonstop.

Out of his peripheral vision, Mark spotted Kamryn sprinting close behind Petra, firing two guns at Chang.

Axel sailed by Mark at cyborg speed. He hurled a grenade in front of Chang, turned left to lob another at the giant ship in front of Emeryx. "Dive!" he shouted, grabbed Mark, and dove for the ground.

Two bone-jarring explosions erupted. Twin fireballs sent red hot flames into the air. Waves of heat seared across Mark's backside. Clods of dirt, tarmac, and underbrush flew skyward, then rained back down in a dusty, suffocating cloud.

Ohashi was Mark's first thought when his senses returned. They must stop the AI—at all costs. He stumbled to his feet. His right hand had a death grip on the gun, the left covered his mouth and nose to avoid breathing scorched air.

Axel pulled Mark forward through the smoke until a shadow flashed in front of them.

Emeryx—burned and mangled. One arm hung by wires, but it still held Ohashi draped over its shoulder. Without warning, it kicked out at Axel, failed to connect, struck Mark's hand instead. His gun went off, shooting Emeryx squarely in the left eye—a one in a million shot. The AI staggered backward, recovered, and disappeared into the overgrown foliage.

They ran after it, then stopped short.

Six large figures broke through the tree line. Androids. The ghostly white humanoid machines marched toward them. A nanosecond later, twice as many appeared.

Axel pulled Mark in the opposite direction, shouting, "Everybody—back to the ship—NOW!"

As they sprinted away from the oncoming horde, Mark commed Malone. "Emergency liftoff in ten seconds!"

Axel glanced over his shoulder, pitching a grenade dead center into the throng gaining on them.

Kamryn and Petra rushed ahead from the left. They leapt aboard the ship, flanked the hatch, and began shooting at the androids.

From above, heavy air pressed against Mark. Gusts whipped debris across the scarred tarmac. He looked up.

The cavalry had arrived. Better late than never.

A huge TMD warship commenced firing at the platoon-sized troop of androids. They fell like dominoes under the close-range streams of green plasma melting them into distorted clumps of metal.

Mark jumped through the hatch, shouting, "Nguyen, scan for a moving thermal signature in the trees! Then tell Dimitrios they took Ohashi, and she's the one who designed the SRVL system!"

Axel threw Fulton's bloody body into the ship, climbing over him to shut the hatch. "Liftoff."

Everyone hit the deck before gravity forced them down.

"Too many thermals in that rainforest," Nguyen said. "This sorry-ass scanner can't tell which is Ohashi's."

When they could stand, Russell followed behind everyone as Axel carried Fulton to the MedLab. "Kamryn, get ready to pump a shitload of Quazar into this worthless piece of crap. We need to know where the AI took Ohashi."

Mark stopped Fulton's blood flow by injecting a clotting agent, then applied WoundX powder to close the three bullet holes before he slapped on bandages. He had to ensure Fulton made it through the interrogation, though he no longer cared if the man lived or died. Rescuing Ohashi was the only thing that mattered. She must be brought back home. To family. *His* family.

Overcome with remorse, Mark swallowed past the lump in his throat, blinking back the tears. If he'd been a better shot, maybe…no—now was not the time for recriminations.

Finished, Mark moved back beside Petra, sliding an arm around her for support.

Kamryn inserted the needle of truth serum into Fulton's carotid artery and pressed the plunger down. Axel cracked open a vial of AZ2 under his nose. In Fulton's condition, it took more than a couple whiffs to bring him around. They grew antsy when his eyes didn't open.

"Wake up Fulton." Kamryn jabbed her finger into a clean white dressing on his chest.

Fulton groaned as he regained consciousness. Dark red blood seeped up through the opened wound.

"How many ships do you have in Indonesia?"

More groans. No verbal response.

"How many ships and where are they?" She stabbed her finger twice as deep into a different wound.

"Two," he whined.

In Fulton's impaired state, the Quazar was having a delayed effect. Since others had died while being questioned under the non-military grade street drug, his interrogators might literally have a deadline.

"Where?"

"At the plant." Fulton's speech came out slow, hesitant, as if in a dream. "And on my property near the Kapuas River."

Kamryn covered her mouth to whisper, "You get that, Malone?"

"Affirmative. We're researching…wait…got it. On our way."

Mark raised both hands to stop the proceedings. "Hold on a sec. I have a couple questions."

Kamryn signaled for him to take over.

"Fulton, what's in Jixi, China?"

"The Zhū Corporation," he replied, slower than before, "with four more ships."

Surprised at the number of additional ships, Mark focused on asking specific questions to get the answers he needed. "How are you connected to them?"

"We're partners," he paused, "in claiming Enceladus as a private holding."

Mark shouldn't have been stunned, but he was. For confirmation, he asked, "Saturn's moon?"

"Yes."

After recovering, Mark continued. "You said 'four more ships.' Explain how many have left and when."

"Five left a month ago." Fulton's voice wavered now. "The last four leave tonight."

Mark posed one last question. "What cargo are they transporting?"

Fulton's tone was weak and fading. "My mining equipment, Chang's androids, Stepanov's weapons."

Mark's head slumped to his chest, overwhelmed by the sheer magnitude of Fulton's new intel.

An oppressive silence lingered in the MedLab as everyone tried to digest how this would change space exploration—or even who *ruled* in space.

"Not our problem," Axel said. "Retrieving Ohashi is." He pointed at Mark and Kamryn. "Suit up."

Leaving the MedLab, Axel turned to Petra. "Strap Fulton down. Do what you can to keep him alive because *I* plan to kill him when we get back. And you're Russell's bodyguard. Make sure nothing happens to him, or we're all dead."

Chapter 24

The weapon locker became the ship's nerve center as three people inserted themselves into suits of armor. The sound of metal being snapped closed echoed over and over. Weapons were checked, gauntlets and helmets locked on, HUDs synced to Nguyen's real-time data feed of thermal signatures, along with a diagram of Fulton's property.

Petra stood by the hatch, ready to release two drones. Russell waited on the opposite side to secure the door.

Nguyen's voice filtered into their helmets. "The ship is a personal transport vessel, six-passenger Perseus model—fast, but short-ranged. No heat signatures aboard—yet. We'll go dark and hold an overwatch position no more than five seconds away. Can't land, so you'll have a twenty-foot drop. Bring Ohashi home."

"Copy that." Axel took point, the first, most exposed position. Mark secondary, ready to assist either the person in front or the one behind. Kamryn always had their back as the rear guard. They crowded around the hatch.

Nguyen counted down. "Three…two…one…Go!"

Russell swung the hatch open. Petra let the drones loose in a pitch-black sky.

As he had many times before, Axel stepped off the threshold into midair, plunging straight down through an overgrown jungle of trees. The military had designed AntiGrav gel boots for this specific purpose. Jumps from a height of twenty or thirty feet were safe, provided the soldier had adequate training on landing procedures. He came down in a solid *thump*, knees bent, and stayed low to get his bearings. Crouched in attack mode, he waited while green HUD readouts inside his helmet linked to the drones. A red dot showed his current location in proximity to the yellow dot on Fulton's ship.

Mark, the novice in this maneuver, came crashing to the ground, a tree branch wedged under his arm, and fell face first ten feet away from Axel.

Despite the seriousness of their mission, Axel chuckled, watching Mark pick himself up. "That pitiful 3.2 landing won't win you any medals." Axel didn't see it, but he felt the dirty look Mark gave him.

Kamryn, the expert, glided between trees, barely rustling a leaf, and landed with a soft *thud* to join them.

Their helmets displayed eerie green x-rays of nearby underbrush, plus all three heat signatures.

Axel led his trio toward the yellow dot. With no other thermal signature visible, it seemed they'd arrived before Emeryx. He prayed the AI showed up soon—with Ohashi. Chang had hightailed it in the other direction, no doubt to split up her pursuers, yet could circle back to meet Emeryx here at the ship. Their helmets were incapable of identifying AIs or androids, only humans, so they moved forward through the underbrush, careful to be as quick and quiet as possible.

Mark spoke first, in a near whisper, although his voice fed into their helmets. "My gut's telling me I need to remind you about what happened at HQ."

Kamryn said, "How's that?"

"We can't underestimate Chang. She left a booby-trapped AI for the military to find. It blew up the R&D complex and killed twenty-two scientists, plus military personnel for one purpose: to destroy any research that might rival or exceed hers. Really, just an updated version of the old Trojan Horse ploy. She expected it would set us back years, giving her the upper hand on Ganymede. If the TMD mounted an attack, she planned to be ready with her army of androids—an effective but contemptable plan."

Axel snorted. "Sounds like you *admire* the despicable Miss Chang."

"Absolutely not. She scares the hell out of me. I watched her pull a steel bedframe off the wall, rip a toilet out of the floor, and dismantle a shower—all in under a minute. She's a Human-AI hybrid, by her own design, who is highly intelligent, immoral, and *lethal*. A disastrous trifecta."

"Amen to that," Kamryn muttered in a spiteful tone.

Their trek continued in silence, with everyone scanning for any sign of another thermal reading.

Axel stopped. "Ship. Fifty yards to the right." Inside his suit, the hair prickled on the back of his neck.

A blunt object smashed into him from the side.

Axel went airborne, sailing backward into trees. "Ambush!" He extended his arm, made a fist, and engaged the plasma gun built into the arm of his suit. It threw a constant stream of bright green plasma toward the oncoming attacker. The android split apart like a sliced tomato. In the plasma's afterlight, scorched android halves lay at odd angles on the ground.

He heard a howl, snapping his head in that direction to see Kamryn on the ground. Axel moved, but not quick enough. Androids tackled him from opposite sides. The enormous force knocked the air out of him, even inside the suit. It would have killed him if he hadn't been in armor.

Two androids had him in a fierce vise grip. Flashes of his fight with the AIs clouded his mind.

Oh, hell no. He'd done this dance before and damn near died. Not this time.

Axel reverted to soldier mode: fearless, relentless, fixated on destroying his enemies. He had a score to settle. Bolts from both his arms cleaved the androids in half. Once freed from their grasp, he vaulted over the pieces to help Mark and Kamryn.

They stood back to back, surrounded by a mountain of dismembered parts. Their arms bristled with streams of green light that slashed through the darkness, hacking off limbs and toppling trees.

Axel went on offense. He hadn't wanted to alert Emeryx or Chang by using grenades, but an army of machines grossly outnumbered his people.

"Grenades!"

Mark and Kamryn hit the ground as Axel threw one after another all around the fight zone. Explosions lit up the forest, shook the ground, and halted the onslaught of androids—for the moment.

"To the ship! They know we're here!"

All three crashed through underbrush, running flat out for the yellow dot displayed in their helmets.

Within seconds, a faint red dot appeared. It advanced from the left and was much closer to the ship than they were.

"Ohashi." Axel poured on extra speed to bulldoze a trail.

"I see," Mark said, racing in his wake. "The androids were sent to stop us so Chang and Emeryx could get away."

"Since that plan failed," Kamryn said, "there has to be another trap. Watch for Chang or the AI—"

A large, misshapen form dropped out of a tree, landed on Kamryn's back, and threw her to the ground.

"Get off me, dammit!"

Axel and Mark turned to help her, recognizing Emeryx as the attacker. Firing plasma was not an option. Both grabbed their slug-throwers to unleash a hail of bullets at the AI.

Although missing one arm, it didn't quit. Instead, Emeryx wrapped its legs around Kamryn's middle and started bashing its head into Kamryn's faceplate.

Oh, no you don't. They already had Ohashi—they weren't getting anyone else. In a surge of raw Von Radach power, Axel grabbed the AIs remaining arm, and wrenched it out of the socket, cables and all. After a full backswing, he let loose with an incredible strike to the AI's skull. It popped off the torso, electricity from ripped wires sparking in the darkness as it spun end over end like an Old Earth football, way over the trees.

"You okay?" Mark asked, extending an arm to help Kamryn up.

"Yeah, but there's tiny spiderweb cracks in my faceplate. It may rupture."

"C'mon." Axel pushed them forward. "Chang must have Ohashi. We need to reach her ship before she takes off."

***

Rane Thorson's self-satisfied grin had grown into a genuine smile. His ship had docked with the dead-in-space *Stellaria*. A Level 6 Protocol was in effect, which required full armor for everyone boarding the ship as protection against the hidden dangers of bioweapons. Spec Op soldiers were first on the runaway vessel. Thorson would follow with the military specialists. After they finished inspecting the cargo and gave the "all clear," the civilian doctors would be allowed to board.

"Sir," Loomis said, "Lieutenant Ortiz reports our RAM-XT microwave pulse did its job by shutting down life support. Every crew member they've found so far is unconscious."

"Excellent. Now restrain the entire *Stellaria* crew, then restore their life support systems. Clear the bridge and engineering of personnel. Stuff them all in the galley if you have to, and put the captain in their stockade—alone."

Thorson left the bridge in the capable hands of his XO and descended two levels to the main airlock, where he donned a shiny black suit and helmet. He signaled to Lieutenant Riddhi and her ten-member team in their Hazmat yellow armor. "Lead the way."

As armored troops cleared each section, they posted guards at every hatch. Riddhi and her team moved judiciously through the passageways, using industrial-strength scanners to check for a multitude of toxic substances—to include NuroKac, Zdeth, and Sorak.

Upon finding the lab, Hazmat team members went into overdrive, securing deadly pathogens in black boxes made for transporting lethal substances.

Thorson moved to the adjacent area where cryopods with children were stacked four deep in row after row. His gut churned with thoughts of the fate these young people had narrowly escaped.

"Has Stepanov been found yet?"

"Yes, sir," Ortiz responded. "You may want to come look at this, Captain."

"On my way," Thorson said, glad to leave the unnerving scene of children in stasis.

Since her quarters were all the way forward, it took the captain's escort a while to deliver him to Stepanov's cabin. He shouldn't have been in such a hurry. The sight that met him was horrendous.

Trashed.

A caustic acid had obliterated the computer hardware, processor, screens, every peripheral.

In the middle of the floor lay what might be Stepanov's remains. The lumpy, tan liquid had the consistency of mineral oil. It might have been human at some point, but not anymore.

"Sir, do you think this is a suicide?"

No, he did not. The muscles in Thorson's jaw tightened. "Get someone from Hazmat up here A-*SAP*." Thorson did suspect this was Stepanov's last-ditch effort to escape justice. He'd read her file. Her history pointed to homicide, not suicide.

A yellow suit of armor breezed in the door with a toolbox full of electronic equipment. "Sir, Sergeant Lockwood, reporting as ordered, Captain."

"You got here quick."

"I was on the bridge, sir."

Thorson pointed at the puddle. "These are Natalya Stepanov's quarters. I need to know if those are her remains. If it's not, I don't care if we're here until my hair turns gray, I'm not leaving this ship without her—dead or alive."

"Yes, sir." Lockwood knelt beside the remains, scanner in hand. "Do we have her DNA?"

Ortiz made a quick trip to the bathroom, returned with toothbrush, towels, and a silk robe.

"Sir, I can't tell you how long it will take," Lockwood said. "But I will give you a definitive answer soon as I have one."

"Excellent." Thorson motioned to Ortiz. "In the meantime, let's take a closer look at the cryopods. I have a hunch this sneaky bitch is trying to pull a fast one."

***

Neither Mark, Kamryn, nor Axel encountered more androids or other enemies while tearing through the jungle undergrowth. As they burst into the clearing, a large yellow dot displayed in their readouts—its source, a lustrous gray ship no more than fifty feet away.

To their right, a faint red dot darted out of the trees—Ohashi, carried by Chang.

Axel faded back into the jungle, Kamryn on his heels.

Mark continued forward, slowing to a stroll. At a complete loss for how to proceed, he winged it and prayed he didn't get Ohashi killed.

"Hey there," he said, waving as if they were old friends.

Chang stopped in her tracks. "I'll snap her neck like a toothpick if you move a micron closer."

She hadn't threatened to shoot Ohashi...perhaps she didn't have a weapon.

Then Mark remembered she *was* a weapon.

"No problem, I'm fine here." He thumbed up his faceplate and gave her a big toothy smile, one she could recognize even in the dark.

"You—Dawson?"

"Yep, it's me. John and I stole some suits from those guys and ducked out when they weren't looking."

Axel climbed up on the ship's aft section. His voice whispered into Mark's helmet. "You're doing great. Keep it up."

Chang edged toward the ship, one arm holding Ohashi's limp body like a shield, the other with a death grip around her neck. "That's a lie. I saw you shoot Wade."

Axel disappeared over the far side of the ship.

"Okay, I did—and I'd do it again. By the way, my name's not Dawson."

"Who the hell are—"

Mark decided a lie was safer than the truth. "I'm General Dimitrios' nephew, Brett Russell. I volunteered to go undercover in Rheinholdt to find out all your dirty little secrets. Worked pretty good, too, don't ya think?"

Kamryn moved up on the ship now, following Axel's path. They must have a plan to disable the ship, keep it from taking off.

Chang kept sidestepping closer to the hatch.

Mark could not allow her to get inside with Ohashi.

"You know...there are warships all over this sector. If you try to take off, I'll send them your coordinates and they'll shoot you down."

"Then she dies, too."

"Collateral damage." Mark made a passing gesture with his right hand to keep her attention away from Axel's location. "Another innocent bystander. I don't even know who she is."

"Another lie!" Chang screamed. "She designed the SRVL system that makes military ships untraceable."

"Okay, you're right again," Mark said to pacify her. He changed tactics, slowly raising both arms and pointing them at her. "We can cut the bullshit now. I'm not letting you get on that ship—with or without her. I've got two bolts of plasma with your name on them just waiting for you to make a move."

"You're bluffing." Chang's tone was spiteful as she repositioned Ohashi to take the full brunt of his threatened attack.

"The hell I am," he snapped. "Uncle Eli will have my ass in a sling if he finds out I could have stopped you and didn't."

Chang wavered for an instant.

Mark caught the flicker of doubt on her face. He was making progress. Time to press ahead.

"If I hit you—fine. If I accidentally lop off one of her arms, the TMD will give her a new one. Or, I can blast holes in your thrusters before you liftoff. So, am I bluffing, and are you stupid enough to try me?"

Chang sprang for the ship. Her movements were so fast they blurred.

No-no-no! Mark ran after her, but aiming on the run didn't guarantee a precise hit.

The hatch opened.

He fired twice. Green energy streaked through the night. Intense flashes slammed against the hull.

The hatch closed.

Mark raced toward the ship, yelling, "Axel, I couldn't stop Chang. She got inside and took Ohashi." Fueled by rage and a gut-wrenching sense of failure, he raced after her. The ship's hull showed his two blasts had punctured holes through multiple layers of metal. He was afraid of damaging it further with Ohashi on board. "Axel, Kamryn—do you copy?"

Without warning, the ship jolted upward. A foot off the ground at first, then gained momentum as it rose straight up, climbing higher and higher to clear the tree canopy.

"Axel, the ship's taking off. Do you copy?" Mark watched, terror-stricken. "*Axel*, do you copy?" Fear gripped Mark's heart. The TMD would surely blow that ship to subatomic particles, killing his friends along with Chang.

A voice boomed in his helmet. "Run—Mark—run!"

Chapter 25

As ordered, Mark ran. Aided by the suit, he made it to the tree line in one-third the time than he could have on foot.

A horrendous sound reverberated through the air. The shock wave made him stumble. He spun around. Off in the distance, a TMD warship hovered high overhead, red beacons pulsating on its underside.

Large pieces of Chang's ship spun outward in all directions. The entire back half—destroyed. The front section began a 45-degree nosedive. He couldn't take his eyes off the crippled spacecraft as it plunged into the trees. A shower of flaming parts fell to the ground. As small fragments zinged past, he closed the faceplate to his helmet.

Mark was beyond devastated. Frozen in the moment. Unable to accept the reality that his friends could be—

No…he couldn't put a name to it. Could not face it.

He stood transfixed by the fireworks. But while most fiery chunks faded, one remained steady. It descended in a straight line.

His HUD display identified them as dots. Red dots. *Three* red dots. Thermal heat signatures!

Mark ran toward the landing coordinates shown in his helmet. Jagged hunks of smoldering metal littered the terrain. He watched the red dots drift downward, now able to glimpse Ohashi sandwiched between two black suits of armor. The lump in his throat threatened to choke him.

When their boots hit the ground, Mark let out a whoop. "Nguyen, everyone's here. Come and get us."

Seconds later the bronze craft hovered a foot off the ground. They climbed aboard. Russell made himself useful at the hatch. After liftoff, Petra helped remove helmets and gloves.

"Where is that sonofabitch?" Axel marched to the MedLab, unbuckled a terrified, screaming Fulton from the pod, and flung him to the deck. His wounds leaked blood as he curled into a fetal position on the floor.

When Kamryn laid Ohashi on the pod, everyone moved back. No one seemed to breathe.

Mark passed the scanner over her from head to toe. "No wounds, but traces of a paralytic, which seems to be wearing off." With great tenderness, he smoothed Ohashi's hair away from her face to kiss her forehead. His voice cracked as he whispered, "You're going to be okay, I promise."

The room chilled. Something terrible was going to happen. Russell receded into the background. Mark watched and waited.

Axel signaled Petra to record and Kamryn to put Fulton in a chair. He and Kamryn—two black armor-clad monsters—took positions on either side of their prisoner.

Fulton cringed under the pure hatred radiating toward him.

Axel nodded to Kamryn. She snapped his chin up with her left index finger. Axel slapped Fulton hard enough to scramble his brains.

He yelped. Blood sprayed across the room. Red streams leaked from both sides of Fulton's mouth. His eyes looked crossed. Fulton should have been glad Axel had used his human hand—the cyborg one would have killed him.

Kamryn popped an AZ2 under his nose.

Fulton regained awareness of his situation. Fear spread across his face.

Axel began patting himself down as if searching for an item. "I can't find my knife. Ah, I remember. *I left it in Chang's neck.* May I borrow yours, Sergeant Fleming?"

"Certainly, Sergeant Von Radach." Kamryn removed the knife from its casing on her thigh and handed it to Axel.

"I will remove your right eyeball—"

Wade Fulton unceremoniously pissed himself. Whereas he couldn't look at them a moment ago, his eyes were glued to them now.

"Or…" Axel flipped the knife in the air, catching it a millisecond before it landed blade down in Fulton's leg. "I will beat you half to death. Then, space you over the ocean. If you don't die before you hit the water, the sharks will rip you apart."

"Unless," Kamryn said, "you tell us how to stop the Zhū Corporation."

"They won't stop." Fulton's eyes flicked from Axel to Kamryn. "They already have a legion of androids on Enceladus. What you don't know is this was their idea from the start. They approached me with the plan to claim Ganymede. Helped finance it. Chose Stepanov and Chang as my partners. Zhū always planned to use it as a way station for Enceladus."

Mark stepped between his friends. He had to know. "Why? For what reason? What's on Enceladus?"

"Ezontium," Fulton mumbled. "An isotope they think is the answer to FTL travel."

Russell choked. He'd remained silent until the mention of Ezontium.

Everyone focused on Russell.

His only comment: "It's classified."

***

Thorson ordered a full-scale investigation of *Stellaria's* hold, including each cryopod. They were to be checked, images taken of the occupants and logged into inventory.

"Ortiz, start from the back, the ones farthest away. Make it thorough, but be quick."

Thorson was antsy. He paced. The longer he stayed on this ship, the louder his gut warned him of an as yet nameless threat.

"I need to speak with *Stellaria's* captain."

Ortiz called for a corporal who escorted Thorson to the brig. He waved the armored guard away, intent on speaking with the woman who sat behind bars.

Her head was in her hands, elbows on her knees, with shoulders slumped as she stared at the floor.

Employing his catch-more-flies-with-honey tone, he said, "Captain, my name is Rane Thorson. Might I have a word?"

"Certainly, Captain." She looked up. Short dark hair, accented by the signature streak of white framed her haggard features.

Thorson immediately recognized the woman. "Brisa Rylak. It's unfortunate we meet again under these circumstances."

"Indeed, Captain. And much more unfortunate than you imagine."

Under different circumstances, he would have thumbed up his faceplate to establish a personal rapport, but he resisted. "I'm listening."

"No reason to sugar coat this, Thorson. We're all dead. Stepanov has murdered my entire crew. It may take a while before we succumb to her alchemy, but we will die, nonetheless." Rylak's deep worry lines and the dark bags under her eyes contradicted her stoic tone.

She pressed forward to described how the crew had been hired for an exploratory mission to Ganymede without any prior knowledge of the ship's payload. Near Mars, Stepanov had ordered a course change. Everything had gone downhill from there. Rylak had several run-ins with Stepanov and finally installed a hidden camera in Stepanov's lab, where she observed her making aerosol for the cylinders. Fearing for the crew, Rylak had a cyber specialist hack into Stepanov's files, where records were found of the crew's altered inoculations. Rylak confronted Stepanov, demanding an antidote. A dispute ensued.

"She stunned me and disappeared. When I returned to the bridge, the power went out...and here we are."

On the surface, Rylak's story sounded sincere. Her physical appearance more than supported her claims. Thorson's skeptical nature, however, warned him to proceed with caution.

"I appreciate your willingness to share this information. I've inspected her quarters. All the files have been eradicated. I'll order DNA samples of your crew and get a contingent of scientists to work on an antidote."

"I won't hold my breath." Rylak brushed the white lock of hair off her brow. "I don't know what's in the cylinders, but take my word for it—Stepanov is not only unscrupulous, but as treacherous as they come."

"Do you think she'd commit suicide?"

Rylak let out a sarcastic hoot. "Never. That move's not in her play book."

On Thorson's return trip to the hold, he commed Ortiz. "Order everyone to stay buttoned up. No helmets or gloves removed. Get Hazmat searching for cylinders. Absolutely no personal contact. Quarantine them." Next, he ordered DNA samples from the prisoners, with instructions to the lead MD back on his ship with the updated information on the enemy crew. He might turn this around and get accolades for saving them, at least until their trial on Terra.

Entering the hold, Thorson dismissed his escort.

"Ortiz, how's the inventory coming?"

"Finished, sir," he said, motioning for the captain to follow him. "I have a surprise for you." Ortiz led Thorson to the rear of the stacked cryopods. "According to the pod's data retrieval system, Emiko #46, a twelve-year-old female of Asian descent, was the original occupant. What do you see now?"

Ortiz keyed a code into the pod's darkened faceplate. An interior light switched on, illuminating an adult human in stasis. Thorson smiled like a Cheshire cat. "Aha! The elusive Miss Natalya Stepanov—in perfect condition—not dead at all."

"Your orders, sir?"

"What would you do, Ortiz?"

"Sir, she wanted to go to Ganymede so bad, I think we ought to send her there."

"What a great idea—no…we can't. We *shouldn't*."

Ortiz grinned. "Maybe we can get the Martians to…"

Thorson admitted it sounded tantalizing. "Put her in the brig next to the captain and record everything." His smile returned. "If they don't kill each other, it'll be a miracle."

***

Everyone took turns sitting with Ohashi on the return trip to HQ. After *MAVREK* landed, a medic treated Fulton's wounds to ensure he'd live through further ISD interrogations.

The crew went straight to Major Torance for complete scans. It felt like old home week having everyone together again.

Then the fun ended.

General Dimitrios ordered the entire crew, including Malone and Nguyen, to undergo a medical halo interrogation. The whole Mavrek crew flat-out refused, instantly contacted their attorneys, and made it clear they'd rather go to the Stockade than be interrogated.

Acting as a buffer, Brett Russell convinced his uncle to forego the interrogation in exchange for statements outlining each person's involvement and let it go at that. But, of course, under penalty of imprisonment, they swore not to divulge any Classified intel, which encompassed everything within the last three weeks (except the Gérard Incident, and only because it, mercifully, never came up).

Russell accompanied the group back to their ship. "This has been one hell of a ride," he admitted to Mark. "I've never known anyone who did half the stuff you guys do."

"You have no idea," Mark said. He enjoyed bragging about his friends. "Axel and Kamryn were in the Armored Unit. Two of the most dangerous people on the planet—in or out of armor. Petra and Ohashi were cybers in the same unit. They can find anything or anyone and can code faster than you can talk. Malone and Nguyen are former Space Command pilots. I've seen them do barrel rolls in a spaceship to out fly pirates. They're my friends, my family. I trust them with my life."

"Well, Hot Shot, you're the only scientist I know who has a Silver Star. Uncle Eli said he gave it to you himself."

"Axel has one, too."

"You're the head honcho here, even if you don't want to admit it. I saw your records. Your cybernetics work is cutting-edge, but you live aboard a ship and travel around the solar system…doing *what*, exactly?"

"You don't want to know."

On the contrary, Russell *did* want to hear about all the hair-raising, down and dirty, shoot-'em-up escapades he'd been a party to, but Mark wasn't telling.

"I know you killed the officer who shot Uncle Eli," Russell said with a healthy dose of respect.

"Yeah, and I ended up with an augmented ear for my troubles."

"You shot Fulton right in front of me. It was like watching an Old Earth gunslinger. Then you put on armor and went to rescue one of the crew."

"*Family*. We're family."

"The general wants to offer you a promotion, plus a coveted spot on the research team of your choice if you'd re-up for at least two years."

"No way. I have everything I need, go wherever the hell I please, and don't have to answer to anyone." A thought flashed in his mind. "Except, I *would* consider a Consultant's position, plus a few perks. And I get to pick my assignments." He had one specific destination in mind: Saturn's rings—Enceladus. The instant Fulton mentioned it, Mark had thought of nothing else.

"Well, he won't be happy, but I'll tell him."

Nearing their ship, Alexis Nguyen drooled when she got a close look at the new Phoenix IX model Interceptor spaceship. She scowled up at Mark. "What I want for Christmas is a new ship—black and armed to the max."

"I'll see what I can do, Alexis." He gave the small woman a hug. "Tomorrow is Christmas Eve, so let's point our sleigh toward home. We all have trees to trim."

A high-spirited excitement percolated through the ship as Mark contacted his parents with the news he and Axel would be home soon. Kamryn let her father know she'd be in Calgary within hours. Ohashi was eager to spend Christmas in New Zealand, where her twin sister and parents were waiting. Likewise, Petra had three younger siblings and a widowed mother still expecting her in Saint Louis. Their absent crew member, Dr. Eva Jackson, remained on the speaker's circuit—in Monte Carlo, of all places. She'd traded her Caribbean holiday for a European excursion.

After dropping off Petra and Kamryn, the ship got quiet. Almost *too* quiet. Mark wanted to spend some one-on-one time with Ohashi before they arrived in Portland. In the ship's hierarchy, Axel would always be the Sergeant, the father figure,

Mark the big brother who hugged and joked with the women—Kamryn, not so much. After this near fatal episode with Ohashi, Mark needed to know she'd returned to the unflappable, self-possessed cyber warrior who tolerated his kidding with an eye roll and a smirk.

The galley seemed like the perfect place for a chat.

"Ohashi," he commed, making lots of searching noises. "Where's the coffee?"

She strolled in, opened a cabinet, and pointed to a stack of pre-measured bags.

"Nooo, *my* coffee."

"We're out. It seems everybody likes yours better." She popped open a bag of regular, poured it in the machine, and pressed a button.

"Do we have cookies to go with the coffee?" he asked, knowing all the women on the ship were cookie fanatics.

Her eyes lit up. She reached behind a row of tall items, pulled out a half-eaten bag of triple chocolate chippers.

"Well, you little sneak."

She winked. "I'll hide it somewhere else next time."

They sipped coffee and munched cookies until Mark said, "I've known you for a year and a half and still don't know your first name."

"O."

"That's a letter."

"No, it's my name. O Hashi. My twin sister's name is A Hashi."

Mark struggled not to look dumbfounded, or worse—laugh.

"It's a family tradition. Started generations ago. I hated it as a kid, now I don't mind." She finished her coffee, set the mug down. "I think it's sweet, but you don't have to do this, you know."

"Do what?" Mark wondered if he looked that transparent.

She gave him a genuine smile. "I'm fine. No broken bones, no missing limbs, no bullet holes." She tapped her temple. "I've always been strong-willed. A little introverted, but with a defiant streak. My years with the TMD taught me to channel the defiance to inner strength.

"There is one thing, though," she added. "Your remark…uh, how did it go? 'Collateral damage. Another innocent bystander. I don't even know who she is.'" Ohashi waggled her finger at Mark. "I was paralyzed, not unconscious. I heard every word." She punched him in the arm, a good one, too.

"Aw, come on, I had to keep Chang talking while Axel and Kamryn broke into her ship."

"I also heard Fulton telling you about the Zhū Corporation on Enceladus. Any chance that's next on our list of vacation stops?"

Not quite able to keep the excitement out of his voice, he asked, "You up for it?"

"We all are. With an army of androids, the TMD will need a Cybernetics expert. Can you wrangle—um,…I mean finagle an invitation out of the general for us to tag along?"

"It's *finesse*, Ohashi. Mark has a talent for *finessing* Dimitrios into things the general later regrets."

Mark glanced over his shoulder to see Axel leaning against the wall.

"You been there the whole time?"

"More or less."

"You in, too?"

"Vacation on Enceladus? Sounds nice this time of year. Besides, have you ever known me to turn down a good fight?"

Where once Mark had been satisfied with the status quo, his view of the cosmos had done a complete reversal. Where once he'd judged Axel to be an adrenalin junkie, now he found himself craving the same rush of exhilaration. Where he had once been timid about space fight, this ship was his home, and he had traveled farther than most. He longed for a new challenge. Without understanding why, he recalled a quote by Carl Sagan, a preeminent astronomer and exobiologist of the twentieth century: *"If we continue to accumulate only power and not wisdom, we will surely destroy ourselves."*

With regard to the debatable existence of Ezontium—a well-respected, albeit, unproven hypothesis claimed that a second island of stability exists in elements. Humans lived on one island—from hydrogen to lead, plus a handful more elements that existed naturally but were mostly radioactive. It was entirely conceivable that an as yet untested radioactive isotope might hold the answer to FTL travel, or something equally significant. A great many scientific discoveries happened by accident. Who's to say this wouldn't be the case on Saturn's tiny moon, Enceladus?

Mark began to think aloud. "When the Prime Council learns the extent of Zhū Corp's crimes to obtain Enceladus, they will order Dimitrios to mount an offensive against any forces on Enceladus. It will neutralize efforts to exploit Enceladus either for Zhū Corp's benefit or to the detriment of humankind. If Ezontium is there, and if it's the answer to future space travel, it should unilaterally be claimed by Terra and Mars—a joint venture for the benefit of the entire human race. *Not* the private property of a murderous corporation."

Again, Ohashi asked, "So, are we going?"

"I'll see what I can do."

Ohashi jumped up, scrounging in the cabinets until she produced a tall, cherry red box. By its size, only a bottle of booze could be inside. "Merry Christmas."

The golden logo was unmistakable. "Namuzko brandy. How did you...?"

"I sent a message to Mars asking Gaige Rayburn to ship a bottle. We got a case."

With fond thoughts of Rayburn and his distillery, Mark poured three fingers into his mug before he passed the brandy around. When they arrived in Portland, he had a good buzz going. His college drinking had taught him the five stages of drunkenness: smart, good looking, rich, bullet proof, invisible. His current state of mind warned him to stay away from the last two.

In Portland, Ohashi offered to take a commercial ship to New Zealand, but the pilots refused to hear of it. Before departing, Mark gave her a lengthy squeeze, and planted a kiss on her forehead. Not prone to outward expressions of affection, Ohashi and Axel broke protocol by sharing a tender sendoff which included a bunch of whispers and head nods. Her eyes were moist, but no tears were spilled.

Outside the spaceport, big, fluffy snowflakes drifted down, sticking to everything as he and Axel grabbed a cab. They traveled over a maze of streets trimmed with decorations and festive lights that glowed in the dark. At last, they stood in front of the house, watching smoke curl out of the chimney, sparkles of red and blue flickering in the windows.

Home.

Mark sighed. He looked up into the heavens. Snowflakes landed on his face as they had when he was a child. A lump rose in his throat, followed by an enormous wave of gratitude. His friends and family were safe. He thanked all the gods in the universe.

"Brother," he laid a hand on Axel's shoulder, "we're home."

**

On a bright, clear morning, seven members of the Mavrek team walked out of TMD Headquarters toward their new ship. As equal partners in Mavrek Enterprises, they had voted to sell three ships to purchase the non-military—but armed to the teeth—cousin of the Phoenix model Nguyen had fancied. The badass black Saber V Interceptor, with a large silver M-7 emblazoned on its tail, sat on the tarmac, last in line for liftoff.

They were officially part of the TMD's squadron of six warships to Enceladus. Two MMC ships would join the contingent as they passed through Martian space. The Terran Prime Council's directives were non-negotiable: neutralize Zhū Corp's holdings, whatever the cost.

Sometimes space was a nasty business, a lesson each one of them had learned the hard way. Mark Warren had suffered the loss of his brother, Eric, and the assault on his father. Axel Von Radach had two cyborg limbs and still mourned the death of his soulmate, Colonel Maeve Sorayne. Every member of the Mavrek crew had been shot, lost a body part, or been kidnapped, but they were still together and Mark Warren loved them all. This is what they did. This is who they were.

Interior lights dimmed to dusky blue.

Excitement level in the cabin shot up a notch.

One by one they harnessed in, exchanged head nods.

Nguyen announced, "*MAVREK 7*, Saturn bound. Liftoff in five…four…three…"

We have gone through hell together,
fought together, laughed together,
almost died together,
we are more than friends, we are family.

Thank you for reading
The EDGE Trilogy

If you enjoyed the escapades of the Mavrek characters, please take a moment to leave
a stellar review!

Help other science fiction readers and tell them why you enjoyed reading.

ACKNOWLEDGEMENTS

All the characters in this novel wish to thank the author, Andria Stone, for giving them a voice, and allowing them to romp through the galaxy.

The author wishes to thank Ranee Stemann and Amanda Ryan as Beta Readers, Jack Llartin as Editor, and Kate Rauner as Technical Consultant, who all helped shape this story. Their time, care, and influence were invaluable.

Made in the USA
Columbia, SC
18 February 2019